Chances for Serendipity

NATALIE CHUNG

For you, dear reader. Don't be afraid to take chances.

CHAPTER 1

16 YEARS OLD

"Oh no. You're kidding me, Liz." I squinted against the blinding sunlight, trying to glare up at my friend. "Why are we here?" I gestured at the grey building in front of us. A building I hadn't set foot in for more than a year.

"Let's go out," she'd said yesterday afternoon when she'd dropped by my family's bakery. I'd expected we'd do something like browsing dresses on sale or sampling desserts at a cute cafe. I mean, her invite had implied something fun. At least, I thought it had.

Liz shrugged. "It's been a while since you've gone to the sports centre. I thought you'd want to visit while we have school holidays."

I closed my eyes and reached for patience. Liz had good intentions, but she didn't know how much this place could possibly hurt me. If I let myself get caught up in the memories... "No thanks. I think I'll pass. I forgot I need to finish my maths homework." Despite it being the summer holidays, I still had several work booklets to do for tutoring school. Not fun.

Liz groaned and hooked her arm around mine before I could bolt back to the train station. I squirmed in her grasp. My sweaty clothes already clung to my back, and her added body heat was not helping. Nope, nope.

She presented me with a perfect, puppy-dog-eyed face, her brown eyes rounded and bottom lip pouting. "Come on, Miss Gloomy. Don't be a party pooper. Moping at home all the time isn't going to make you happy."

"So?" I challenged, my arm straining in her steel grip.

"So, you need some fresh air. Besides, you've never played tennis here in December. I heard that some famous tennis players come to practice here this time of year. You know, off-season and all."

I stopped struggling, suddenly as still as a statue. "Really?" My heart rate spiked at the idea of meeting an Australian tennis star in the flesh. But... My mind crashed back down to reality. Liz habitually omitted important details to suit her agenda. For all I knew, "famous tennis players" could mean absolute unknowns who won local tournaments. Why would anyone remotely famous train in Sydney? Most of them wouldn't be living here.

My eyes narrowed. "How would you know? Have you seen someone famous?" Liz played tennis at the centre at least twice a week. Or she had when I used to go.

"Nope, but my sister works at the centre now."

I flailed in her grasp. "You never mentioned that before."

"Well, you ditched tennis club for a year."

I winced at the unexpected bluntness in her voice, and she grimaced.

"Sorry, I'm not blaming you. But a lot has changed, you know. They did a huge renovation on the building. Just come in and see."

She dragged me to the entrance like a disobedient dog on a leash. I considered a game of tug of war with her, but my sore arm already sagged in her unrelenting grip. "Fine," I said. Since we were already here. And, okay, I'd admit the slim chance of seeing a tennis star would be a dream come true.

The double automatic doors slid open, and we walked through. A blast of cold air immediately engulfed me. I sighed in relief at no longer baking outside in the hot summer sun. Liz finally released me, and I took the opportunity to unstick my clothes from my sweat-drenched body. Ugh. Gross day to be out, but summer wasn't getting any cooler.

With some of my discomfort gone, I focused on my surroundings. The same old potted plants as before still lined the sides of the corridor, but it now opened up to a more spacious lobby with a large front counter. A flowy banner hung across the counter, the words "Summer Fun —Join a Sports Club!" emblazoned in block letters. I breathed in the strong smell of fresh paint. They really had renovated this place during my long absence.

A girl sitting at the counter looked up and waved. "Hey, Liz. Didn't know you were dropping by today. Who's your friend?"

Liz nudged me in the shoulder. "This is Serendipity."

"Serena," I immediately corrected.

Liz rolled her eyes. "Yeah, yeah. I heard you clear as air, Sere," she said, putting extra emphasis on my nickname by making it rhyme. "Anyway. Sere, this is my sister, Ellie."

I lifted a hand shyly in greeting. "Hi."

I'd never met Liz's sister before since she went to a different school than us. She looked a lot like Liz, with her thin, pointed nose, rosy, freckled cheeks, and brown hair pulled back into a high ponytail.

"Hi, nice to meet you." Ellie stuck her hand out and I shook it. "Feel free to look around, but some areas are off-limits without a pass."

"Sere's a club member too," Liz interrupted. "But she'll need a new pass. She bought a two-year membership last year. You can check the system."

Ellie's mouth made a wide O shape, her large eyes somehow looking bigger as she stared at me. "Sorry, I've never seen you around before."

Liz frowned, and I didn't miss her sideways glance at me. "I told you before. She took a one-year break."

"Oh, why?"

My lungs constricted, choking on the reply I'd prepared over a month ago in case anyone asked this exact question. "I—I, uh—"

Liz let out an exasperated breath and shot Ellie a pointed look. "You never listen, Eleanor." She wound an arm around my waist and guided me away from her sister. "Come on, Sere. Let's go."

"But..." I shook my head and cleared my throat. "Don't I need a new pass?"

"We can do that later. Let's just use mine to get in."

Leaving no room for arguments, she steered me through the left corridor. I marvelled again at the changes. The last time I was here, yellowing wallpaper had peeled off the edges of the dingy wall, and everything, from the outdated carpet to the dusty corners, had been more than a little run down. Now the freshly painted walls depicted stylish murals of tennis players I knew by name.

As we passed a realistically drawn Steffi Graff and Andre Agassi, I whirled toward Liz. "Please don't tell me this is what you meant when you said I'd see someone famous."

"Yeah, sure." Liz waved at a painted rendition of Roger Federer in front of her. "Sere, meet the one and only Swiss maestro."

I made a *pfft* noise which she returned with a cheeky smile as we moved on.

At the end of the hallway, we reached a door that required membership access. She withdrew a pass from inside her backpack and swiped it through the card machine. The faint sound of a click emanated, and she pushed the door open.

"Woah," I said at the sight I beheld.

Four—yes, *four*—tennis courts were set up side by side in one long line. There used to be only two! Distinct, white lines of paint marked the blue-floored hard courts. Three of them were occupied by people of various ages.

In the court closest to us, an older couple hit the ball over the net to each other with soft strokes. The next one down had four middle-aged adults. My eyes darted after the ball as they rallied in quick succession. The last one, at the far end, had a man feeding balls to a young guy who returned them with impressive drop shots.

"Cool, hey?" Liz said, beaming at my reaction.

"Liz..." My breath hitched.

In my depressed state these last few weeks, I'd refused to go anywhere outside. I'd been content with wasting the school holidays away in the confines of my home and my family's bakery. Or, as Liz had said—moping. She hadn't wanted that for me and had done everything possible to convince me to do otherwise. I'd all but spat in her face for it.

My eyes watered, and I turned, tugging on her shirt sleeve. "I'm sorry I was mean to you."

Liz's lips pursed as she blinked several times. Rubbing her eyes with the heel of her hand, she mumbled, "Silly, you weren't mean. I just feel bad 'cause I can't help you much." Then she wrapped her arms around me and squeezed me hard as I buried my face in the crook of her shoulder. I was a terrible friend, bagging her out for bringing me here, claiming I was no longer interested in tennis. But that wasn't the truth. I'd just forgotten how much I loved it here.

Now I remembered. The thud of the ball landing on my racket. The non-stop running to reach the ball in time. The laughter despite not always winning...

Liz released me and eyed me carefully. "Do you want to play for a bit?"

A choice. She wouldn't force me if I wasn't up to it. I stared longingly at the one empty court and then at the occupied ones. In the group of four, a lady laughed as she launched a backhand winner into an open area of the court. The other three players clapped approvingly with their rackets.

My heart skipped a beat as I turned to Liz and nodded.

She grinned. "Lucky I booked this court for half an hour."

Geez. How far ahead had she planned this?

"I'll grab us rackets. You wait here."

She returned a few minutes later with two rackets and a canister of tennis balls. I took a racket, letting the familiar weight settle in my hand. This one had a different grip to my own racket, but that was to be expected with mediocre rental equipment.

I experimentally swung the racket, practicing all the strokes. Forehand. Backhand. Forehand volley. Backhand volley. I couldn't believe it'd been a year since I'd played. "I'm going to be really rusty."

"We're not playing in a tournament." She rapped me gently on the head with her racket. "Just have fun."

Have fun. It was the reason I'd decided to go out today. Well, I'd expected something a bit less demanding, but...

I did a once-over of my attire—a slim-fitting tank top, shorts, and some worn-out sneakers. Not exactly tennis-worthy, but at least I wasn't wearing anything impractical like a tight skirt or sandals. "Let's go serious."

Liz raised her eyebrows, hands on her hips. I called it her Judgy Bird stance. "I won't go easy on you just because you're rusty."

"Good." I started my warm-up routine, stretching out my legs. "You can serve first."

"How are we gonna play this? I don't want to sweat too much."

That made both of us. "First to four games wins?"

"Okay."

I jogged to the other side of the court. While she took her time to do quick stretches and get ready to serve, my eyes were drawn to the fast motion of a tennis ball on the court beside us—the one with the middle-aged man and young guy. The man fed balls to the guy who crouched in front of the net, volleying them back over. Not a match. Practicing? Maybe they entered local doubles tournaments together.

"Oi, Sere!" Liz waved frantically, catching my attention. "If I was playing a hundred percent seriously, I would've just hit you with an ace."

Oops. I got into a return stance, legs apart and knees bent.

Liz bounced the ball several times. Then, throwing the ball up, she raised her racket behind her shoulder. As the ball reached the peak of its toss, her racket snapped out. I barely had a chance to blink as it shot over to my side.

I reacted automatically, racket reaching for the ball. With a reverberating twang that shook my arm, it ricocheted off the racket strings in a high arc.

I gasped in horror as the ball flew off-tangent—and struck the young guy on the next court over. Straight in the back of his head.

"Oww!" The guy cupped his head and whipped around, searching for the source of his pain.

"I'm sorry! I'm so sorry!" I had barely played yet and I was already embarrassing myself. "Are you okay?"

His gaze landed on me. "Yeah, I'm fine."

I studied him while he rubbed the back of his head. He looked around my age, but he stood almost a head taller than me, with eyebrows furrowed and full lips pressed together. His thick, dark brown hair curled at the ends. My face burned hot when his curious eyes pinned me with a returning stare.

Oh. My. Gosh. Out of all the people to accidentally hit, it had to be a good-looking guy.

"Aiden!" his older companion shouted.

I jolted backward as the man ran over to our side of the net. He tilted Aiden's head forward, examining where the ball had hit him. "You should watch where you hit the ball, girl."

"I'm sorry." My fingers plucked at my racket strings. Could I shrink into a corner and hide?

Aiden swatted at the man's hand. "Geez, it's not her fault. I'm fine. Stop making such a big deal."

The man huffed, parting masses of Aiden's hair this way and that. "Your head is important. Any damage to your brain—"

"I can still play tennis, even with a couple of lost brain cells," Aiden retorted, shoving the man's hand off his head. "Chill."

The older man grumbled, unable to take no for an answer. "Your mother will be furious."

Aiden scoffed. "You don't know anything about my mum."

"One hit is all it takes to get someone killed."

"You're being an idiot. I'm still standing, aren't I?"

I fidgeted uneasily, still wishing I could disappear from this awkward exchange.

"Fine." The man threw up his hands. "Let's take a break."

"About time." Aiden stalked to the benches on the other side of the court, leaving the man trailing behind.

Liz made her way to me, laughing as she held a hand to her stomach. "Did you really just hit a guy in the head? That in itself is a talent."

"I told you I was rusty." I wanted to simultaneously throttle her and bang my head against a wall. She'd watched the scene unfold and had chosen to stand aside instead of coming to my aid. Though I knew she didn't have to stand up for me, I was used to her being my shield in confrontations. She had no problem back-chatting and offending others. Me? I avoided anything that involved angry people and fights.

She snorted, folding her arms and glancing at the two guys now sitting on a bench by the back wall. "You really are something else."

"Blame it on your serve, *Lizbeth*."

"Oh, we are so not going there, *Serendipity*." Liz's lips pressed together in a thin line.

There was a heartbeat of silence.

"Lizzzz," I said, already giving up on using her proper first name. A bubble of laughter burst out from me.

Liz smiled. "It's been so long since I heard you laugh. But I'll be having the last laugh when I kick your butt and win four games to none."

I punched her lightly on the shoulder. "Watch it. I'll be the one to win."

"We'll see about that."

We proceeded to play it out. Liz continued serving well, though a couple were faults, luckily. She won her game without me hitting another person, thank goodness. Then it was my turn to serve.

I'd never been that great at serving, to be honest. A pins-and-needles sensation spread along my fingertips as I bounced the ball. I swore I could see from the corner of my eye that the guy I'd hit earlier, Aiden, was watching me. I didn't dare look to properly check.

"Did you forget how to serve?" Liz shouted.

All of a sudden, I felt more eyes on me. Great, Liz. Now you've gone and done it. If that guy hadn't been looking at me before, he definitely was now.

I gulped, trying to calm my nerves. One breath. Two. I kept bouncing the ball and gave myself a pep talk. *Remember how you used to do it. You can do it again. Muscle memory and all that.*

Instead, my brain chose to push another memory onto me.

Nice shot, Sere, the familiar voice echoed in my head, followed by the ghost of a hand high-fiving mine.

I froze as a hiccup made its way out of my mouth. The ball I'd just bounced flew past my outstretched arm, missing my palm entirely. I stumbled forward to catch it in mid-air.

Gah. Don't think about the past.

I shook my head. *Focus.* I was serving. Or trying to, very badly.

I chucked the ball up and swung at the highest point of the toss. A resounding off-feeling vibration coursed through my arm as the ball hit part of the racket frame.

The ball flew straight into the net.

I grumbled as I went to collect it. My shorts lacked pockets to hold any extra balls. Why couldn't I get anything right today?

For my next serve, I didn't even bother to bounce the ball. I straight-up flung it high like I knew what I was doing.

Except my racket hit nothing but air. The ball grazed my arm before dribbling to a stop on the ground.

"Double fault!" Liz yelled.

"Bright observation, Liz!"

She grinned, curving her hands around her mouth like a speakerphone. "Love–15!"

"Stop embarrassing me!"

"You're doing a good job of that yourself!"

From the benches behind Liz, Aiden threw his head back and laughed. His older companion wasn't next to him; he stood with a mobile phone pressed against his ear, his attention elsewhere. At least someone was completely unaware of my incompetence. But that meant Aiden was most likely laughing at me.

I slapped my thighs. *Get a hold of yourself, Serena Tsang!* Who cared if he laughed at me? I would show him. I went to pick up the ball again. Maybe the ball hated me, or maybe I hated the ball. Maybe we both hated each other. It didn't matter.

Squeezing the ball tight, I willed it to forget whatever grudge we had against one another. *Let's do this.* Less force, more accuracy. Emotions could make or break you. In my case, frustration was breaking me. I needed to be calm.

I relaxed my shoulders and straightened my arm, palm facing up. When I tossed the ball, I imagined it to be like a rising ocean wave. Calm. Smooth. This time when I hit the ball, it sailed over the net and into the service box. By sailed, I meant it was slow. Horribly slow. But I'd done it! A proper serve.

That was where my positivity ended. While I was distracted by my small success, Liz returned the ball with a forehand that blitzed past my left side.

"Love–30," she announced in a sing-song voice full of glee.

She broke my game fairly quickly after that. I tried to be more aggressive on her serve, but she held easily at 40–15.

Miraculously, I managed to hold serve in my other games, but that was my only victory. Being down a break, Liz eventually took the win.

"Nice game," she said, high-fiving me.

We went to cool off by the benches on my side of the court. Good thing it was further away from the bossy man and Aiden who were both still at the benches on the opposite end of the court. As cute as Aiden was, I'd already made the world's worst first impression on him.

Liz repeatedly tugged on her shirt collar, airing herself. "I'm going to the bathroom," she declared. "I need a cool shower. Plus I have to check on something."

A shower sounded glorious, but I hadn't brought any spare clothes or bathing essentials. Guess I'd live without one until I got home.

As Liz left, my attention drew to someone walking my way. Oh my gosh. It was Aiden.

Relax, Serena. Maybe he was going to the bathroom too. Not like he would come and talk to me after I hit him in the head.

I averted my gaze, fumbling through my backpack for my drink bottle. Finding it, I took a gulp of water—and nearly spat it out.

Aiden had covered the distance from his end of the other court to the end of mine in a matter of seconds. His eyes locked onto me, dashing all my hopes of avoiding him.

CHAPTER 2

"Hey." Aiden waved at me with his drink bottle. "Do you always hit people in the head with a ball, or am I just the unlucky one?"

"I, uh," I stuttered, clutching tightly onto my own drink bottle like it was my only lifeline. With Liz gone, it kind of was. He spoke in a light manner, so I was pretty sure he wasn't going to sue me or anything dramatic, but... I had no idea what to say. Did he want me to apologise? Beg for forgiveness? Get even and let him hit me in the head?

He pushed back his tousled, damp fringe, his lips quirking into a lopsided smile. "Guess I'm the unlucky one, then."

Nerves stirred in my stomach when he dropped onto the bench beside me, bathed in a strong fragrance of deodorant with an underlying hint of sweat. I hoped he wasn't planning on staying awhile to make idle conversation, because I was *really* bad at that. And I didn't want to embarrass myself any more than I already had today.

"Aiden!" his older companion shouted from across the court.

"Can't ever relax, can I?" He groaned and tilted his head forward to massage his neck. When the man called out again, Aiden yelled back, "Chill, I'm taking a break!"

"Didn't you take one?" I asked.

"Yeah, because he thought I'd injured my head."

I winced. "Sorry about that."

He waved it off. "It barely hurt. Don't worry about it." I opened my mouth to protest, but then he added, "You know what hurts though? Watching you try to serve. No offence."

Surely I wasn't *that* bad. "I'd like to see you do better." As soon as the words tumbled out of my mouth, I wanted to face-palm myself. Geez. Why did I say that? There was no doubt he could serve better than me. From the way he'd practiced earlier, it seemed like he played tennis a lot. He might've even been better than Liz.

He smirked and extended his hand. "You want a demonstration, then you've got a demonstration." Confidence radiated in his every word. "Lend me your racket."

I reluctantly handed it over. When he blinked at me, still waiting, I belatedly realised my stupidity and passed him two tennis balls. My skin tingled at the contact of his warm fingertips brushing against mine.

He pocketed one of the balls and rolled the other against his shorts as he walked to the baseline of the court I'd been using. I followed him, keen to see just how good he was.

"You should get some new balls. These are so fuzzed up."

"They're not mine. We're renting."

"Oh." His nose crinkled. "Guess they'll do since we're not playing."

His right foot slid closer to the white paint of the baseline in a sideways stance, the racket gripped in his left hand.

"Leftie?" I asked.

"Yep. *Quiet, please. Player is ready to serve,*" he said in a voice that mimicked a standard chair umpire.

A giggle escaped from my lips at the accuracy of his imitation, and he smiled in response.

Without further ado, he tossed the ball in the air and swung the racket like a whip. The ball hit smack-bang in the middle of the strings and whizzed over the net in a blur of yellow-green, then barely clipped the white line marking the middle of the tennis court. An ace down the T.

"Wow." Just wow. That was the only word that would come out of my mouth.

He turned to face me again, grinning at my wide-mouthed gape.

"You're *good*." No, not good. He was great. Brilliant. Unless that was a fluke. "Do that again!"

Aiden raised his eyebrows, but he plucked the other ball from his shorts pocket and repeated the manoeuvre. This time, the ball curved into the left corner of the service box.

I clapped my hands. "You're like a pro!"

He wiped his forehead with his wristband. "I'm not that good. Tennis for pros is a whole other world. It's a life commitment until you retire."

"But a life playing tennis professionally seems like a great job." Travelling the world, seeing the sights, playing in front of crowds. Plus being paid to do all that. It was as nice as I imagined life could be.

His jaw tightened as he handed me the racket. Then he crossed to the other side of the court and collected the balls.

I went to sit on the bench by the wall, wondering if I'd somehow offended him. Was he jealous of professional tennis players or something?

When he came back, he dropped the balls into the open canister. "Most tennis players don't choose that life," he said suddenly. It took me a moment to realise he was continuing the conversation from before. "Who chooses to start playing tennis when they're only three or four years old?"

I considered his argument. "True. But people aren't three or four years old when they're playing in Grand Slams. By then, I'm pretty sure they should know whether they like tennis or not."

"You reckon? How about the players who smash their rackets?"

My face scrunched in distaste. "People shouldn't do that. A racket is meant to be your partner in tennis. It'd be like kicking your friend in the head. Not to mention how much a racket costs."

I'd worked my butt off a few years ago, doing house chores and odd jobs for neighbours, eventually accumulating enough money to buy a racket. The mere thought of destroying such a valuable possession didn't sit well with me. "I mean, tennis players get sponsored, but normal people pay a lot for one."

"I never thought of it that way." Aiden folded his arms, gnawing on his bottom lip. "So you think all pros play tennis because they like it?"

"Or they do it for the money." Who knew?

"How do you know if you actually like something if you've been doing it for so long? It just becomes a part of your life."

That was a good point, but it was also a question I could answer with utmost confidence. "Try living without it. If you feel like you can't, and keep thinking about it even when you're not doing it, that probably means you really do like it." I'd learned that the hard way after I'd stopped baking a few months ago.

Aiden drummed his fingers along the edge of the wooden bench. He made a humming noise that sounded like approval. "Where did you learn such good advice from?"

"My dad."

Oh, crap. I hadn't meant to say that. I mean, it was true in a loose, indirect way. Plus it sounded too obnoxious to say I learned it myself. But I hadn't meant to mention Dad.

Aiden chuckled, oblivious to my mistake. "Your dad sounds wise. I'd love to meet him."

"I..." My throat locked up, refusing to let me speak. I took a big swig from my drink bottle and swallowed, then grit my teeth together, trying to suppress my rising desire to curl up and cry. Breathe in. Breathe out. It wouldn't do me any good to drown in a flood of tears. Knocking a fist to my chest, I mumbled, "He passed away this year."

"Oh God, I'm so sorry." Aiden clamped a hand over his mouth. His other hand rubbed the back of his head in the same spot I'd hit him in earlier.

"Are you sure you're okay?" Changing topics was usually a tactic I employed to deflect someone's sympathetic intentions, but in this case, I also hoped I hadn't bruised his head.

"What?"

I pointed to his hand still touching his head.

He dropped both his hands into his lap and looked at them in surprise as though they were separate entities with their own brains. "Oh, yeah. I'm fine. I should be the one who's sorry. That was so insensitive of me."

"It's okay..." I couldn't fault him for not knowing. "I'm the one who mentioned him first."

Aiden's body slumped against the wall, head bowed. After a prolonged period of awkward silence, his head snapped up, startling me. He straightened and scratched his nose, giving me a sidelong glance. "Do you want to tell me about him? If you feel you can, that is. I know talking can help sometimes. If not, I'll just apologise a hundred more times like an idiot."

Tell him about Dad? "My dad..."

He nodded at me in encouragement. I didn't think he was prying—not really. My school counsellor *had* actually told me to share my sorrows when I felt I could. I'd never really tried to though. I didn't want anyone to pity me or act awkwardly around me. But Aiden... There was something about him. It might've been the fact that he was a stranger, or that it was the first time in ages that I'd been out instead of moping at home. Whatever it was, I found that I did want to share something about Dad with him.

I gulped, looking away from him and focusing on the empty tennis court.

In what felt like a lifetime ago, Dad and I had come here on weekends for social club tennis. We'd mainly used the free-with-membership synthetic grass courts outside. Though during the hotter days, we'd booked the expensive indoor court. We'd been the father-daughter duo that everyone knew. Then we'd stopped coming.

I inhaled deeply, working on steadying my breathing. My chest throbbed painfully. Rather than ignoring it, I acknowledged it. Yes, it hurt. Yes, it wasn't fair he wasn't here. It wouldn't be the same anymore without him. It would never be. But if I wanted to honour Dad—to remember him with a smile, rather than with tears—I could share one piece of his life with someone.

"My dad's the reason why I like tennis a lot. Even though I'm not that good at it. He was the biggest tennis fan. We used to go see the Australian Open every year."

We'd stopped that tradition after his health had deteriorated. This year, we'd watched it from a crappy TV in a cramped hospital room. A sharp pain in my ribs surfaced at the memory. I fumbled for words I could use without my heart breaking into pieces. "But I don't think I'd want to go anymore. It'd just make me sad without him there."

Oh no. I'd blabbered without realising it. I'd never told anyone this. Ever. Not even Liz. Way to go, Serena. Not like a stranger would be interested in my life's woes. He probably only asked to be polite, and now I'd overshared.

But Aiden nodded solemnly, placing a hand on my shoulder, his grip gentle and warm. "I can understand why he loved it so much. It's a really great atmosphere. I hope one day you'll want to go back."

I shuddered and let out a breath, releasing all the tension I'd held in. "Maybe."

I was about to ask if he'd been there too, when he said, "You know, I don't even know your name yet."

I paused at the sudden change in topic. "Uh, Serena."

"Woah. Like Serena Williams?"

"Something like that." He didn't need to know my real name was unnecessarily longer and dumber.

"I'm Aiden."

"I know. Your friend kept saying it."

Aiden glared at the man. He was on his phone again. "He's not my friend. He's my dad."

"Oh..." I hadn't drawn the comparison between them. Aiden's tousled hair and angular nose mirrored nothing on his buzz-cut-haired, pudgy-nosed father. "He seems to care about you a lot."

"Not really," he said in a tone that warned me not to discuss this any further.

Oh-kay, I wouldn't step on that landmine then.

Luckily, Liz came back at that moment. Her damp hair frizzled in a voluminous heap around her face. She wore a different top than the one she'd played in, and some exercise shorts.

Dumping a large plastic box near my feet, she collapsed onto the bench. "Ahhh." She stretched her arms out, her joints cracking. "Fun Day is going ahead."

So that was what she'd been checking on. Fun Day happened every weekend. Club members brought in their children, and the centre let them play for free. Liz regularly joined in, teaching kids how to hit tennis balls with small rackets over mini nets. I'd watched a few times last year, but my lack of confidence and excuse of playing with Dad had meant I'd never joined in.

Liz eyed Aiden. "Hey. Is this the same guy you knocked out with a ball?"

"I did *not* knock him out."

"Well, it did really hurt." Aiden laughed at my concerned expression. "Joking." He turned to Liz. "I'm Aiden."

"I'm Liz." She gave me an odd look—bugged out eyes and flared nostrils—while Aiden had his back to us, sipping from his drink bottle. What was she trying to tell me? Did she have a problem with him? But her face relaxed when Aiden faced us again, and she said, "I'm starving. Didn't you promise me egg tarts, Sere?"

"Oh, right." I rummaged through my bag and dug out a plastic container. "Here."

Liz cracked the lid open. The yellow tops of the tarts glistened, just waiting to be devoured, encircled by flaky, golden crust. She pushed her nose up close and breathed in deeply. "Ahhh, my one true love."

I snickered, snatching the box away from her. "They aren't *all* for you." I turned to Aiden. "Want to try one?"

He hesitated, his eyes shifting to where his dad was still preoccupied with a phone call before landing back on me. "Okay." He shuffled closer to me. The movement jostled my arm as I scooped a tart out from the box and handed it to him.

I observed him from the corner of my eye as he took two quick bites, chewed, then shoved the rest in his mouth in one go. "Tchs owd."

I bit the inside of my cheek to stop myself from laughing. "What?"

Aiden chewed the rest with his mouth closed and swallowed. "It's good. Where did you buy these?"

"Sere made them. Her family owns a Chinese bakery." Liz butted in before I could reply, grabbing a tart from the container. Unlike Aiden, she savoured every bite and licked the remaining crumbs off her fingers.

"Wow, you made them? That's so cool." Aiden's "wow" was similar to mine when I'd seen him hit an ace. Which was ridiculous, because anyone could make an egg tart if they took the time to learn how. Not everyone could hit an ace.

"It's not that hard," I said.

Liz made a grab for another tart. "She says that, but it's not true. Trust me, I've tried."

She'd only tried once, so that hardly counted. "With enough practice and persistence, anyone can do it."

"It's not that simple." Aiden frowned, and a crease formed between his eyebrows. "It takes skill and dedication in whatever you do."

"I guess so." Why was he so fired up?

His frown deepened. He scooted closer to me until we sat shoulder to shoulder. Raising his index finger, he gently poked my cheek. "Give yourself some credit, Serena."

I held his gaze, suddenly hyper-aware of the lack of space between us, of his casual touch that made my insides flutter. Up close, I noticed his eyes were hazel with specks of forest green. A little mole marked his skin next to the bridge of his nose.

"If you two lovebirds are done chatting," Liz interrupted, "do you want to participate in Fun Day?"

A wave of embarrassment washed over me as I turned to her. "I don't know." I'd never tried teaching kids tennis before.

"Come on, it'll be fun," Liz insisted, pulling on my arm. "Hey, Aiden. You'll join, right?"

Aiden's eyes flitted to the other end of the courts, where his dad was, then back to us. "Wait a sec." He dashed off to his dad, and I watched as he said something and pointed in our direction. After their short exchange, his dad went back to talking on the phone and Aiden returned.

"I guess I don't mind joining in." He shrugged. "But only if Serena joins in too."

"Me?" I felt my cheeks flush as I regarded his expectant smile. "Okay," I agreed before I thought too much about it.

"Yay!" Liz practically leaped on top of me and choked me in a tight embrace. "They should be here soon." She glanced at her watch and, as though her words had been a cue, the door of the room burst open.

A bunch of children rushed inside like a tidal wave. Like a literal natural disaster—pushing and shoving each other, screaming excitedly.

Oh boy. What had I gotten myself into?

CHAPTER 3

A middle-aged lady walked ahead of the children. I recognised her as one of the coaches who often held practice sessions in the club. "Follow me, please!" she yelled out over the boisterous kids. She led them to the court Liz and I had played on. The centre must've reserved it for Fun Day. "One line here!" She gestured with her arm in a wide arc.

The children assembled into a crooked line of sorts. Some of the kids looked as young as five, while others could have passed as ten or eleven.

Liz leaped up from the bench and went straight to the coach. The lady's thin lips curved into a smile as she saw my friend, and they started chatting.

"Get that for me, will you, Sere?" Liz's loud voice echoed as she turned to point at the plastic box she'd set down earlier near my feet.

I hefted it up, and my arms strained as I pulled. It was a lot heavier than it looked.

Seeing me struggle, Aiden hopped off the bench and grabbed it.

"Thanks." I sighed and rubbed my sore arms.

"No problem." He lifted the box with relative ease, the muscles in his arms bunching up. We walked to Liz and the coach, and he set the box down. "What's in here?"

"Kids' rackets," Liz said. "The centre obviously isn't loaning out real ones to the kids."

"Fair enough." He pried open the lid, took out a little racket, and waved it at the line of children. "Who wants to play tennis?"

The room filled with the screams of eager children. The coach glowered at Aiden in disapproval.

"Okay, everyone. I'll need you to split off into four teams." She directed each child in the line to Liz, Aiden, me and then her. By the time she finished, we each had four children. "You know what to do." The coach ruffled Liz's hair, making her messy curls even more dishevelled than before. "I'm leaving you in charge, Liz."

"Yes, Coach Ava." Liz saluted her. "Sere, let's do it. Practice racket handling, then one at a time with the ball."

She rattled off some more detailed instructions to Aiden while I huddled my group together. Okay, I could do this. Kids couldn't be that hard to teach, right? I'd seen Liz do it plenty of times.

"Hi, everyone. I'm Serena, and I'll be teaching you some tennis today."

The four kids cheered—one girl and three boys. The girl looked the youngest, around five or six years old. She clung to an older boy who she called Kyle. Siblings? The remaining two boys appeared to be around the same age as Kyle.

I gave each child a small racket. Grabbing one for myself, I instructed the kids on the basics of swinging the racket and how to hit a ball. We did this all without the tennis balls. A swarm of kids running everywhere, armed with tennis balls, was a huge no-no.

"Like this?" The little girl's racket whooshed over her head, and her double ponytails swished along with the movement.

"That's too high, Mia," Kyle said. "Like this." He perfectly copied the same stroke I'd demonstrated to them.

Mia squinted, concentrating hard as she tried to mirror Kyle's movements. After about five tries, her form improved.

"Yep, like that," I said. The other two boys watched us, then also correctly replicated the swings. Satisfied, I let them practice by themselves for a minute, ensuring they were all far enough apart to avoid whacking each other.

With a moment to myself, I snuck a glance at Aiden. He stood in front of his group of children, confidently showcasing a proper forehand with the kids' racket. Kind of hilarious. The small thing looked like a toy in his hand, and was made even more ridiculous with the addition of a mini net. But the children watched, mesmerised, as he hit a tennis ball over the mini net.

Kyle tugged my arm. "Coach, can I do that?"

All the children in my group stared longingly at Aiden and his display. I contemplated ignoring him and going about my own routine, but the kids would probably still get distracted by him.

Sighing, I approached Aiden and tapped him on the shoulder.

"Hey." His eyes glinted. "Want to be my guinea pig?"

My mind conjured up the image of the small squeaking pet. "What kind of experiment are you thinking of?"

"Help me demonstrate." He smiled, unfiltered happiness visible on his face. It was such a contrast to the look he gave his dad. My eyes swept to the other side of the room where his dad still held a phone close to his ear, his mouth moving rapidly.

Aiden elbowed me. "So will you help?"

I turned my attention back to him. "Uh, yeah. Sure. My kids are getting bored anyway." I called my group over. Mia reached us first, ponytails flying like little wings on her head, the boys following close behind.

"Are we going to play for real now?" one of the boys asked, eyeing Aiden bouncing a ball in his hand.

Aiden shook his head. "Demo first. Stand on the other end of the net," he said to me, pointing with his racket.

I power walked there. *Please don't tell me what I think he's planning is true.*

"Okay, good." He raised his hand with the tennis ball, signalling his intention to start. Oh, heck no. He really did plan to play a game with me. With kids' rackets and a mini net.

"Are you sure—" I started, but never got to finish, as he dropped the ball and hit it. It sailed over the net. Yep, sailed over like my not-so-brilliant serves from before, except purposely slow as opposed to accidentally slow.

The ball made contact with my small racket's strings, the weight light on my wrist. We were using those squishy, beginner, red-yellow tennis balls. I redirected the ball back over the net toward him. He returned it with a perfect forehand that glided it back to me.

The children gasped, looking on in awe. As if they were watching a Federer vs. Nadal match instead of two teens playing with kids' equipment. We continued for several more hits. Aiden ended it by dribbling my last slow return with his racket, flawlessly catching the ball in his other hand.

"Show off," I muttered, but smiled. It was hard not to be impressed when he did it like that. So effortlessly.

The children clapped, and I joined in on the applause.

Aiden stared at us in disbelief, as though he didn't think his display warranted such a reaction. Then his lips stretched into a wide smile. "Okay, who wants to play?"

"Me, me!" all the children screamed out.

"Form a line, please. And no pushing! Everyone will get a turn."

Surprisingly, the children listened. Within ten seconds, we had nine children filed in a single, neat line that would have impressed kindergarten teachers.

Then, one by one, they took turns with Aiden, learning how to drop the ball and hit it over the net. He was a natural with the children, guiding them step by step on the correct grip and stance, never getting irritated by their mistakes. Praise came easily from him. "Good work," "nice one," "awesome shot" and so on. Was he secretly a tennis coach?

He only had some difficulty when it was Mia's turn. After the third ball she tried to hit to me thumped into the net, she stomped her feet. "I can't do it!" she howled in frustration. "It's too hard!" She threw her racket, making it clatter onto the floor.

Aiden picked it up. "Try again." Crouching to her eye level, he handed her back the racket. "And don't throw your racket again. The racket is your friend. You don't hurt your friends, do you?"

"No," Mia said sulkily.

I stifled a laugh at his reuse of my "rackets are friends" reasoning.

"That's right. You have a good swing, but you need to change it so that your racket faces up more. Like this." He tilted the racket in her hand to a forty-five degree angle. "Try this and you'll get it right over the net."

"Really?"

"Yep. Don't move from that position. I'll feed you the ball, okay?"

Mia's face scrunched. "But I don't want to eat the ball."

He laughed. "What I mean is, I'll drop the ball and you hit it."

He did just that, and this time when Mia hit the ball, it soared over the net to me, straight for my chest. I caught it cleanly in my hand.

"I did it! I did it!" Mia cheered. Aiden held his hand up and she high-fived him.

Coach Ava passed by, giving us both a nod of approval. "Good job."

He was doing such a good job, it wasn't long before Liz dumped her group on us too. "Thanks!" she said and dashed off.

I was mulling over Liz's disappearance when Coach Ava told me to take a break, replacing me as "guinea pig" on the other side of the net. I rested on the bench, back leaning against the wall, and took large sips from my drink bottle.

"Sere!" I heard Liz say before I saw her. "Look what the sports centre got." A baby blue plastic camera sat in her outstretched hands.

"Nice." As long as she didn't use it to take photos of me.

Fortunately, she bounded off and snapped photos of the children instead. The parents had apparently given her permission on the basis that each kid would keep their respective photos.

I resumed my post as "guinea pig." Soon after, parents started filtering in to collect their children.

Mia and Kyle's mother was the last to arrive. She thanked Aiden profusely once Mia chattered about how much fun she'd had. Aiden brushed off her thanks, rubbing the back of his head awkwardly like he didn't know what to do. At least, I hoped that was why he rubbed his head. I still wasn't sure if he'd lied about it not hurting.

"Bye, bye, Coach!" Mia said before she ran off after her brother and mum.

"Bye!" Aiden waved at her until they disappeared behind the door, then blew out a breath. "That was actually a lot of fun. Good job."

"You too."

Liz ran up to us at that moment, lifting up the camera. "Obligatory Fun Day photo!"

Oh, no, she didn't dare! Heartbeat racing, I prepared to smile just as she snapped the photo.

Once the photo finally finished printing, she handed it to me with a huge smile plastered on her face, oblivious to my personal torment. I groaned, flapping the film up and down. I was going to look dumb in this photo, wasn't I? When the image cleared, I was proven to be correct. My face was in a strange, off-guard, half smile.

Aiden leaned over my shoulder to peek. "Haha, you look so out of it," he said, his breath tickling my neck. My face grew hot. Easy for him to say. He grinned easily in the photo like he'd been born ready for the shot.

I dangled the photo in front of Liz, but she only laughed. I growled at her. "I want a better one, Liz!"

"No can do," she said. "One photo each. But Aiden can get a nice one with you."

"Wait, no—"

"One, two"—I smiled, giving a peace sign—"three!"

This time, I felt a bit more confident that I looked less awkward. But before I could peek, Aiden grabbed the still-blank film and fanned it in the air. He gave a satisfied smirk at the cleared image, then shoved it into his shorts pocket like a lollipop he wasn't going to share.

I gawked helplessly at him, my eyes darting between his face and his pocket. "Let me see!"

"*Nope*," he said, making a pop on the p for emphasis.

"I'll swap you for it." I held out my own failed instant photo.

"Why would I swap mine when it's better than yours?" he asked, as though we were trading Tazos in chip packets. I would have laughed if the question didn't irk me so much.

No amount of pleading changed his mind. If anything, I think he had fun watching me get riled up.

Just when I was thinking of resorting to tackling him, his dad marched toward us. During our play session with the kids, he'd disappeared somewhere. But now that he was back, I had the sensibility to not draw his attention. By the grim, serious expression on his face, he looked half a second away from chewing someone out.

"Aiden! Time to go!" he called out.

Aiden groaned, but stood up from the bench and shrugged at me. "Well, that's my cue." He pulled out the photo of us from his pocket. Pressed between his thumb and index finger, he waved it like a tantalising prize I'd never have a chance at winning. "See you later!"

"See you," I said. "You're showing me that photo next time!"

"Sure," he agreed, laughing. I watched as he retreated with his dad out the door.

Next time. When would that be? Tomorrow? Next week? I should have asked for his number, but that felt a bit too much like I was asking him out.

Oh well.

If only I'd known how far off next time would be.

CHAPTER 4

TWO YEARS LATER
(18 YEARS OLD)

A blast of hot air warmed my face as I opened the oven, releasing a great puff of steam. The smell of freshly baked buns permeated the air. My stomach gurgled as I inhaled the scent and withdrew the tray of pineapple buns to examine them. Crispy, golden-brown crust gleamed under the kitchen lights, each bun flawlessly round and plump.

Mmm, perfection.

I switched off the oven and used my arm to wipe away the beads of sweat forming on my forehead.

While waiting for the buns to cool on a rack, I washed the remaining dishes from this morning's baking. A lot had piled up, thanks to my experimentation on a perfect strawberry-chocolate custard tart. I grimaced at the stack of bowls and spoons coated with layers of chocolate and custard. So far, all my tries had resulted in a tart with too much chocolatey taste overwhelming the strawberry and custard flavours. I'd made a bet with my brother that I could get it right within a week. Good thing I had four more days to prove him wrong.

I was drying the last of the washed utensils when the soft tinkle of bells from behind the kitchen door alerted me to a customer entering our shop. I glanced at the clock on the wall. 9:00 a.m. on the dot.

Mum greeted the customer before it became a conversation in rapid-fire Cantonese. Something about how long it's been and asking what each other's children had been up to. Mum's favourite topic. Normally, I had to ask her to repeat herself if she said anything when the kitchen door was closed, so they must've been talking pretty loudly for me to hear so well.

After washing and drying my hands, I checked on the pineapple buns, raising a hand over them and meeting lukewarm air. Good. Pulling on some disposable gloves, I transferred the buns onto a plastic tray and treaded to the kitchen door connected to the storefront. I pushed it open with my shoulder and swept past Mum and the customer —one of our regulars, Mrs Wong—while they gossiped.

"Max graduated this year, top of his class," Mum said proudly. Mrs Wong *oohed* and *ahhed* as Mum flicked through photos on her phone.

I snickered quietly to myself. My older brother, Max, *had* graduated top of his IT course, but he'd repeated a year due to failing several classes. Mrs Wong obviously didn't know that. The only gossip Mum ever left out was stuff that reflected badly on her. Otherwise her mouth's boundaries knew no limits.

I lifted open the door of a windowed case with the label "pineapple buns" and inserted the plastic tray inside, then straightened the buns into neat lines with a pair of tongs.

"Sere, there you are," Mum said. "Do you remember Aunty's son, Ben? She tells me he's looking for someone to help out at a tutoring school."

"Good morning, Aunty." Mrs Wong wasn't my real aunty, but that was what we called Mum's close friends in Cantonese. "Tutoring school?"

Mum's statement sounded harmless enough—get a new job and befriend a guy—but what she really meant was something like, *Hey Sere, you should take this job and befriend this fine young man and get together with him.* "Too bad I already have a tutoring job."

The day Mum stopped plotting to hook me up with one of her friend's sons would be the day I got married to one of them. And that was so not happening. What if I dated one of them and we broke up? The last thing I wanted was for Mum to blame me for one of her favourite customers dissing our shop because of a failed relationship with their son.

I hurried back to the kitchen before Mum could tell me more about what a great guy Mrs Wong's son was. Sighing, I placed the tongs on the kitchen bench and folded my arms.

What else could I do to avoid the two gossiping mums? I surveyed the room for any other task to perform. Eyeing the one oven still turned on, I peered through the window. Egg tarts occupied every inch of the tray, their middles still glistening in liquid form. Other than these, everything else we'd started baking this morning was done. My cousin Lee would also be coming soon to do some more baking.

I yawned, removed my gloves, and threw them in the bin. "I'm going out," I announced to nobody in particular as I climbed up the stairs to the second level where we lived. Slipping off my thongs at the top of the stairwell, I walked barefoot toward my room.

"Hey. Dippy," my brother called as I passed by his bedroom.

I backtracked to him, surprised to find the door open. It'd been closed when I'd gotten up this morning. "You're awake." How was he not sleeping? Or had he not slept at all? That was the more probable answer. Max was the worst night owl who ever walked the earth. Sometimes I went to the toilet at 4:00 a.m. and he'd be up. "Mum's gossiping about you again."

"Yeah, you know she loves me." He sat at his messy computer desk, mashing keys on his keyboard. His eyes stayed glued to the computer monitor, as they often did when we spoke. I envied his multi-tasking abilities. "Are you going shopping? Bring back some of that Greek yoghurt that's still on special this week."

That was why he'd called me? "Anything else, Your Majesty?"

"That's Gor Gor to you." Ever the stickler for being called an older brother in Cantonese.

"I'll call you that when you start acting like one."

His black-framed glasses caught the light as he spun around in his chair to scrutinise me. "Hah. Guess you don't want me to pick you up from the train station anymore."

Oh crap. Walking home alone late at night did not sound the least bit appealing to me, especially during summer. "Sorry, Gor Gor." I clasped my hands together to implore him.

He nodded in approval. "That's more like it, Dippy."

I rolled my eyes, making my way to the edge of his unmade bed. The mattress dipped as I lowered my weight on it, and something uncomfortable poked my bottom. I jumped up to find a pair of rolled-up socks I'd accidentally squashed. "Gross." I dangled them in the air.

"Those are clean."

"Better be."

"What a Dippy," he said as he turned his attention back to his computer screen again.

I'd long since stopped bothering to ask what preoccupied him for all hours of the day on his computer. He always came up with vague explanations that made no sense like, "I'm envisioning this app that'll cut the cost of groceries every week if I tweak the code to *blah blah*." Blah

blah being the part where the rest of his words went through one ear and out the other. Then, when he saw my clueless face, he'd say, "Don't ask if you don't care, Dippy."

Funny how I had to call him Gor Gor, but he got to call me a silly nickname like Dippy. Where was the fairness in that? Not to mention... "How come Mum doesn't try to throw you into a relationship?"

He shrugged half-heartedly, tapping away on his keyboard. "Who'd she try to set you up with this time?"

I tossed up the pair of rolled-up socks and caught them. "Ben or something. Mrs Wong's son."

"Pah. Don't think you'd like that guy. Saw him with her last week. Kind of screams posh."

"Nice to know." I'd never seen the guy and wondered how someone could possibly scream posh. Rich clothing? Condescending speech? I was happy not knowing, but I was willing to bet I'd see him soon if Mrs Wong and Mum had anything to do about it. "I'll need you to cover for me for Mum's lunch break today. I'm busy."

"Sure, *busy*. You don't start uni for another three months. What could you be busy with? You just want to avoid Aunty's son. Don't blame you."

I hurled the socks at his head, but he ducked and laughed. "Don't forget my yoghurt, Dippy."

Pushing my trolley down the fresh produce aisle, I glanced at my phone, marking off the pork mince on Mum's shopping list. Next was sugar. Ten one-kilogram bags of them. Normally we got it shipped to our shop directly from our supplier, but they'd upped the price this month, and Mum said with the specials at supermarkets this week, it was cheaper to buy in-store.

But... Crap. I'd totally forgotten. Without Max's car, I wasn't capable of bringing ten bags, plus all the other groceries, home by myself—even with the help of Mum's pulley shopping trolley bag, currently tucked safely beneath the supermarket trolley. I used to bring the supermarket trolleys home until they installed those annoying slots where you had to insert a dollar coin to use them. The last time I'd taken one home, someone had nabbed it after I'd left it out front. Probably someone who had wanted to make a quick, free buck. I guess I couldn't really blame them. Mum would've done the same thing.

The best I could do now was get three bags of sugar and ask Max to pick up the rest on another day this week after he finished work. Should be able to carry that much on my own. With that settled, I steered the trolley in the direction of the baking aisle.

I was strolling through the newspapers and magazines section when my eyes caught on a flash of something familiar. I stopped short, my gaze snapping to a magazine.

No way.

I plucked the magazine off the shelf and examined the front cover.

The huge title read, "Exclusive Interview with Teen Tennis Sensation, Aiden Andale" accompanied by a photo of Aiden that took up half the cover's space. He wore full tennis gear, complete with a racket in hand, posing as though in the middle of hitting a backhand. A cool, one-handed backhand. He had a smile on his face that wouldn't have existed in a real tennis match.

My heart skipped a beat, and I thought of the last time I saw that smile in person. Two years ago. Had it really been that long already?

My mind went back to that day, moments after he'd abruptly said goodbye. Liz had squeezed my shoulder hard and whispered loudly, "Don't you know who he is?"

"No? Why would I?" Did he go to our school or something?

"He won the Junior Boys' Australian Open this year!"

My jaw dropped. "No way."

"Yes way. Told you you'd see a famous tennis player, Sere!"

I shook my head at the memory, bending the flimsy magazine in my hands. Had he expected me to recognise him back then? Maybe it was better that I hadn't. Though, why did it matter? Not like I was ever seeing him again.

But that didn't mean I wasn't interested in reading about him. Aiden was known as a notoriously private person. He had no social media accounts and usually never gave personal interviews, so this would be my only chance to know more about him outside of his tennis career.

I traced a finger over the magazine cover. Plastic sealed the entire magazine along with the free drink bottle it came with. I contemplated throwing it back on the shelf and walking away. I considered it for a few seconds.

Yeah, right. Who was I fooling? I'd regret it for the rest of the day if I didn't buy it.

Sighing in defeat, I chucked the magazine on top of my pile of groceries. It was worth it. The magazine came with a drink bottle that normally retailed for eight dollars. My inner frugal approved. But my traitorous heart knew the real reason why I was conning myself into buying something I would usually never take a second glance at—I was a big snoop who wanted to know more about Aiden Andale.

I tried to ignore this fact as I continued gathering all the items on my shopping list, pausing in between to dump a tub of my brother's favourite Greek yoghurt in the trolley. When I was satisfied I'd checked everything off the list, I headed to the self-checkout. Being early had its perks, because the queue was practically non-existent.

I'd scanned through half of my items when a screeching noise overrode the *beep* of the scanner. I turned to see a lady in the checkout beside me, rocking her baby in a carry sling. The baby wailed non-stop as the lady scanned her only item, a container of baby formula, through the machine. I observed her from the corner of my eye as I continued to check out.

"Oh, for goodness' sake. Where is it?" The lady took off her backpack and shoved her hand around inside it. She did this for the next few minutes while I finished up and paid for the groceries.

At this point, I was fairly certain she must've forgotten or misplaced her wallet. If my no-nonsense mum was here, we'd definitely have walked away by now, with her tattling to me in Cantonese, *This is why we should take care of our things*. But she wasn't here.

Live a life with no regrets. That was what I'd promised myself after I lost Dad. Past-me would've hung my head down and walked off, with or without Mum. But this was present-me now, and I wasn't going to leave without seeing if I could help.

"Excuse me. Are you okay?"

The lady craned her neck up to look at me. Her eyes were rimmed red with heavy dark circles, no doubt from having to attend a young baby day and night. "It's nothing, hon. I think I must've left my wallet at home. I'll just have to go and—"

Another cry from her baby interrupted her. She bobbed up and down, making soft soothing sounds. While she was preoccupied, my eyes slid to her checkout screen highlighting the total—thirty-five dollars.

"You didn't bring your phone?"

"No," she said, despair written all over her face. "I left it charging at home by accident."

So she had no other way to pay or withdraw money from an ATM. At this point, I still had the option to say, *Oh well, that's too bad. Good luck*, and walk away. Except I didn't. Instead, I withdrew my wallet from my handbag.

She put out a hand to stop me. "Oh, honey. It's fine. Don't worry about it."

Her baby's cries told me otherwise. "Doesn't your baby need that formula?"

"Yes, but I can drive home and back."

"That sounds really inconvenient for you." *What with the baby and you looking half-dead.* "Don't they have strictly limited supplies for formula?" I knew that didn't apply to all formulas, but recent news was all about people buying the stuff out everywhere.

The lady nodded. "Yeah...actually this is the first store in a while that's stocked this one." She bit her lip. Her baby was now silent, as though he or she, too, understood the gravity of the situation.

Well, that did it. "I'll pay for you, then. There's no need to go back and forth."

"But, hon—"

I ignored her, rescanning the formula—stupid self-checkouts auto-cancelled after a few minutes—and then pressed on the "Pay Now" button. I tapped my credit card and watched as the receipt printed out.

"Here you go." I deposited the large can of formula into the lady's arms.

Tears filled her eyes. "Oh, thank you so much. You're a sweetheart." She pulled me into a one-armed hug, her baby making a gurgling sound while squashed between our bodies.

I patted her back awkwardly, not used to praise, before taking a step back and smiling at her baby.

"Daisy says thank you too," she said, tickling the baby's chin. "I'll pay you back today. I promise you. Can I get your contact details?"

"Oh, don't worry about it. If you have to come to me, you'll just be going out of your way all over again."

"Nonsense. Do you live nearby? I can drop in when I pass by."

I considered this. "Yeah. My family owns a bakery about five minutes' walk from here."

"Perfect!"

"But there's no rush. Please only come if it's convenient for you. And you can sample some of our buns too." If the lady liked them enough to buy some, that might make Mum forgive me if she found out I'd paid for a random person's groceries. I still hoped she never found out though. I crossed my fingers that the lady would come during Mum's break or odd day off when Max or I went on duty instead.

I pulled out a small business card from my wallet and handed it to the lady.

"'Tsang's Bakery,'" she read. "'Hong Kong-style baked goods.'"

The glossy blue surface of the card shone as she turned it over. A simple design, courtesy of my brother and the time he dabbled in graphic design, only to decide he didn't hold a single creative bone in his body. Still, all the details were there. Phone number, address, email.

"Oh," the lady said. "My sister lives close to your shop. I'll call her up. I'm sure she can drop by later to pay you back."

"Yeah, sure. No rush."

The lady beamed at me. "Thanks again, hon."

CHAPTER 5

"Hi, you must be Mrs Tsang's daughter?" The guy who walked into the shop looked like he could've been sponsored by a high-end sports brand. The same fancy logo decorated everything he wore, from his cap, to his crisp black T-shirt, all the way down to his fluorescent yellow shoes.

Was he who I thought he was? "Yeah. You are?" I asked, feigning I had absolutely no idea.

"Ben Wong."

I schooled my expression into nonchalance, trying not to burst out in a fit of inappropriate laughter. My brother was spot on with his vague description. Screams posh indeed. "What can I help you with?" I asked in a calm voice betraying nothing of my inner thoughts.

He scratched his head, barely rumpling his short hair. He had one of those stylish undercuts that needed fortnightly trimmings to stay neat. "My mum said you were interested in a tutoring job?"

Seriously? Mum and Mrs Wong really one-upped me this time. "Nope. I already have a tutoring job. Thanks for asking, though."

"Oh, okay..." Ben looked around helplessly. "My mum also said you guys have great buns, so I thought I'd drop by."

"I see." Awkward. Max had seen him before at the store, so this wasn't Ben's first visit. I gave him the benefit of the doubt. He was probably giving himself an excuse to stay, so he wouldn't make himself look dumb for coming here all the way for nothing. Wait till I told Max about this.

Speaking of Max, I was going to kick him for refusing to take my shift during Mum's two-hour lunch break. This was all his fault. Mum accepted his excuses of having some important project to do, but I didn't buy it. He practically lived, breathed, and slept with his computer when he wasn't at work. He could definitely spare two hours of a day to help.

But no, he knew this would be torture for me, so *of course* he let me do it instead. The fact that Mum complied —despite her usual habit of lecturing him to get out of his room—should've raised my suspicions.

"Uh, which buns do you recommend?" Ben's question startled me from my thoughts.

Can you please leave? You're wasting your time, I wanted to say. But I couldn't be blatantly rude to a so-called customer. I pointed to an assortment of different bun pieces scattered on a tray at the counter, toothpicks sticking out of them. "Try some."

He picked one up. "What's this one?" He popped the piece into his mouth before I could respond.

"Char siu bao," I said. Barbecue pork bun.

"It's nice," he said, then went to pick up a piece of red bean bun next.

"Yeah." No kidding. What was this Ben guy doing? Was he trying to scope me out? Ask me for my number? Or just pretend to not know anything about buns and buy some? Forget kicking Max for this. I was going to pummel him instead and then make him cover my next ten shifts as payback.

Just when I thought this would be the beginning of a long nightmare, the shop bell jangled, bringing in a fresh draft of wind and an unfamiliar lady.

She surveyed the shop before her eyes settled on me. "Hi," she said. "I'm looking for Serena."

"Yep, that's me." Did I know her? I stared intently at her tired eyes that blinked back at me. Her hair was in a messy ponytail, sunglasses perched atop her head. Nope. I was certain I'd never seen her in my life, but—

"Thanks so much for helping my sister buy the baby formula today."

Oh. That was why she looked questionably familiar.

"I'm Rose Miller." She held out a hand and I shook it.

"Rose..." The lady I'd helped at the supermarket had introduced herself as Iris before we'd parted ways. I thought it was cute she'd named her baby after a flower too. But to think her sister's name was Rose...

"Yes, I know. Iris, Rose, Daisy," she said. "Everyone mentions it, so I'll clear the air. No, I don't have any daughters, and if I did, they wouldn't be named after a flower." She laughed to herself. "Iris just wanted to continue the tradition."

"That's cool though." It was way cooler than being named Serendipity. No offence to Mum.

"Isaac," Rose called, turning around. She took hold of a little boy I hadn't noticed behind her and shifted him in front of her. "This is my son, who I didn't name after a flower."

I laughed. "Hi, nice to meet you." A familiar-shaped bag was slung over his shoulder. "You play tennis?"

Isaac nodded stiffly, his hand moving to grasp his mum's arm.

"That's cool. I do too." Only occasionally nowadays, but I still enjoyed it.

"He's very shy," Rose said. "Isaac, tell Serena who your favourite tennis player is."

I bent down to look into his deep brown eyes. He averted his gaze to the floor. I waited for him to say the name of one of the top, ageless pros like Nadal or Djokovic.

"Aiden Andale," he whispered instead, so softly I had to strain my ears to hear.

"Oh," I rasped out.

Bells chimed on the door again, breaking my concentration, and I looked up to find Ben Wong gone. *Goodbye I guess, and I hope to never see you again.*

"Who do you like?" Isaac asked me, louder this time.

"Hmm." That was a difficult question. Out of the WTA, my favourite player to watch was Hsieh Su-wei, with her cool double-handed forehand and variety of shot-making tactics. But if we were talking on a more personal level, I supposed it would be pointless to deny it. "I guess my favourite is Aiden Andale too."

Isaac's eyes lit up at my answer. "He'll win a Grand Slam soon," he said matter-of-factly.

"He probably will," I agreed, not to appease him but because it was most likely true. The way Aiden was playing now, he could be winning multiple Grand Slams soon.

"He won two titles this year." Isaac listed the names of each title, Aiden's opponents, and even the scores. I gaped at him in stunned silence, wondering how such a shy boy could suddenly turn into a talking tennis encyclopedia.

"I want to meet him again," he continued.

Wait, what? "You've met him before?"

"Yeah! He's so cool. He has the best backhand! I wanted to ask him to teach me, but Daddy said I shouldn't ask because Aiden's a busy person." His smile dropped into a pouty frown.

"Isaac," Rose said with a laugh, ruffling his hair. "Looks like you've made a new tennis friend. But you need to get home and have a bath. Why don't you pick out a bun to buy while I have a chat with Serena and then we'll go?"

Isaac's frown persisted as he said, "Okay," and trudged off to look at the shelves of buns.

Rose gave me an apologetic smile. "Sorry. It's actually amazing to see him talk so much to someone. I wasn't lying when I said he's shy."

"No problem," I said. "I love talking about tennis."

"That's great to hear because that's all Isaac talks about." She shook her head as though she wished otherwise.

"Mummy, I want this one!" Isaac said, pointing at the tray full of cocktail buns.

"Okay, munchkin. Let's see what else we can get."

Ten minutes later, Rose and her son left the bakery with a small bag of buns while I stared at a fifty dollar note in my hand. Since I'd used my own money to pay for the baby formula, I swapped the fifty for a twenty, ten, and five in the cash register and stuffed the bills into my pants pocket for safekeeping.

The rest of my shift flew by, as uneventful as possible, with a handful of customers coming and going without drama. Mum returned at 2:00 p.m. on the dot.

"Thanks, sweetie. There's a letter for you. I forgot to tell you before. I left it on the dining table," she told me as she took my place at the counter.

"Okay. Thanks, Mum."

I bounded up the stairs, two steps at a time, wondering what kind of letter someone would send me. My shoulders sagged in disappointment when I got to the table and discovered a standard letter of farewell from school, reminding us to return all our school library books, something I'd already done long ago. I stuffed the letter back into the envelope and dragged my tired legs toward my room.

On the way past Max's room, I couldn't resist shouting, "You're dead for making me take the shift."

"We'll see about that after your failed strawberry-choc custard tarts," he shot back.

Oops. I'd forgotten the details of our bet. The loser took all shifts during Mum's lunch breaks for the month, excluding the days we had work. Not fun. But I couldn't motivate myself to start another test batch of tarts right now. The prospect of having to clean up again made me woozy. Maybe after a nap.

I collapsed onto my bed, intent to crawl beneath the blanket and rest. As I threw the covers up and kicked my leg over, something sharp dug into my skin. "Oww." My hand searched blindly for the offending object, and I grabbed it.

It was the magazine. I'd almost forgotten about it.

Getting into a more suitable sitting position, I ripped open the shrink plastic and pulled out the mag. It smelled nice. Not as great as freshly baked buns, but still nice.

I flipped through the pages until the full-paged interview of Aiden popped up. A large photo of him in a plain white T-shirt and shorts took up the two-page spread. Casual. Cute. Laughing. Holding someone's hand.

My heart lurched to a stop as my eyes jumped to the girl next to him in the photo. She had waist-length, strawberry-blonde hair. And she was beautiful. With rosy cheeks and a smile showing pearly white, perfectly straight teeth. Not an eyebrow hair out of place over her big, doe-like eyes. Model-like beauty. She probably was one. A lot of pros dated them after all.

Off to the side of the image, next to the loved-up couple, were the words, *She's my biggest inspiration on and off the court*, accompanied by huge quotation marks. What did that mean? I scanned the page to get more context.

Q: Aiden, who would you say is your biggest inspiration?

A: My girlfriend, Tammy (Tamara Patrickson). I'm the luckiest guy alive to have met the most gorgeous girl ever. She works hard for her job, and that teaches me to work hard for mine as well. If I ever need help, she's there for me. What would I be without her? I don't even know. All I know is that—

I closed my eyes, gripping the page so hard that it crinkled. Taking a deep breath, I let go and slapped the magazine shut. *You're being an idiot, Serena.* I opened my eyes again, unable to look away from the front cover of the mag.

Aiden Andale. The current youngest tennis player in the ATP top-twenty rankings at the tender age of eighteen years old. He'd made it as far as the quarter-finals in the US Open this year. There had been speculation about him having a girlfriend, but he'd managed to keep it all under wraps. Well, not anymore.

Until now, I'd convinced myself I was a big fan, not some love-sick girl crushing on a celebrity.

I walked to the bookshelf in the corner of my bedroom. Dragging out a thick album from the top shelf, I placed it on the bed and riffled through it until I reached the middle of it. My thumb slid over the plastic covering the tiny instant photo. Me, with my awkward half-smile, and Aiden with his broad grin.

My stomach clenched tight as I stared at his smile in the photo, trying not to compare it to the smile he'd worn in that magazine with the beautiful girl. Maybe I should have asked him for his number back then. Maybe we would've been best friends by now if we'd stayed in touch.

Ugh. What was wrong with me? Following any news about Aiden Andale. Now I was jealous because he had a girlfriend? Meanwhile Mum tried to set me up with her customer's sons.

I closed the album and went to slot it back onto the shelf. Then I crammed the magazine onto the bottom row of my bookshelf. I would urge Liz to take it away from my prying eyes next time she came over. Far, far away.

Be more positive, Serena. It wasn't all bad that I'd bought the mag. I did get a free expensive drink bottle. Plus I got to see Aiden Andale happy and in love. If I could see that as a positive. Maybe one day, I would find that kind of love with someone too.

I slumped back onto my bed, pulled the blanket covers over my head, and squeezed my eyes shut.

I could only hope.

CHAPTER 6

ONE YEAR LATER
(19 YEARS OLD)

The last thing Dad made me promise him before he passed away was to study hard and be happy. Had he meant if I studied hard, I would be happy, or as two separate things? Study hard, but also be happy? Whatever his stance had been, he wasn't here to tell me now. Mum's stance, however...

"*Aiya*. You should stick it out for a few more years," she told me for the hundredth time.

After locking the front door of our shop, I flipped the sign so that the "Sorry, We're Closed" message was visible from the outside. Then I pulled the blinds shut. "What if I really don't want to, Mum?" Like, really, *really* didn't want to?

Mum collected all the empty trays from the transparent display cabinets, leaving me to get all the leftover buns from every other cabinet. She stacked the trays onto the counter and gave me a reproachful glare. "You'll regret quitting just to make life easier. You'll be making a big mistake, Serendipity Tsang."

She only ever used my full name like that when she meant business. She was basically saying, *You're stuffed if you do this.*

She was probably right.

I sighed, picking up the remaining red bean buns with a pair of tongs and dumping them into a plastic bag. We'd sell them tomorrow for a discounted price. I dropped the bag onto the counter on top of the trays.

"Even if I finish my law degree, it'll be hard to find a job. Maybe it'll be better if I just help out at the bakery more?" Though the workload wasn't easy, I'd choose baking any day over boring lecture slides and sleep-inducing research assignments.

"What are you talking about?" Mum's voice rose to a higher pitch. Uh-oh. "You want to drop out to work at the bakery?"

"Never mind." Good thing I didn't mention more of my great ideas, like my silly childhood dream. That would never go down well. "I was just joking." No, I wasn't, but I had to change the topic while I could. "By the way—who was that guy who came just before closing time? He seemed really friendly."

Mum's face instantly brightened, her eyes rounded and eyebrows arching high. "That was Kelvin Lee. His mum comes to the bakery a lot too. He's studying at the same uni as you, you know."

I paused as my tongs clamped around a sausage bun. "Are you trying to set me up again?"

"No. He's a nice boy, and you two could be good friends."

Yeah, right. Good friends, my ass. She was setting me up. I placed the bun into the plastic bag. "Can you stop trying to find me a guy, Mum? I can do that myself if I wanted to."

"But I can find you a nice Chinese boyfriend—"

I raised the pair of tongs to point at her. "No, Mum. Just no."

"But you're lonely and—"

"No." I groaned. "I can do whatever I want with uni and whatever I want with guys. Stop being a busybody."

Mum exhaled loudly, glowering at me. It was the same kind of look she made when she took buns out from the oven and found that one wasn't perfectly presentable. A showcase of eternal disappointment. "Fine then." She pointed threateningly at me. "Live a lonely life by yourself!" She stormed off and slammed the kitchen door shut, leaving me to mull over what had just happened.

Live a lonely life? Was that how she saw it? Between Mum's expectations and my promise to Dad, there wasn't much room left for a guy in my life. Besides, I wasn't desperate. Maybe if I was twenty-nine, not nineteen. Why was she so adamant to play matchmaker? Ugh.

I packed the rest of the unsold food by myself. A few minutes into my angry bag-stuffing, the kitchen door creaked open. I half expected it to be Mum, back for round two, but it was Max who slipped in, his hair sticking up in odd directions. Freshly woken from his nap, no doubt. Lucky him.

"What happened?" he said, stifling a yawn. "I heard Ma shouting." Max liked calling our parents by their Cantonese equivalents, just like he preferred me calling him Gor Gor. Ma was Mum, Ba was Dad.

"Sorry to wake you from your beauty sleep," I sneered.

"Meh." He waved a hand dismissively. "Any more sleep and it would've been a nightmare."

"Reality looks pretty much a nightmare anyway." I shoved the last of the buns into another plastic bag and carried the whole tray of them into the kitchen.

Max followed me. "What's got you in a twist, Dippy?"

"Uni, Mum, *life*," I muttered, placing the plastic bags of buns into the cupboard.

"Uni," he repeated in disbelief. He adjusted his glasses and squinted at me. "Thought you were acing uni, unlike me."

"Acing it doesn't mean I like it." I stalked back to the storefront and hefted the empty trays to bring them to the kitchen. I chucked them in the sink and started scrubbing one furiously, a pathetic outlet for all my frustration.

"Woah, take it easy," Max said after I'd cleaned three of them at top speed. He helped stack the washed trays on the dish rack. "Why don't you like uni?"

"It's not what I thought it would be." And I hadn't really known *what* I'd wanted to do fresh out of school, so the obvious choice had been to take something academic to make Mum happy. Except that had backfired now.

"So what do you want to do? Drop out?" Max asked.

I massaged my temple with a wet hand as a throbbing pain began to form. "Maybe. I don't know. Mum's already countering everything I say."

"Obviously," he said. "You need to butter her up first before you break the news."

"Butter her up? What's next? Put her in the oven?"

"Ha ha." He slapped me on the back. "Welcome to the real world, Mui Mui." Little sister. Of course the only time he called me that was to make fun of me—not that calling me Dippy wasn't making fun of me. But he tended to use Mui Mui whenever he wanted to highlight that I was the younger, inexperienced one.

I huffed out an exasperated breath, put the last washed tray on the dish rack, and made my way to the staircase. The telltale thumping from behind told me Max was still following. "Speaking of the real world, what's got Mum in a temper today?" Despite her constantly finding new guys for me to "befriend," I'd never once set her off so badly for telling her not to. Something else triggered her mood. Unless it was the combination of me wanting to quit uni *and* not wanting a boyfriend.

"Don't you know? Not very observant, Dippy."

We reached the second floor landing and I headed for our smaller kitchen. "What is it? Another Mr Zheng vying for her affections?"

A year ago, a persistent single man Mum referred to as Mr Zheng had visited our shop daily, chatting her up. But unlike her playing the wingman in my love life, Mum was happy being staunchly Team Forever Alone when it came to herself. Or more like Team Never Betraying Dad. Last December, Mr Zheng had left our bakery, shoulders sagging and empty-handed. I hadn't seen him since.

Max collapsed into a dining chair. "Hah, maybe. But that's not what's bothering her."

I pulled open the fridge and scoured for a simple meal to heat up, finding takeaway boxes with some leftover steamed fish, tofu, and rice. That'd do. I scooped some of each into a bowl, set the timer to microwave the food, and then rounded the kitchen bench toward Max.

"So," I said, plopping into a chair beside him, "what's bothering Mum then?"

He shook his head, took off his glasses, and rubbed his eyes. Without them on, he looked strangely different. Like another person impersonating him. My brother but not quite my brother. "You really don't remember? It's their wedding anniversary today."

A painful lump of guilt tightened my chest. "Oh my gosh. I'm an idiot. I totally forgot." Mum always got extra emotional during special occasions like anniversaries and birthdays without Dad. That explained everything, especially the whole "live a lonely life" part she'd shouted.

"Hey," Max said. "Did Ba make you promise him something before...?" He trailed off, unable to finish.

Before he died. That was what he didn't want to say—or couldn't say. Sometimes Max had more trouble expressing his feelings than me. His way of coping was sitting in front of a computer screen for hours until he fell asleep. Yeah, not healthy. "Did Dad ask *you* to promise him anything?" I questioned in return.

Max's throat bobbed. He slid his glasses on again, back to looking like himself. My not-so-brotherly gor gor. "That's not important," he said so quickly that I picked it up as a lie. "What did you promise Ba?"

With the way he brushed off my question, I doubted he would spill anything to me. Yet he still expected me to share things with him? Typical. But I'd learned some time ago from a certain someone that sharing feelings actually helped. And who knew? Maybe sharing with him would convince him to share with me.

Pain twisted inside me as I thought back to the last time Dad spoke properly to me. "I promised him I would study hard." And be happy, something I still tried to figure out the exact meaning of.

"Hah. Study. At least one of us is doing a good job then."

"What—"

The microwave beeped.

I jumped up to retrieve my food, all the while trying to decipher Max's words. What did he mean? What had he promised Dad? Something he hadn't been doing a good job of... To make sure Mum stayed happy? I could help him with that. Unless it was to hook up with Kelvin Lee. That was another story.

And it wasn't like I was doing a good job keeping my own promise. Study hard, yet here I was telling Mum I wanted to drop out.

As I carefully took the bowl out of the microwave with a hand towel, steam rising out, I imagined Dad's reaction to my predicament with uni. Encouraging Dad would say, *You can do it, Sere.* Discouraging Dad would say, *Your ma's right, Sere. Think about what you're doing.*

Which version would he say if he were here now? I placed my meal on the dining table and slumped back in my chair. My breath came out in uneven gasps, catching Max's attention. His eyes bored into mine, a sad, knowing look in them.

"I miss Dad," I choked out.

Max turned his face away, staring off into the kitchen. Did he also picture Dad cooking there like he used to every day?

"Me too, Dippy," he finally whispered. "I miss him too."

I stretched my legs out under the desk and rolled my shoulders. How long could two hours possibly last? Very long if it was this lecture, apparently. One hour in and it felt like a lifetime had passed.

Angling my neck around the tall guy sitting in front of me, I scrambled to copy the notes, my fingers typing on my laptop keyboard at lightning speed. Our lecturer was explaining new boring terminology. With the notes, at least I could search the terms up afterwards. At nine in the morning, it all sounded like "blah blah blah" to me.

As soon as I'd jotted down the last bit of his explanation, the contents of the projection screen faded into the next slide. A daunting new heading materialised in large font. *Group Assessment 1 (weight: 30%)*. "Now, I've made it easier for everyone by grouping you randomly into pairs," the lecturer began.

Grouping? Randomly? Oh, no. Not this. Randomly assigned group assessments were the worst. It was like a lottery. You had a slim chance of winning a good group member, but you'd more likely lose and get the useless ones who contributed nothing.

"If you log in to your accounts on the student portal, you'll find your partner's name under the allocated assessment folder."

The lecturer droned on as I opened up an internet browser on my laptop and navigated the student portal, searching for the dreaded group assessment. After several clicks of my mouse, the guidelines of Assessment One popped up on my screen. A few words stood out to me on the core list of objectives marked off for a high distinction. Because a HD was, as always, my aim.

Shows advanced ability to work together as a group. Essay highlights all required information in significant detail. And on it went.

Whose brilliant idea was this? An essay written by two random people together. Great start to the uni year. Not. Could I quit now? But I still hadn't come close to an idea to "butter Mum up" as Max had put it. At the rate my ideas were going, I may as well put myself in an oven to roast.

Chairs scraped as students got up, putting a hold on my thoughts. Was it time for a break already?

"Where's Greg?" someone yelled out.

Nope. They were just finding their randomly assigned partners.

I scrolled back up on my laptop to look for my own partner's name.

Group 16:

Harrison, Jeremy

Tsang, Serendipity

Oh no. It was one of those confusing surnames that could be first names. I hoped I wouldn't accidentally call him Harrison.

"Are you Seren..."

My head jerked up.

A guy towered over me. He was cute, with the kind of boyish face that looked like it could belong in those teenage boy band magazines Liz used to read. His fringe fell just above his eyes, a hesitant expression on his face. He glanced down at his phone. "Serendipity?"

"Uh, yeah. Are you Harrison—I mean, Jeremy?" I bit my tongue at the exact slip up I'd feared making. What was wrong with me?

"Yeah." He grabbed the chair from behind him and dropped into it. "You have a long name."

I winced at the reminder. "Just call me Serena."

He raised his eyebrows. "But that's not your name."

"Call me Sere then."

"Sere," he repeated. "That's funny. Everyone calls me Jere. We rhyme."

Sere and Jere. We did indeed. What were the chances of that?

"It must be fate, hey?" His lips parted into a wide smile. "So, how do you want to start this assessment?"

I pursed my lips. We could go about this like everything was normal, but it wouldn't be fair if I didn't share the truth with him first. "I might quit," I said.

He blinked at me. "Already? Do you really not want me as a partner?" He chuckled, but I could hear the nervousness behind it. Maybe his last group had let him down, and he was scared I was about to do the same.

"Uh, no." My cheeks heated under his gaze. "I mean, I might drop out of this course. I've been thinking about it." The cut-off to drop without the penalty of a withdrawal fee was tomorrow. "I'll let you know tonight."

We exchanged mobile numbers and then the lecturer continued on with the slides.

"See you if I see you," Jeremy said when class ended. "I hope you don't quit."

At least one of us knew what to hope for. I didn't even know myself anymore.

Tunnel lights blurred by as the express train surged full speed ahead. My eyes drooped and my head swayed. I was on the brink of dozing off when a sudden, persistent vibration in my hand jolted me wide awake. My eyes shot open, and I blinked blearily at my screen. *Gor Gor,* the caller ID read.

Prickles of apprehension made their way up my arm. Max never called me. Ever. Unless I didn't answer his texts, and those were usually requests for specific food items when I was out shopping. I hit the answer button and held the phone to my ear.

"Hello?"

"Sere!" Max's panicked voice blasted from the phone, making me flinch. The last time he'd called me Sere instead of Dippy was probably when we were kids, a sure sign that things weren't normal.

"What's wrong?"

"Ma—" Static screeched in my ear, cutting off the rest of his sentence.

"Ma what?" No answer. "Hello? Max? Helloooo?"

Fuzzy sounds were my only response, and the call abruptly ended.

He called again a few seconds later. My heart thundered in my chest as I answered. "Hello?"

"Can you hear me now? Ma fainted and she hit her head." This time, his voice rang clearly on the other end. "God, I—" He let out a strangled noise.

I tried to process his words. Mum fainted? She'd hit her head? "Is she—is she okay?"

"She's still unconscious and—I don't know. The paramedics are taking us to the hospital."

Paramedics. Hospital. The two words never sat well in my mind, particularly hospital. I normally avoided going to hospitals at all costs, intent on burying the bad memories of Dad far into the deepest depths of my mind.

But there was no other choice now.

"Which hospital? I'm on my way."

CHAPTER 7

Mum's pale face peeked out above the covers of a white blanket, her eyes peacefully closed. It didn't help ease my anxiety though. Fear dug painfully into my ribs as I recalled what the doctors had said.

Stable. They'd said she was stable for now. We would only know the extent of the damage when she woke up and they did a scan on her head. Stress had been the most likely factor in her fainting. "She needs a calm, stress-free environment," the doctor had advised us.

Guilt tugged at me hard. Had I been the direct cause for Mum fainting by stressing her out? *Please let her be okay. Please, please, please.* It was a mantra I recited for well over an hour while Max stared at Mum, sighing loudly every few minutes. I could sense what he was thinking without him saying it.

We'd lost Dad. We couldn't lose Mum too.

Seeing the hospital again after all this time didn't help either. The stark white bed sheets, walls, and drapes... everything the same way it'd been since my last visit here. The ghost of these memories haunted me, like I was a tightly wound ball of yarn ready to unravel. All it would take was the small pull of that beginning thread, the one I'd always hid. I thought before coming here that if I tried hard, I could hold the memories all in and hide that thread.

I was wrong. The thread had been yanked on as soon as I'd set foot inside the hospital and the heavy fumes of disinfectant assaulted my nostrils. Even now, that smell wouldn't let up. I saw Dad everywhere here—like I saw him in the house, but the house was different. The house had good memories. The hospital had bad ones.

Dad lying on the bed headrest sluggishly, his eyes half open. Dad opening his mouth to speak, the words a breathless struggle. And in the final stages... Dad, unable to breathe, strapped to a ventilator.

My breathing thickened, a lump forming in my throat. It was a near-impossible feat to dislodge those memories from my mind.

Soon, voices and squeaking wheels told me dinner was here. The food trolley lady left Mum's meal sitting on the bedside table—a metal dome on a tray, with a popper of orange juice and small yoghurt.

My stomach let out a low growl at the sight of the food. "We should get something to eat." Or do anything to take our mind off the gloom and doom.

Max glanced at me with tired eyes but didn't say anything.

"Come on, Gor Gor." I got up and pulled his arm. He reluctantly stood. "When was the last time you ate?"

"This afternoon. I didn't get to eat dinner when I came home because—" He shook his head.

Because Mum had fainted before then. He'd told me he'd been chilling in his room after coming home from work. He sensed Mum wasn't feeling well and told her not to worry about cooking, but she insisted. Then he heard a thump and rushed to find her on the floor of our kitchen.

Thank goodness Max had been home. If he hadn't...

I pulled on his arm again. "You must be starved. I'm starving, and I haven't eaten since lunch either." I dragged him with me to the door. "Let's go eat something. There's nothing else we can do here but wait anyway."

About half an hour later, we trudged our way back to Mum's room from the hospital cafeteria with full stomachs. Max hadn't said much to me, but I didn't expect him to. He probably took things a lot worse than me, having spent more time in the hospital with Dad. More time here meant more bad memories. While I'd been stuck at school at sixteen, Max had already started uni, so he'd had a bit more freedom to visit Dad. Lucky or unlucky? Who knew how he saw it now.

When we got to Mum's room, I came to an abrupt stop. Soft, incandescent lighting shone from behind the curtains around Mum's bed. My heart sped up as I hurried to pull apart the white drapes.

Familiar warm brown eyes met mine.

"Mum!" I yelled out at the same time Max said, "Ma!" I resisted the urge to crush her in a hug, and instead grabbed her hand and gave it a small squeeze. "You're awake."

"How are you feeling?" Max asked.

"Not too bad, sweetie." She gave us a small, tired smile. "Sorry for worrying you both."

I stayed with Mum in the hospital that night. She'd convinced Max to go home and bring back some things for her tomorrow. He probably wouldn't have left otherwise. After Mum did all her scans, the doctors told her to take it easy. There wasn't much more we could do. We needed to wait for the results and rest, but I sensed Max felt guilty for not being able to help Mum more.

She relaxed now in a hospital gown, the head of the bed raised so she could sit up. "Can you pass me the remote, sweetie?" As I handed it to her, a brief image flashed—Dad asking if we could watch the Aus Open on TV. My stomach did somersaults as Mum pressed the power button and the TV screen flickered on.

"—stunning win at the Indian Wells yesterday. Tell us all how you've been feeling after the victory."

My whole body stiffened as the view panned from the reporter to the interviewee at her side.

Aiden Andale grinned on the screen. "It means the world to me. It's one of the biggest tournaments around. Everyone dreams of achieving something like this."

The interviewer asked more questions while my mind reeled at the news. Aiden had won the Indian Wells? I'd seen him advance through the second round, but after that... I'd gotten distracted by uni and Mum.

"He won a tennis tournament? He looks so young," Mum said.

"Yeah, he's my age. He was born in the same year as me." He was about six months older than me, according to Wikipedia. Yes, I'd Googled him after I'd spilled my guts to him that day and realised I'd known next to nothing about him. Now I knew more about him than he knew about me. If he remembered me at all, that was.

"Is he a new Australian player?" Mum asked. Unlike me, she didn't follow tennis. She'd only held a mild interest whenever Dad rambled on about it, so I wasn't surprised she didn't know about him.

"He's been around for the past two years. He's won four titles so far."

"Wow."

"He made it into the fourth round of the Aus Open this year," I went on, "but his best run is quarterfinals in the US Open. Even though he lost that match against a top-ten player, he took it to five sets."

Mum squinted at me. "You sure know a lot about him. *Do you like him*?" She said the last part in Cantonese, like it was a secret she wanted me to divulge.

"No!" My cheeks burned. Maybe I'd spoken too much like a proud mum. Oops. Sure I still admired him, but that was more as a tennis player, not as a romantic love interest.

Mum chuckled, and I was relieved to see that her fainting episode hadn't dimmed her spirits further. "Why do you know so much, then?"

"I—I know a lot about many tennis players." Somewhat the truth, but I didn't know a lot, to the extent of birthdays and the number of titles won, about most players. I paused, feeling guilty for the lie. "Well, actually... I met him before—at the sports centre." Nobody else except Liz knew, mainly because I didn't think anyone else would care since they didn't watch tennis.

"Really? You met a celebrity?" She gawked at me, then shifted her gaze to the TV, probably assessing Aiden's looks. She nodded her head slowly as if to approve. "Did you ask for his autograph?"

"I didn't know who he was until after."

"Aww. Your baba would've been jealous."

I sucked in a breath at the thought. He'd always cheered for the Aussies when we'd seen live matches at the Aus Open. "Yeah, he would've."

Our thoughtful silence was filled by the voices on the TV. Mum had considerately turned the volume down, but I was right next to the TV, allowing me to hear everything clearly.

"Lately, we've noticed you use a new catchphrase after you win your matches. How did you come up with your tagline 'embrace the unknown'? What's the meaning behind it?"

"It means to go for it," Aiden said. "Follow your dreams, even if you don't know what's waiting for you next."

"What advice do you have for people who want to follow their own dreams?"

"Persevere," he said. "Do what you want. Go for it with everything you've got."

What should I do if I can't do what I want, Aiden? What do I do if what I want is to quit my law degree, but it goes against my own mum and hurts her in the process? What if I don't want to stress her out and risk her health? Those were the words I wanted to ask him.

But Aiden Andale only continued smiling at me from the TV screen. My phone rumbled in my jean's pocket, and I pulled it out to see a preview of a message from Jeremy Harrison. I unlocked my phone.

Hey Sere, did you make up your mind? Are you dropping out?

My hands shook as I typed my answer.

Hey Jere. Yep, I made up my mind. Not quitting. Let's work hard to get a high distinction.

Chapter 8

Two years later
(21 years old)

My hands burned under the heat of the fish and chips box I held. After setting it onto a table full of condiments, I grabbed the tomato sauce, its nozzle splattered in leftover bits of dried red. I squeezed the bottle, producing a pathetic squirt of sauce that barely covered the chips. Squeezing harder, the bottle let out a hollow burble, releasing nothing but air.

Ugh, forget it. It was as empty as my stomach. Giving up, I swiped a few napkins, cupped my fish and chips box with them, and strode off to find Liz.

The outside of Ken Rosewall Arena bustled with activity. Everywhere I looked, people milled about, some holding giant tennis balls waiting to be signed.

I made a beeline for an area packed with lawn chairs, my sneakers squelching on the grass. Cutting through a mass of people queuing in front of a food truck, the undeniably delicious scent of cinnamon doughnuts wafted into my nose. Yum. Maybe I'd get some later.

Thankfully, the rest of my way was relatively clear of people and didn't involve any more mouth-watering scents. I caught sight of Liz waving at me and hurried over to her.

"Good thing the match is delayed for another fifteen minutes," she said as I relaxed onto the lawn chair beside her.

"Yeah." Just as well so we could eat first. I dug into my fish and chips, swirling a piece around my tongue. Mmm.

In between bites of my meal, I glanced at a giant LCD screen towering in front of us. On screen, they played a repeat of the women's finalists receiving their trophies.

In the distance, partially obscured by the LCD screen, stood the gate doors that led into that very arena. The plain grey outside was rounded with jagged upside-down steps that expanded outwards. It wasn't the same as Rod Laver Arena in Melbourne, but it was the biggest tennis arena in Sydney. And when the next tennis match started...

"I can't believe we're seeing Aiden Andale live," Liz said, as though she'd read my mind. "Seems like yesterday when we met him at the sports centre."

My stomach did a wild flip, and I found myself unable to respond. Stupid. It was just a stupid reaction from my body. I blamed it on Liz. She'd given me a ticket to these finals as a Christmas present. I'd been all too happy to go with her—before I'd known who would be playing. Last night when I found out who'd made it through, I'd called to cancel on her.

"Cancel on me, and I'll message Aiden Andale on his social media all about your crush on him in high school," she'd said. "I have plenty of photos of that cute scrapbook page you had of him—the one with the adorable red hearts you drew all over."

I'd mentally face-palmed at the reminder. Why, after all these years, had Aiden Andale decided to create social media accounts? Did he look at his private messages? Probably not, but I still didn't want Liz to message him that embarrassing photo. I'd done that shameful scrapbook page in secret in Year Eleven. Liz had found it hidden between the pages of an old chemistry textbook on my shelf a few years ago. My seventeen-year-old self's fangirling was like a hardened piece of bubblegum under a school desk. Gross and impossible to pick off.

And so here we sat, waiting for the match to begin.

"So how've you been, girl?" Liz offered me some of her gravy-smeared chips, but I declined with a shake of my head. She raised her brows as if to say, *Your loss.* "Feel like we haven't hung out for ages." Pulling a particularly long chip from the pile, she ate it whole.

"What are you talking about? I went to your place last month."

She leaned closer to me, hand braced on the edge of her lawn chair while she chewed and swallowed her food. "*That* doesn't count," she said sternly, pointing at me with her plastic fork. "Jerky was there. I don't like being a third wheel."

"*Jere*," I corrected, resisting the urge to roll my eyes. I couldn't understand for the life of me what she had against him. Judgy Liz would always be judgy. "How's your family doing?" I asked, intent on steering the conversation away from me.

Liz lay back, resting her arms behind her head. "Okay, I guess. Same old, same old. Glad I could come out today and take a breather."

"How's Ellie?"

"Ellie," she muttered, "is so damn selfish." She avoided my eyes as she said this, tilting her head up to look at the slowly darkening sky.

Selfish? "How—"

"Our men's finals match will begin in approximately ten minutes," a voice proclaimed on the speakers.

Crap. I cut into my fish and shoved a large piece into my mouth. After several minutes of us devouring our food, Liz's last remark swam back into my head. *Ellie is so damn selfish.*

That couldn't be right... A vision flashed in my mind—Ellie, with hollow cheeks and a wan smile. "She's in remission, so please be gentle," Liz's mum had whispered in my ear, as though speaking loudly about it would somehow physically hurt Ellie.

"How is your sister selfish exactly?" I asked Liz, who was presently dabbing a chip in a generous slab of gravy stuck to the side of her takeaway box.

Liz's nostrils flared, and she narrowed her eyes at me. "I don't want to talk about her."

"But you sound like you need to vent."

"Oh, you have no idea." She popped the gravy-drenched chip into her mouth and licked her lips clean.

"Tell me then. I won't judge." I speared a big portion of my chips and munched on them, waiting for her to speak.

"You'll *totally* judge me," she said in sharp dismissal.

Not as much as you judge me, Liz. Out loud, I said, "Come on, how is she selfish? Does she constantly change the TV channel? Make fun of your mistakes? Dob on you to your parents? Steal your clothes?" That was all I could come up with when I imagined an annoying older sister. Well, Max actually did all those things, minus the clothes. An annoying older brother couldn't be that much different than an annoying older sister, right?

Liz scowled. "No. I know she went through a lot and it wasn't easy. Don't get me wrong. But Ellie's always been a bit self-absorbed, and now it's a lot worse. She's acting like she's a little spoiled princess all the time now. Whatever she wants, she gets. If she wanted to come here"—she swept her hand out—"then she'd get tickets from Mum or

Dad, no questions asked. They force me to drop everything for her. But the other half of the time, they basically drop everything for her themselves anyway." She gobbled down a mouthful of chips, leaving me to think about what she'd just divulged.

She'd mentioned missing out on a lot of things last year. Uni graduation, participating in a prestigious art exhibition, a big trip around Europe with uni friends... Was that what she was holding against her sister? That did suck, and maybe I'd been a bit judgy about her attitude, but still—Ellie could have died. Didn't Liz care about that enough to forgive Ellie for being a little selfish?

"Let's talk about you instead," Liz said suddenly.

"Me?" The topic I was trying to avoid? "No thanks."

"Yes, please," she retorted. She got up from her lawn chair and perched on the side of mine, pushing me aside to give her enough space to sit. "This is the whole reason we're out together."

"It is?" That was news to me. Weren't we here for her? She loved tennis more than me after all. I mean, sure she'd bought a ticket for my Christmas present, but I thought that was so I had no way of getting out of going with her.

"Yeah, Sere. You're studying your butt off at uni as usual. And now you're too busy to hang out with me even though it's technically uni break."

"I'm not trying to avoid you, Liz. You could always come see me."

"I did. I came to the bakery last Saturday. Some other girl was working there. She said you were out." Liz said this in an accusing tone, like it was my fault I happened to be gone the one time she decided to drop by without notice.

"Oh..." I'd watched a movie with Jere that day.

"What's going on? Don't you always take your mum's Saturday shift?"

I shrugged. "Busy now. No time. Plus she has Ming now. That's the new girl you saw." A semi-lie. Mum and I weren't on good terms right now. Skipping my Saturday duties last weekend was probably the most rebellious thing I'd done since dropping Extension Two Maths in Year Twelve against Mum's wishes.

"But you love the bakery."

A clear fact I didn't need to be reminded of.

I shrugged again. "I still help sometimes during the week." A definite lie this time. At the rate I was going, the feeling of flour beneath my hands would be like a distant dream I'd made up. But until Mum apologised for her behaviour lately, I wasn't doing anything in the bakery for her.

"Attention, please. The men's finals are about to start. Please head to the allocated gate number assigned on your tickets."

With that warning, we scrambled to collect our belongings. As we made our way to the arena, other thoughts soon overshadowed our discussion.

Somewhere nearby, Aiden Andale was preparing for the match. I would finally see him again, and I didn't quite know how I felt about that. Over the years, I'd gradually gotten over the fact that I'd once met a famous tennis player. But every so often, he appeared on a TV ad during the Aus Open or random articles popped up on social media, and I obviously couldn't avoid them.

It felt kind of weird to see him like that. Sort of like personally stalking an old friend on Facebook who I'd lost touch with—not that I'd stalked Aiden Andale recently. I still followed his tennis matches every now and then, but that was about it.

Maybe to anyone else, it wouldn't be weird following him on social media. But to me, it felt like that would be inviting trouble when I had a boyfriend. Not that Liz believed me. She loved nothing more than to push the idea of me liking Aiden into my head. Even after I started going out with Jere, it was like a habit that she couldn't—or wouldn't—break. Just like now.

"You totally still have a crush on him," she whispered in my ear after we took our seats in the arena.

"D-do not!" I spluttered, shielding my mouth with my hand. Despite telling her the truth, she gave me the most incredulous look while snickering. If she saw me laugh now, or so much as crack a smile, she'd call me a liar. Luckily, our row was practically empty, besides a couple sitting on the other end of it, or else I'd probably melt in a puddle of embarrassment right about now.

My gaze shifted to the court below, desperate to find something that could distract me. Far up high in the cheapest tickets section, courtesy of Liz, we got an unhindered view of the court from the side where no umpire's chair blocked the way.

"*Sairrr*," Liz said, drawing out my name in a sing-song voice. She flashed me a saccharine smile that reminded me of the Cheshire cat. "Did you know Aiden is single now?" She wagged her eyebrows suggestively.

How did she even know that? "He could be secretly not single."

"Nah. Guys like him flaunt it when they're not single. Plus it's all over social media. Tamara Patrickson is now dating some actor. She broke up with Aiden at the end of last year."

My throat suddenly felt dry. I cleared it, then said, "Well, it doesn't matter. *I'm* not single." And even if I was single, what kind of life would I be living, liking a celebrity who'd probably forgotten about me a long time ago? Pretty pathetic way to live. Besides, he didn't seem like my type—overconfident, always smiling, and social. I didn't know if that was a media-front personality, but it sort of screamed fake to me.

"Don't settle for Jerky," Liz said, and just like that, all thoughts about Aiden Andale evaporated from my mind.

Irritation surged through me. "His name is Jeremy, and I don't care if you don't like him. He's my boyfriend, so the least you can do is try to be nice, like he is to you."

I wasn't joking when I said Jeremy was nice. Nicer than nice. The kind of guy who would help a lost pet find its home or put a few coins in a charity donation bucket. Our names matched too. Sere and Jere. That was like fate, right?

I could envision it now. We'd start a law firm together and have two kids—one boy and then one girl. Or was one girl, then one boy better? Well, whatever. It didn't matter the order or gender.

The point was that Liz was wrong about him. She thought we weren't a good match. When I asked her why, she didn't supply me with a more elaborate answer. I had enough of that crap coming from Mum.

Last month, I'd invited him home and didn't remind him to take off his shoes before coming in. His shoes tracked marks for Mum to clean up. Then he hit the nail in the coffin by declaring he was a proud vegan, refusing to eat anything Mum politely offered him.

Mum also wasn't so happy I'd decided to try going vegan with Jere. Yeah, maybe it wasn't such a great idea to try it when my home smelled of non-vegan baked goods, but Jere was worth it. Actually, he would probably have a heart attack if he knew I'd caved and eaten fish and chips. But that was beside the point. The point was Mum shouldn't be so harsh with her opinions about Jere. And until she apologised, I wasn't doing any bakery duties.

Maybe Liz took my statement seriously, because she finally shut up after that. I turned my attention back to the court below. Cameramen were at the ready on the sidelines, training their cameras toward the crowd. No further announcements had been made yet about the players coming. What was taking so long?

Soon enough, Liz and I needed to tuck in our legs to let multiple people through. Eventually, our row filled up completely.

"Hey, Sere..." Liz's serious tone caught me off guard. I faced her directly to regard her change in mood. Her lips thinned, slowly transforming into a grimace.

"What is it?" I whispered.

She shook her head. "Nothing. I mean, I'm sorry I upset you. I was just teasing... I'm—I'm glad that we could hang out today, you know. I wasn't sure when we'd get a chance to again since you're always so busy all the time now. And —"

"Ladies and gentlemen." We jolted in our seats, our attention usurped by the announcer's voice blaring through the speakers. "We apologise for the delay. But it's finally time! Please welcome your Sydney International finalists!"

CHAPTER 9

"Our first finalist is a newcomer to this tournament, ranked sixty-seventh in the world. From Italy—Vincenzo Monetti!"

Polite clapping echoed throughout the arena. A stately tall guy walked through the courtside entrance, his face a blur from this distance. The LCD screen hanging above the court zoomed in closely to reveal a baby-faced youngster. According to articles I had read yesterday, he was eighteen years old. A few whistles came from a corner of the audience waving Italian flags with matching painted flags on their cheeks.

"And our second finalist, and no doubt home-crowd favourite, ranked twenty-fourth in the world. I give you—from Australia—Aiden Andale!"

Deafening cheers erupted over the arena. My gaze inevitably locked onto Aiden as he strolled out through the same entrance. Like Monetti, I couldn't see his features from this far away. *I don't need to look closely,* I told myself. *I already know what he looks like.* But my eyes betrayed me by slowly wandering to the LCD screen again.

My breath caught in my throat as he sat at his designated bench and pulled out a new racket from his tennis bag. A blue headband pushed back his mussed, dark brown hair. Matching blue shorts and a white shirt completed the look. Somehow, he didn't look too different from the first time we'd met. Seeing him was like a big blast into my past.

The sound of a phone camera went off—Liz taking photos. She continued snapping more while they warmed up. It wasn't until she leaned into me, and I saw my own eyes widen in surprise on her phone screen, that I realised what she wanted.

"Selfie," she said, swivelling around to tilt her phone up behind my shoulder.

I twisted to face the camera, automatically posing with my signature peace sign and closed-mouth smile. A bit of the court showed from behind our close-up faces.

"Perfect. New profile pic." She grinned, and I couldn't help smiling too. For as long as we'd had Facebook, Liz's display photo had always been one of her and me.

We settled back into our proper seating positions just as the match began. "Players, ready to start. Andale to serve."

I watched with intent focus as he bounced a ball. Tossing it up, he flung his racket out like a whip—just like the first time he'd demonstrated to me. The ball ripped diagonally across the court.

I didn't dare blink as Monetti stretched out his racket to return it. Aiden hit a forehand back—the perks of a leftie. Monetti's feet slid to reach the ball. But Aiden had already anticipated the direction and hit a clean, one-handed backhand into the empty crosscourt.

"15–Love," the umpire called out.

The crowd applauded like mad, clapping along with the thumping of drums. I joined in on the raucous applause.

The game sped by. I couldn't tear my eyes away. Aiden hit an ace, then got his next point off Monetti's return that went out wide.

The set went on with nothing major happening, both sides equally matched—until the momentum changed at 3–3. It was Aiden's service game. His first serve hit the net, and Monetti predicted his second serve, returning it straight past him to win the point.

Aiden's mentality must've suffered a blow, because after that, he hit another fault, and his second serve wasn't that great again either. He got caught off guard in the direction of the return and hit the ball out wide. 0–30.

The next point was a long rally that had Liz and I clutching onto each other. Fortunately, it ended with an unforced error from Monetti netting the ball, and we heaved a sigh of relief.

But that didn't last. The scales tipped back in Monetti's favour when Aiden hit a double fault under pressure, setting the game to 15–40.

Not good.

"Come on," Liz whispered. Her hand latched onto my arm in a death grip.

I would've told her to loosen up, but I was just as wound up on this next point. As Dad used to say during these crucial moments—it was make or break.

My heart thudded erratically with every moment during that next point. From Aiden's nerve-wracking first serve let, to the next serve that zoomed to the edge of the service box. Monetti's quick reflexes caught the ball and returned it. The rally went on for a dozen more seconds, the pace finally changing when Monetti hit the ball and it barely flew over the net. A drop shot!

Aiden raced toward it, shoes squeaking to a stop just in time to catch the ball on his racket. The ball arched back over the net.

And then Monetti lobbed the ball up high.

No!

Aiden pivoted, running back. But it was too late. The ball was already too far ahead. It bounced onto the baseline before Aiden could reach it. Or did it?

"Out!" a linesman yelled.

Monetti raised his racket, signalling a challenge.

Everyone clapped in time to a steady beat as the challenge flashed on the screen, an overview of the ball's trajectory going in slow motion, zooming into a bird's eye view close-up to show—

IN.

The ball had clipped the line by what looked like an ant's width—barely a millimetre in.

The crowd howled, and I clenched my teeth together. No way. No freaking way.

"Crap," Liz muttered, body sagging as she finally let go of my arm. Yeah. She was going to leave me a bruise for sure before this match was over.

I squinted at Aiden on court. He stared at the successful challenge, shaking his head.

"Game, Monetti," the umpire announced. "Monetti leads, four games to three."

Aiden stalked to the bench, his racket posed high above his head. His arm trembled. Was he going to break his racket? No doubt his boiling emotions were bursting to explode. I mean, who wouldn't be mad at losing their game that way? But, just as quickly, his arm dropped limply to his side. He wrapped his hand into a fist and hit his thigh. Once. Twice. Three times.

Dropping onto his bench, he threw a towel over his head. He stayed like that for the full one minute and thirty seconds of the changeover break.

"Time," the umpire said.

I sucked on my bottom lip as he chucked the towel off his head and went to his side of the court. *Come on. Don't give up. You'll have a chance to break back.*

I inhaled deeply through my nose as Monetti threw the ball up and served—

And Aiden delivered a flawless backhand return. The ball went back and forth, a long rally in the making. I stared, transfixed, as Aiden returned the ball relentlessly, never letting his guard down. It was like Monetti was hitting against a brick wall. Whatever frustrations Aiden had let out with his fist-smacking and towel-covering worked. He ended the twenty-five shot rally, hitting a winner at a wicked angle, impossible to reach from Monetti's baseline position.

Monetti faltered on his subsequent serves, the pressure to hold his game undeniably weighing on his mind. Soon enough, the score reached 15–40. Two break points for Aiden. Two chances for him to change the tides.

"Go, go, go," Liz said, her hand clamping onto my arm again.

Monetti served fast this time, aiming down the T. But Aiden was faster. Legs split wide, bouncing on the balls of his feet, he immediately twisted to hit a perfect one-handed backhand. It flew straight onto the singles sideline before Monetti could react.

"Yes!" Liz screamed.

The crowd went wild. Liz pulled me up with her, and we jumped up and down like hyper children, cheering and laughing.

"Game, Andale," the umpire said. "Four games all."

It was a whirlwind of a set after that. Aiden gained more confidence and momentum on his break back, and whatever slight advantage Monetti had disappeared. He crumbled on his next service game, losing it to let Aiden take the set 6–4.

During the second set, Aiden got a head start, winning his own first service game and then breaking Monetti's service game to lead 2–0.

Eventually, I didn't bother looking at the score anymore, simply mesmerised by watching the game itself. A hypnotically induced trance of following the distant yellow-green blur of the tennis ball, the loud bouncing of the ball smacking the surface of the hard court.

"What?" Liz hissed suddenly.

I tore my gaze away from the match.

Liz held her phone to her ear. A voice sounded on the other end, too muffled for me to hear.

"I'm busy right now. No. I know. Obviously... She doesn't need—" Liz rolled her eyes, curling a strand of her hair around her finger. "Now? No. It's always about her, don't you see? I'm in the middle of watching a tennis match. You're..." She paused to listen. "Ugh! Fine!" The words seethed through her teeth.

She slammed the phone down on her thigh and jabbed the end call button. "Freaking hell," she muttered.

"What's—"

"Don't ask," she cut me off, glaring. I cringed, causing her face to immediately soften. "Sorry. I wanted to enjoy today, but of course I can't. I need to go home."

"Now?"

"Yeah, because *someone* can't be left by themselves for five freaking seconds."

Was she talking about Ellie? Although tempting to ask, it wouldn't help the situation. If she wanted to talk about it... "Text me when you get home."

"Sure. Sorry again." She said one last farewell and promptly left when the gates opened during the next changeover.

I quickly texted Jere.

Hey babe, can you pick me up later? Liz had to leave.

As the rest of the match went on, I couldn't get into it again. My head felt strangely heavy after Liz's phone call, and the mugginess of the closed arena bore down on me. Had it been this humid the whole time?

I shifted restlessly in my seat, constantly checking my phone. Jere still hadn't texted me back after twenty minutes. I called him, but it went to voicemail. Thanks to the match delays from the rain this morning, it was already nearing midnight. He'd probably fallen asleep already. But that also meant no trains going home by the time this match ended.

Well, here goes my last resort. I messaged Max.

Can you please pick me up from the arena? Liz had to leave early.

I saw him pop up online and start typing an answer.

If you promise not to skip any more of your Saturday shifts.

What the heck? I didn't have much of a choice. Jere wasn't answering, and I wasn't going to call a taxi or driving service to pick me up. That would cost way too much.

Fine.

I waited as he typed again.

K what time then?

I looked at the current scoreboard: 6–4, 3–1, 30–15 on Aiden's serve. The match would most likely be Aiden's win with straight sets, so I told him to drive now. I yawned. Waiting too long for him would be torturous when I was halfway to falling asleep.

Sure enough, before I knew it, the score reached 5–3, on Aiden's serve. 40–15. Pretty much game over. Match point. Not that you could see it on Aiden's face or in his movements.

He stood with a serious focus as though this would just be another serve, not potentially one that would end the match. Straight-faced. A true pro. He tossed the ball, back arching, racket snapping back.

Bam. The ball shot over the net and down the T in a flash. Monetti's racket didn't even touch it—he hadn't had time to react.

An ace.

Shouts and clapping washed over the arena as Aiden threw his arms up in celebration.

"Game, set and match. Andale wins two sets to love, 6–4, 6–3."

"Embrace the unknown!" Aiden yelled into the microphone.

Everyone cheered and hooted. The large LCD screen mounted high above the umpire's chair displayed Aiden's face as he held up his translucent, vase-like trophy.

"First, I'd like to say congrats to Vincenzo. He played really well this week to make it to the finals, real top-level. Today I was the luckier one, but I'm sure he'll continue to do well in the Australian Open next week."

Vincenzo gave a polite nod.

"Next, I want to thank my team. My dad, for coaching me. My physio, Trev, and my trainer, Mike. I wouldn't be able to do all this without their help. Thanks to the ball kids, the sponsors, and organisers of this event. Nothing would be possible without you too.

"Man, what a great start to my year. I was born in Sydney, so to win the actual Sydney International...it means the world. So thanks everyone for coming out today. I appreciate all your support. See you in Melbourne next week."

Melbourne next week. My heart threatened to burst out from my chest at the painful reminder. Dad had loved Melbourne Park and the Australian Open more than anything. What would he have made of Aiden Andale and his victory today? There was only one possible answer.

Happy. Dad would've been happy. And the thought of that brought a sad smile to my face as Aiden lifted his trophy in victory again and I joined in on the applause.

Max's car slowed to a stop on the curb. I opened the front passenger door and jumped in. "Hey, Gor Gor. Thanks for picking me up."

"Meeeh," he said, dragging out the one syllable for as long as humanly possible. "Just make sure you keep your promise. What's up with you and Ma anyway? You're usually the goody-two-shoes."

"She said mean things about Jere, so I'm punishing her."

"Seriously?" He slapped his hands on the top of the steering wheel. "More like you're punishing me. She's making me do those Saturday shifts now. Gosh, Dippy. Grow up."

Grow up? That was hilarious coming from him, the guy who spent ninety percent of his free time in front of a computer. And why was he complaining so much? Mum had recently employed Ming to help out with the baking, so it wasn't like the pressure was all on him. But I kept my mouth shut because I wasn't in the mood to start an argument. "Whatever. I won't skip again."

He huffed. "Better not." Flicking on his right indicator, he did a head check, pulling out of the curb and onto the main road. "Who won, by the way?"

I stared outside my window at the blurry shadows of buildings and trees as we sped past them. "Aiden Andale."

"Woo, go 'Straya," he said like a true patriot. "So was it what you expected?"

"Yeah." I'd predicted Aiden would win. That, I'd expected. But Liz's strange behaviour, her edginess and annoyance at her sister, her abrupt departure after the random phone call—I hadn't expected that tonight at all.

I tried to push aside my worries for her as my brain slowly drifted off. Who knew what our lives were coming to? Maybe Aiden's catchphrase was right. Maybe we should embrace the unknown more. Though how exactly did one embrace the unknown?

CHAPTER 10

8 MONTHS LATER
(22 YEARS OLD)

"Whyyyy? Why would he do that?" I wailed as sad melancholic background music played from my laptop. This was the worst romance movie ever. It shouldn't even have been classed as romance. More like tragic sacrifice.

I paused the video player and let my head collapse onto the bed. Balling my hands into fists, I pummelled my pillow repeatedly like a punching bag. "Useless. Stupid. Idiot." Yeah, I wasn't talking about the movie anymore.

Someone knocked on my door and slid it open, interrupting my tirade. I suppressed a yelp at the dark head that poked in through the gap. "What was that noise? What are you doing in the dark?" Mum's voice closed in on me as she approached. Shadows eclipsed half of her face, the other half lit eerily by the light from my laptop screen.

"Noth-thing," I lied, my voice hacking in coughs midway.

She shook her head firmly. "You should be resting if you're sick."

I made a show of grabbing a tissue and blowing my nose loudly into it. Ugh, no use. One wasn't enough. Grabbing another tissue, I blew some more. When I finally felt like my nose was temporarily semi-clear again, I said, "I am resting. I already slept half the day away."

"Watching a sad love story won't help." How did she—

I turned to my laptop. A still image of the video showcased the pretty, crying heroine clutching desperately onto the fallen hero pierced by his own sword. Oh... I guess it was kind of obvious.

"You're still not over him?"

I winced at her bluntness. She didn't need to say who *him* was. We both knew. "No, I'm over it. I don't need him." I'd meant the words to come out convincing, but they sounded lame and despairing in my scratchy, cold-induced voice.

"That boy was no good anyway," Mum went on, as though she didn't believe me and I needed another reminder. "Didn't eat meat, distracted you from studying, stopped you from helping me, always asking you out and wasting money—"

"Mum!" She was so not helping.

"You'll see. It's better without him." She said it like she was talking about leaving out some suggested extra ingredient in a recipe. What she didn't know was that he'd sunken his way into my heart, became as important as flour in buns. How did I continue on now without the most essential ingredient in my life?

Of course I didn't say all that to her. "Yeah, thanks Mum. It's late. You should go back to bed." I shooed her out, leaving me to drown silently in my sorrows. Or anger. Whichever it was. Probably both.

I moved the laptop to my bedside desk and snapped the lid shut with a sigh. Just as I settled back onto my bed in the welcoming darkness, my mobile phone chimed and a notification popped up.

Liz: Please answer me. Let me explain what...

The rest of the message was hidden from the preview, waiting for me to unlock my phone to view it. I didn't. Because however mad I was toward my boyfriend—*ex-boyfriend*, I grudgingly corrected myself—multiply that times ten for Liz.

A burning hot sensation ignited in my chest, spreading through my whole body like an inner inferno. My best friend. She'd been my best friend. Or so I'd blindly thought. Best friends didn't betray each other. A heavy pain pounded in my head. I clamped my eyelids closed and smoothed a hand over my temple. I totally did not need this drama when I was sick.

Chucking the phone on my pillow, I sprawled my arms and legs out like a starfish. Forget about Liz. She didn't deserve a chance to explain. What was there to explain anyway? Nothing she said would change what had already happened. I hoped she was feeling miserable for what she'd done.

Nope. I couldn't do this anymore. I couldn't be the pitiful girl who wanted sympathy. I needed out.

I slowly peeled myself off the bed, teeth chattering. It felt like a freaking ice age outside the heated confines of my electric blanket. I threw on a woolly jumper and exited my room, padding across the darkened hallway.

Max's bedroom door was closed, no light visible in the small gap underneath between the floorboards. Well, well. Surprisingly asleep for once. Thankfully, he was avoiding me like the plague after Mum told him I wasn't feeling well. I didn't need him silently appraising my depressing behaviour. Mum's take on it was enough to last me a lifetime.

Pitch black surroundings greeted me when I reached the kitchen. I fumbled for the switch and flicked it on. Bright kitchen lights winked to life, stabbing my eyes. I whipped around and blinked several times, slowly adjusting to the vibrance. My gaze automatically went to the kitchen bench, a long shadow cast atop it.

For a moment, I forgot it was my shadow and thought... I shook my head. How could I have thought my own shadow was Dad? My throat swelled up, and I wasn't sure if it was a symptom from my cold or something else. I swallowed once. Twice.

My mind worked in strange ways. I'd made meals in this kitchen countless times over the years. Nowadays, my mind hardly ever strayed to images of Dad. But I felt guilty when I remembered him occasionally, like I was being bad for forgetting him all those other times. And when I did remember him, it hit me hard like a tank. Like right now, I could almost imagine his back from here, wearing a dirty white apron, a plain coloured T-shirt underneath, and tracksuit pants. Dad loved his tracksuit pants. He'd be making something one of us liked. Fish soup for Mum. Steamed spare ribs with black beans for Max. Barbecue pork for me.

My stomach growled at the thought of nice food, and a strong urge overtook me.

I wanted to make something. Anything. What should I make though? That was the big question. A proper meal would have been the good thing to make, but I wasn't in the mood to be good. I wanted dessert.

Egg tarts, maybe? It was one of my favourites in our bakery after all, and I hadn't touched one since trying to stay vegan. But no, that was a dumb idea. Egg tarts were Liz's number one favourite too. Did I want a constant reminder of her while baking them? No thanks.

The pressure in my head built up from thinking about her again. I silently cursed, going to our kitchen drawer with all the meds. Finding a bottle of pain relievers, I popped a tablet in my mouth and gulped it down with a glass of water. Hopefully the pain would subside in an hour if I was lucky.

Now what could I make? Something that wouldn't be too time-consuming and adventurous while I was supposed to be confined to bed. Nothing too filling. Mum had already made me Chinese congee today.

I looked around the kitchen for inspiration. Glass fruit bowls lined the bench. A bunch of ripe bananas sat in one of them. Banana bread, maybe? That was easy enough. My stomach seemed to disagree though. As soon as I picked up a banana and sniffed it, bile rose in my throat. I pushed it down, reflexively gagging. No banana bread then. My eyes trailed over to the next fruit bowl. Apples. That didn't sound appetising either.

What *did* I feel like? I walked over to the cupboard. *Please have something nice I can use.* Mum's stock for the bakery was strictly for the bakery only, so I couldn't go downstairs and take anything, not that there was anything much to take that I'd want to use. It was mainly piles of sugar, flour, and eggs, which I made sure to stock in our upstairs kitchen.

I pulled the cupboard door open, browsing the shelves. My eyes stopped on a carton of eggs. Hmm... I'd felt like egg tarts, but steamed egg pudding sounded nice too. Dad used to randomly make it as a slightly sweet dessert. *Steamed egg pudding it is, then.*

Seeing as I couldn't go without some good music whenever I cooked or baked, I tiptoed back to my room and got my wireless headphones and phone. What would be a good song to put on repeat while cooking? My thumb hovered over my most recently created playlist: Breakup. Yep, I know. I was so original. Whatever.

I hit shuffle on the playlist. A steady stream of music flowed from my headphones. The lyrics hit me deep in my gut as I listened while gathering all the ingredients and utensils. Why did the song sound like me? Why was I so pathetic to cling onto everything when Jere had already moved on with someone else? Was it because I still loved him?

I paused midway through filling a saucepan with water. Placing it down, I took off my headphones and I wrung my hands together, my breathing growing heavy. This time I couldn't stop the onslaught of this week's most horrible moment from playing in my head again.

"Sere, we need to talk," Jere had said to me. We were at his house. He walked me to the sofa and gestured for me to sit.

I sank into the plush leather, but its soft comfort did nothing to placate my worries. "Why are you being so serious?" A list of possibilities rattled off in my mind. Was he arguing with his parents again? Did he fail a subject and hide it from me? Did Mum snub him when I wasn't there?

He stared me right in the eyes. "I need to tell you the truth. I can't hide it from you anymore. It's killing me."

His words confused me. Unsettled me. But it was the tormented expression he wore on his face that grabbed my attention. He was dead serious.

"Killing you? What's going on? What's killing you?"

He turned away from me as if he could no longer bear to face me directly. Chickening out. His next words cut me straight through the heart like a sharp kitchen knife. "I'm sorry, Sere. I—I can't be with you anymore. I love someone else."

No, I had thought at the time. *No, no, no*. Lies. Not the truth. How could he love someone else? He was supposed to love *me*.

Even when all the pieces had fallen into place, after he'd tried explaining how it was *better for the both of us*, I refused to believe him. Even after I lost everything in a single night, I still couldn't bring myself to accept the words he'd uttered. Why was I so stupid? Had I been the only one in love the whole time when he never felt the same way? Why had he ever asked me out and told me he'd liked me in the first place? Why had he let me fall in love with him like it meant nothing to him?

I couldn't banish those thoughts. My chest caved in on itself, and I gripped the kitchen bench, the edges digging into my skin. *Stop thinking about it, Sere. Stop thinking about him*. He probably hadn't thought about me since that night. Probably all he thought about now was *her*. That boyfriend stealer.

Suddenly possessed by an uncontrollable bout of anger, I hurled a tea towel across the kitchen, watching as it whacked a cupboard and flopped onto the floor. Thrown away. Discarded. Just like me. I wrapped my arms around myself, squeezing tight, holding in the sob before it could come out. *Get yourself together*.

I retrieved the towel and folded it back on the bench. Thinking about it all again would do nothing except make me upset. I didn't want to be pitiful. Wasn't that the whole reason why I got out of bed? I needed to stop feeling sorry for myself. Dessert would make me feel better, so I willed myself to cook it.

Setting a saucepan on low heat, I mixed in some sugar with water until it fully dissolved. When that was done, I switched off the stove and went over to the bench to crack an egg. I beat it until it hit a nice, fluffy consistency. I took the milk from the fridge and I poured some into the sugared water. Then I combined the two together and stirred.

By the time I wrapped the finished mixtures with aluminium foil and put them in a steamer, I felt slightly better. Like I could breathe a bit again. "Cooking is the best therapy," Dad once said. He was so right.

A short while later, I took out the finished products from the steamer—three little bowls of pale yellow, glossy, and jiggly smooth egg puddings. Yum. I packed away two in the fridge for Mum and Max, then prepared to dig into my own.

Just as I scraped a spoonful of my egg pudding, my phone beeped. The blob of pudding lay on my tongue, but the decadently eggy taste did nothing to tame the annoyance burning inside me. If this was another message from her—

But it wasn't. A notification from my sports updates app popped up instead.

Andale v Monetti

See live scores now for the US Open

Aiden Andale versus Vincenzo Monetti again? Talk about deja vu. I'd been feeling so unwell and lazy these past few days that I hadn't kept track of the US Open. But this was definitely a match I didn't want to miss.

I dashed to the living room, lit faintly by the kitchen lights, and snatched the remote off the sofa. Powering on the TV, I quickly lowered the volume—I didn't want to wake up Mum or Max—and opened up the TV guide. *Please show them playing. Please, please.* Mum stopped subscribing to the paid TV sports channel after Dad passed away. I supposed it made sense. It wasn't cheap, and the only sport I bothered watching was tennis. But now, I had to rely on good old free TV. At least Aiden was Australian, so that meant they were more likely to broadcast his match.

I scanned through the TV guide. *Australia Today*—nope. *CSI Miami*—nope. *US Open Tennis*—yes! I mashed the remote button, my stomach churning as the screen flickered.

"—hope it's nothing serious. Andale isn't known for taking medical timeouts, so this is a really rare occasion," a commentator said.

Aiden was lying on his back next to his bench. A medical trainer knelt beside him. He grimaced as he talked to them, but whatever he said couldn't be heard on TV. Still, it wasn't hard to guess that things weren't going well when he started gesturing at his leg and the trainer pressed a hand on the spot he'd indicated. What was Aiden suffering from? A cramp? A sprain? It couldn't be a broken bone, could it?

"At five games all in the second set, it will be crucial for him now not to stumble. Especially after losing the first set," a second commentator noted. "Can't be too sure how this will play out now."

Oh no. I looked at the scoreboard on the bottom left of the screen. Crap. He'd lost the first set 6–7. If he didn't secure a win in this set, then it would be two sets to love and pretty much game over.

The scary question was, could he win it? It certainly didn't look positive to me. Not when the medical trainer wrapped his knee in tight bandages. But Aiden didn't falter, despite the pain on his face when the umpire called time. He stood and slowly made his way to the baseline, his leg movements stiff and careful, almost robotic. Instead of walking for his towel or the next ball, he motioned for the ball kids to hand them to him.

It was his serve now. He needed to hold, then either break Monetti on his next game or win the subsequent tiebreak. It was all or nothing.

Some part of me thought I should get my egg pudding and eat it. But I didn't, too afraid to tear my eyes away from the screen for even a second. What if he didn't win this game? Was he going to continue if his injury persisted? A serious knee injury was no joke. Aggravating it could mean taking a long time off tennis.

His first serve fell into the net. So did his second, and my heart seemed to fall along with it. Double fault.

"Love–15," the umpire said.

"Not good. Not good at all," one of the commentators said.

Aiden's head hung low. He spun around a moment later, jerking his chin up at the nearest ball kid. They passed him another two balls.

He took his time bouncing the ball before serving. I could almost feel the tension through the TV. A flutter of nerves rallied inside me. Was he feeling the same? I wouldn't have an inkling of an idea what to do in his position.

As he tossed the ball up and hit it, I chanted, *Try your best.* His serve made it in, and Monetti executed an easy return. Aiden hit it back. It continued for a short while until Monetti made a sneaky drop shot. Aiden ran for it, only to stop halfway to the net after realising the ball had already double bounced.

"Love–30."

Crap, crap, crap.

The umpire called out a time warning when Aiden failed to serve before the shot clock ran out. Boos jeered from off-screen. He raised his hand to silence the dissenting spectators, then limped his way back to the baseline.

"Can Aiden Andale continue the match?" one of the commentators asked.

"That limp says otherwise," the other pointed out.

Yes, that limp said it all. And if it didn't, then his next slow first serve—at only 142 kilometres per hour—said the rest. He'd reached his limit, yet he was stubbornly refusing to go down without a fight.

If there was any sympathy in Monetti's heart, he certainly didn't show it, mercilessly returning the ball and forcing Aiden to run crosscourt. I was sure he would collapse and give up.

He didn't. Like some kind of running machine that didn't feel anything, he went straight for the ball despite the severe pain he must have been in. How did he do it?

Was he crazily determined or determinedly crazy? Maybe he actually had a chance.

No sooner had I thought this, Aiden rolled to the ground, leg visibly spasming, and all my hopes fizzled out. He clutched his knee, making no attempt to stand as his face scrunched in pain. I watched on hopelessly as an organiser came to talk to him. He nodded at something they said, teeth gritted and forehead wrinkled in obvious distress.

After the umpire spoke with the organiser, he announced, "Mr Andale is retiring from the match."

A tear escaped from my eye. Then another. Soon my eyes brimmed with them. Stupid, emotional self. I swiped a tissue from the living room table and blew my nose. Snatching another, I dabbed at my tears. Through the blurriness of my vision, I watched Aiden slouch off the court, his limp more pronounced with each step he took.

"This is the biggest disappointment of the year, isn't it?" one of the commentators exclaimed.

"Not a good day for our Australian," the other agreed.

I choked back a sob as more tears streamed down my face and coughed into another tissue. No, it wasn't a good day at all. Not for him or for me.

Sometimes, life sucked hard, and we just had to learn to live with it.

CHAPTER 11

ONE YEAR LATER (23 YEARS OLD)

"I'm home," I called out at the top of the staircase. I flung my heavy backpack off my sore shoulders and slipped out of my heeled shoes, my toes uncurling in relief at the pressure off them.

"Welcome home, sweetie," Mum said. She lounged on the living room sofa. Loud shouting in Cantonese came from the TV speakers, followed by a cacophony of sound effects. I glanced at the TV screen. Two long-haired men fought in mid-air. An old-style Hong Kong drama. Mum was into those lately.

She angled her head to look at the clock on the wall as I took a seat beside her. "You're late today."

"Mm-hmm." It wasn't anything unusual. Very much the contrary. Late nights were becoming the norm on workdays. I bit down on the need to complain, choosing instead to relish in the best news ever. "But it's holiday time now!" I stretched my arms up and leaned back on the plush cushions on our sofa. My chest already felt ten times lighter. Holidays meant no more big responsibilities, no more shouting managers, and no more late work nights for the rest of the month. Yippee.

Mum's answering smile reflected all the excitement that burst inside me. "You deserve the break. Are you sure you don't want to come with me to Hong Kong?"

"Nah. I told you I'd look after the bakery while you're gone." It was the least I could do. I'd given up most of my bakery duties for the last two years, which had led to Mum hiring her baking assistant, Ming, as a permanent part-time employee.

"I can't wait to work with you again, Sere!" I turned around to spot Ming, Mum's favourite shop assistant and hopefully future daughter-in-law, standing beside Max. She waved a soapy hand at me from the kitchen sink.

"Ming, you're here! You never seem to catch a break." Fresh after finishing work at the bakery and she was still sticking around doing chores. I had no idea how she did it.

Her face broke out into her trademark dimpled smile. "You can blame it on your brother." She nudged Max. He grunted and gave her a pout she ignored. "Made me stay for din."

I chuckled and got up to walk over to her. I swore Ming was our guardian angel in disguise. Up close, she definitely looked the part. Her black hair was currently styled in a short bob cut. The ends curled inward, drawing attention to her oval face and sweet smile. She acted the part of an angel, too, simultaneously alleviating Mum's stress while also encouraging Max to no longer spend his whole life in front of a computer. He hovered beside her now, looking at her like an overly affectionate puppy as she washed the dishes, and he dried and packed them away. Ugh, they were sickeningly cute, but thank goodness Max had found an actual nice girl without any thorns.

"We saved your din for you," Ming said, her chin pointing to the dining table.

I ran my hands through the oily strands of my black hair, and winced at how gross it felt. "Thanks. I'm going to take a shower first."

I did just that, losing sense of time as I lathered shampoo in my long, greasy hair and scrubbed. While I did this, I thought about things I hadn't dared to tell Mum. Particularly, the problems at work which had caused me to come home late.

Someone on my team had stuffed up half the client invoices this week. I'd spent the entire day helping him fix up his blunder. Well, more like fixing it *for* him, because he'd slithered out around 4:30pm without a goodbye. I knew the mistake wasn't my fault, and I could've let it be, but the big boss, Mr Roberts, wouldn't care about whose fault it was. He cared about results. If nobody delivered, then the shouting and blame... Yeah, that would fall on the whole team.

I groaned as I stepped out of the shower and dried myself with a towel, shivering from the coolness of the air on my wet skin. I stared straight into my dry, red eyes in the fogged-up mirror. Would this be the rest of my life after I started my full-time graduate position next year? Wake up early, go to work, get home late, rinse and repeat. Why had I chosen law for my degree again? Oh yeah, because it paid big bucks. Even that was a lie. I had yet to rake in six figures, thanks. Maybe after another thousand years of stress and fixing other people's mistakes. And then what for?

If I was to ask Mum, she'd say, "Save for your future home, your future family!" Hah. Like that was happening. I'd sworn off relationships for a year now, and so far, so good. Mum's meddling tactics didn't work either since I'd steered clear of the bakery. So what future family was she talking about? One with me adopting dogs and cats? Sounded good to me. I could use a fluffy companion like Ming's labradoodle, Teddy. Unlike some guys I knew, Teddy was friendly and loyal to a T.

Ah well. No more whining. I blow-dried my hair, and tried to think of something positive instead. Christmas came in three weeks. Life was great. Until I went back to work. But I shoved those worries into my mental "come back later" pile.

By the time I'd scarfed down my din, as Ming liked to call it, exhaustion had seeped deep into my bones. I sagged into a heap on my bed and took my phone out of my backpack. Tapping it on, I mindlessly scrolled through social media, catching up on the latest gossip.

A few minutes later, my phone beeped. *Warning: Low Battery (5%).*

Ugh, not now. My hand dropped to the floor, blindly grappling for the charger, only to be met with empty air. I poked my head down. Yep, no charger. Max must've stolen it again.

I begrudgingly lifted myself off the bed. Should I tell him off for nabbing my belongings? Berating him in front of Ming would be a hilarious form of revenge. She sometimes joked that I acted as his big sister. But did I really want to annoy Max like that? He would probably end up permanently stealing my charger as payback if I did that to him. Not worth it.

With that decision made, I crept to his room and turned on the light. As usual, my brother failed to clean up after himself. The blankets on his bed were flung haphazardly, half-hanging off the edge. Next to his bed, moonlight streamed through his clear, square window. I snapped the curtains shut before continuing my search. His computer desk, littered with gadgets and a crooked stack of books, was the worst mess of all. I shuddered at a neglected muesli bar wrapper lying next to his keyboard, along with some scrunched up tissues. And beside that—

Yes! My charger! I snatched it up, causing something white from underneath to flutter to the floor. I bent down to pick it up. It was a plain envelope addressed to Max. But what caught my eye was a word on there—renovations.

Instincts took over me and I slipped the letter out from the envelope, unfolding it.

Dear Maximus Tsang,

Thank you for your enquiry concerning your bakery's desired renovations. Below you will find a quote...

My pulse drummed in my ears. Renovations for the bakery? And they totalled... Oh my gosh. Almost forty-thousand dollars.

I stalked to the living room, my fingers numb as I gripped the impossible letter. I needed answers, and I needed them now.

Max slouched back on the sofa, laughing while Ming leaned in to whisper conspiratorially in his ear. She stopped short when she saw me.

"What is this?" I thrust the letter onto Max's chest.

"What—" He straightened before grabbing the letter and looking over it.

"So?" I demanded. If this was what it looked like, he'd been hiding it from me for some time. I couldn't believe it. He was aware of my lingering trust issues. Yet here he was, keeping a huge secret from me. "Why didn't you tell me we were renovating?"

"We're not renovating," he said.

"Liar! Proof right here." I jabbed at the letter he still held.

He flinched and leaned back onto the sofa. "It's only a quote, Dippy. Calm down. Nothing is concrete yet."

"Don't Dippy me! You should tell me if you're thinking of doing something big like this."

"Why? You don't involve yourself in the bakery anymore."

His words were a huge slap in the face, hitting me harder than a physical slap would have. I took a moment to compose myself. *Don't get mad at him, don't get mad at him.* "That's because I have a time-consuming job and—" Why was I even justifying it to him? "That's beside the point. I did heaps to help before, and I'm going to help Ming starting Monday when Mum goes on holiday."

"Yeah, for this month. And then next year you'll..." He trailed off, his nose scrunching. His glasses slid down at the action, and he adjusted them with an exasperated sigh. "Just go to bed. We'll talk more tomorrow."

I growled. I wouldn't let him off that easily. "Let's talk about it now!"

He winced, clamping a hand around my arm. "Stop being so loud. You'll wake Ma up. She doesn't know either."

Wait... "She doesn't?" I exhaled slowly.

"No." He released my arm, letting his hand fall to his lap. "Like I said, it's only a quote. I was looking into ways to help fix up some stuff that's been getting old. You know, like the floorboards in the storefront. But mostly fixing up the kitchen. Ma complains that there isn't enough bench space, and the ovens are getting old. Things are rusting. Etcetera, etcetera."

"Okay. Okay, then," I said.

"Sere, Max wouldn't go through with something this big without telling you first." Ming stood up and placed a steady hand on my shoulder. Her thumb drew circles in the crook of my neck with a gentleness that made me think, *Yep, she's an angel*. Unfortunately, her soft touch alone wasn't enough to alleviate all my anger.

"Wouldn't he? Looks like he was gonna." I dropped on the sofa beside him and glared, not ready to forgive him just yet. The idea of his betrayal by omission still burned deep.

He held out his hands in a gesture of surrender. "If I'd told you early on, you would've told Ma in five seconds flat."

"Would not." Well...unless she asked about it. "Okay, maybe I would have. But I promise I won't now."

Max snorted, and Ming sat back down to give him a playful shove in the side.

I sighed. "Sorry I overreacted. I just—the bakery means a lot to me, even if I don't work in it every day anymore. I mean, the place is literally part of our home. Just let me pay for some of it if we do the renovations, okay?"

"Yeah. Relax," Max said. "You saw the cost. It'll probably take a while to get the money for it, but I'll put some of my savings in too."

"But why are you helping to pay for it?" He should've been saving what he could for his own future home. Sydney housing prices were crazy expensive.

"Uh..." He gulped and scratched his chin. "Remember one time when I asked you if you promised Ba anything?"

"Yeah?" Vaguely. Life had changed a lot since then.

"I promised him some things too," he admitted.

I knew it! I wanted to yell it out, but... I shut my mouth. That would most likely make him reconsider revealing it. I couldn't risk that now that he was so close to coming clean about it.

Max reached for Ming, pulling her close. She leaned into him, her concern evident in her furrowed eyebrows and pursed lips. She knew talking about Dad wasn't easy for Max. Like me, he and Dad had been close. Really close. "I knew you'd want to know what I'd promised him, but I was embarrassed to tell you."

"Why? Pretty sure he wouldn't have asked you to study hard like me." Max had always been bad with his grades, to put it kindly.

"No, of course not." He rolled his eyes, then bit his lip. Contemplating whether or not to tell me. Finally, he said, "He made me promise him that I'd look after the bakery. That I would make sure it stayed alive."

I stopped breathing as his words sank in. Dad had made Max promise him that? All those times... The first few months after Dad passed, we'd even considered selling the bakery... "You—I can't believe you—" I couldn't believe he'd tried to take all that responsibility onto himself without telling me. "You're not alone, you know. Don't just go doing things on your own. No more secrets, okay? We'll do this together."

He nodded slowly. "All right. Together." Then, because he couldn't help himself, he added, "Just make sure you don't tell Ma."

I moved to punch his arm. But before I could, Ming launched herself at us, pulling us into a group hug. The heat of both their bodies enveloped me, calming me.

I should stop worrying so much. Everything will be okay.

CHAPTER 12

"*Mmmm*, these things are *delish*. Like little pieces of heaven," Ming said with exaggerated enthusiasm, licking a smear of chocolate off her lips. Poised in her hand was a half-eaten, strawberry-choc custard tart. It had all been her brilliant idea. After Max mentioned the one baking challenge he hadn't minded losing against me, she'd insisted I make batches of them to sell this week. "Max has made these with me before, but yours are definitely better. The original!"

"Hey, no eating on duty," I said, but I chuckled at her contented smile.

She proceeded to dust her hands over the bin and then covered the tray of tarts with a clear glass dome lid. "This will be a big hit with all our customers. You could open your own shop and only sell these tarts, and I'd come every day, your most loyal customer for life." Her dimpled smile faltered. "Well, maybe not every day unless you make a sugar-free version. I don't want to get high blood sugar."

My cheeks warmed at the praise, and I quickly ducked my head to hide my smile while I wiped the rest of the tart crumbs off the counter and into the bin.

My first week off work was flying by so quickly. It was already Thursday. Since Mum left a few days ago, I relied on Ming to help me. We woke up extra early in the morning so we could get most of the baking done before the bakery opened for the day. Thank goodness for the existence of coffee or I didn't know how I'd manage.

How had Mum done it for the past seven years without Dad? She was Wonder Woman reincarnated or something. Sure Ming helped now, and my cousin Lee worked a few days a week. But most of it was on Mum, and I was beginning to see just how much of her personal life she'd sacrificed to keep the bakery alive without Dad. We should've been giving her breaks more often. If anyone deserved it, Mum did.

Still, I didn't hate all the hard work. Maybe because everyone was so nice. Some of Mum's friends practically squealed at seeing me again. As embarrassing as it was to hear them say Mum talked a lot about me, I was happy to be back, even if only temporarily.

Too bad it wouldn't last. But I would enjoy it while I could.

The bell jingled on the front door as it opened, and Ming and I looked up from our tasks. A tall lady walked in, and her gaze landed on me. Or it looked that way. It was hard to tell with the sunglasses hiding her eyes.

"Am I seeing a ghost?" she said, gasping. Before I could respond, she marched up to us in three long strides and swept me up in an embrace.

"Hi, Mrs Miller," I said into her shoulder and breathed in the strong scent of her lavender perfume.

"Still calling me that? I see some things haven't changed." She squeezed my waist as if to make sure I really wasn't a ghost, then let go of me and took a step back. "For the thousandth time, dear—call me Rose." Her head tilted to the side, and I caught a glimpse of my face mirrored in her sunglasses. "Unless you want me to start calling you Serendipity?"

Nope, not in a million years. "Rose," I conceded. "Long time no see."

Funny how some things worked out. After she'd paid me back for buying her sister's baby formula all those years ago, she kept returning to our bakery. "Isaac is a picky eater, but he loves your buns," she had told me, much to my delight. From then on, she'd been a loyal weekly customer. But with the stress of finishing uni this year and starting part-time work, I hadn't seen her in ages.

Rose removed her sunglasses and tucked them in over her buttoned blouse. "Well, I'm glad to finally see your face again." One side of her mouth curved upward in a smirk, her eyes twinkling with mirth. "Your mum kept giving me excuses for you every time I asked when you'd be around." Then in an eerily accurate impression of Mum, she said, "'My daughter is a busy girl, on her way to becoming a lawyer. She's a hard worker.' I thought they must have locked you inside your work office and thrown away the key."

As Rose prattled on, I took a moment to observe her. Brown curls tumbled down to her shoulders, and an ever-present smile was upon her lips. She always had this motherly feel about her; the way she spoke so amicably without reserve and took a personal interest in everyone. It seemed her friendly chit-chat nature hadn't changed a bit.

"Oh, by the way," Rose said, turning to Ming, "look what I finally got!" She withdrew a magazine from her handbag and handed it to her. "It should be on page thirty-something."

Ming thanked her and flipped through the magazine.

I stared at the two women. "What are you two talking about?" I asked Ming, but she was too busy looking at whatever was in the magazine to reply.

"Don't you know?" Rose asked.

"Nope."

"I'm surprised your mum didn't tell you. I'm helping a friend with the local food magazine this month, and she wanted my take on the best food places in the area. So I asked your mum if we could put Tsang's Bakery in it, and she said it's all fine. She gave me some nice photos of your bakery."

"That's amazing." This could potentially attract more customers, giving us more business.

"Ooh, look at you. You look good in this photo, Sere." Ming flashed a dimpled grin at me.

Blood rushed to my head all at once. My legs were already moving to stand beside her before I could think.

Tsang's Bakery, for all your sweet and savoury cravings, it said on the top of the double-page spread. I skimmed over the text underneath—*family business... Caters to events... An absolute delight*—to where a collage of photos and a few discount coupons cluttered the remainder of the space. Most of them were close-ups of our baked goods like pineapple buns, egg tarts, paper sponge cakes, and barbecue pork buns. That wasn't what caught my eye though.

Oh, no, no, no.

In the middle of those beautiful shots of delectable bakery goods was my face. Granted, it wasn't the worst photo ever of me. I smiled at something off-camera, holding up a pair of tongs in one hand and a tray of egg tarts in another. You could even see the sleek shine on my black hair and the flakiness of the egg tart crusts.

These must've been the photos Lee had taken of our bakery for practice with his expensive camera. That was supposed to have been family photos and shots of the food. Or so I had thought.

I moaned, grabbed a hold of Ming's shoulder, and shook her. "Is it too late to remove me from this thing?"

"I'm sorry. It's already been printed, and they're sending it out today as we speak," Rose answered for her. The sheepish smile on her face didn't look apologetic in the slightest. *Sorry not sorry,* it seemed to say.

Oh well. Hopefully this would help us attract potential customers. We could really use some more.

But why hadn't Mum told me about this free promotion? She usually loved sharing news about free things. "Cafe near the train station is giving away free ice cream," she'd gushed to me a few weeks ago. Yet she hadn't had the time to inform me about this?

An irritating *squeak* emanated from the floor as Rose moved around to collect buns, disrupting me from my spiralling thoughts. *Note to self—tell Max we definitely need to renovate the floorboards.*

I smiled when Rose grabbed a couple of cocktail buns to put onto her tray. Looked like Isaac's favourite hadn't changed.

After several minutes, she placed down an entire tray filled to the max. I punched in the prices and quantity into our cash register, and Ming helped me bag each item by type into plastic bags.

"How's Isaac doing these days? Still playing tennis?" I hadn't seen him for more than a year now. Back in my uni days, when I'd worked in the bakery more often, he'd drop by here for snacks on his way back from school and talk to me all about the latest tennis news. I missed the little guy.

"Good, good. Of course he's still playing tennis. Do you really need to ask?"

No, I should've known that boy would never stop loving tennis.

"But he's still keeping up with his studies..." Her eyes widened. "Oh, that's right! You just reminded me. I wanted to ask for your help."

"My help?"

"Yeah. My not-so-little boy turns eleven next week. Do you remember those tennis ball lollipop things you make?"

My mind conjured up the image of a tennis ball on a lollipop stick. "Oh, you mean the cake pops?" Every year in December for the week Dad's birthday was on, I would make little round cakes layered in chocolate and skewered them on lollipop sticks. Then I decorated them to look like tennis balls. Max had given me the idea to sell them after an experiment with leftover cake mix. Not to sell for a profit, but to donate to a charity that had helped us during Dad's time in the hospital.

He'd said, "If we can help others in need, it'll be worth it." So it had become a sort of tradition, one that I'd carried on for all these years.

"Yes, yes! Cake pops." Rose clapped her hands. "I was wondering if you could make some for Isaac's party."

Hmm, they were pretty easy to bake, and I would be baking them next week anyway. "Sure."

At my confirmation, Rose paid for the food and departed with a kiss on my cheek and a promised invitation to Isaac's birthday party next Sunday.

By the next week, I'd gotten used to the morning wake up and workload, and we were—surprise, surprise—getting more customers in than usual. That magazine was serving us well. But on Wednesday morning, things took a turn for the worse.

"Can you believe Ming is sick? She's *never* sick," I whined to Max, spreading egg wash across the tops of pineapple buns with a brush. They went straight in the oven after I was done. *Hurry, hurry*, my mind screamed at me as I set the timer.

Max stooped over the sink, munching down on his meagre breakfast of jam toast while I stressed about how impossible it would be to run the bakery without Ming. "We won't be able to sell any red bean buns today. Or cocktail buns." She'd managed to bake everything else this morning, but I wouldn't be able to bake what was missing and manage the shop once it opened. "How can she be sick?"

"You forget she's human too. Not your 'secret guardian angel,'" Max said after his mouth was no longer full of toast.

Oh man, I regretted telling him how I called her that in my head. "You're a bum," I said. "You know I'm worried about her. You should check up on her later. Make her some congee."

A joke. Making congee wasn't in his knowledge as far as I knew. We'd been taught all the bakery's recipes by our parents from a young age, but besides that, he could barely cook an egg.

"Hah, funny." He pulled his infamous why-are-you-my-sister-again face at me, but it was soon replaced with a thoughtful look. "Don't worry. She might be able to sleep it off while I'm at work." He picked up his work bag, and I followed him to the storefront.

"Too bad my boss won't let me take time off on short notice. You should ring up Lee. Ask him if he wants to take Ming's shift today," he suggested. Our cousin had taken the next few weeks off to commit to his freelance photography. Who knew if he was even available now.

"Yeah, maybe." But I had no intention of bothering Lee. I could handle this on my own. "See you," I said, watching

Max leave.

I locked the door and returned to the kitchen, noting down the number of buns we'd baked so far for the day. Without Ming, we wouldn't be able to replenish the stock throughout the day. Ming really did pull everything together. I was useless without her.

I trawled my aching feet back to the storefront and deposited a tray of freshly cooked egg tarts into their glass cabinet.

I would not give in to despair. I could do this. No biggie. Even if Ming couldn't come in tomorrow either, if I woke up earlier, I could maybe get most of the usual quantity baked in time.

The cuckoo clock on the shop wall chirped out a long tune, alerting me to the time—9:00 a.m. Oh crap. Time to open up shop.

A frantic urgency swept over me, plunging me into a dazed frenzy. I unlocked the front door and flipped the sign to "Now Open," then rushed back and forth between the kitchen and storefront, setting everything up.

Just as I placed the paper sponge cakes into their respective glass cabinet, the bell on the door jangled. A warm breeze drifted inside, pulling me out of my daze.

"Good morning," I greeted, my voice filled with false cheer. I moved the sponge cakes around with a pair of tongs until they looked more presentable, then turned around, prepared to explain the situation to a regular customer. It was usually the same few who came in before their work hours started. *Sorry, we don't have all the buns out today. One of our workers is sick, so we're a little short-staffed.* But those words never left my lips.

Instead, my entire body jerked to a stop, and I gaped at the familiar face standing in the doorway. My mind took a moment to process what my eyes were seeing.

But it couldn't be true.

It was Aiden Andale.

CHAPTER 13

"Morning," Aiden said, as if it was the most normal thing for him to be here.

I'm dreaming. I must be freaking dreaming, I thought, my eyes tracing over his features. His face—it was the same face I'd seen countless times playing in tennis tournaments, down to the small mole slightly obscured by his perfectly pointed nose.

I only realised I was gawking when his gaze landed on me. *Look away, Sere.* But it was like I'd turned into a statue. Every one of my limbs locked into place, refusing to budge. As though one wrong movement would prove that what I was seeing right now wasn't real.

Seconds or minutes passed. I wouldn't have known which. It was like time had stopped inside the bakery. Then a faint clatter shattered our silent staring contest, bringing me back into motion.

I looked down. The tongs I'd been holding had dropped out of my hands and onto the floor. Oops.

"Let me get that," Aiden said at the same time I stooped to retrieve it.

Before I could react, we collided. A jarring pain shot through the top of my head, and I bit back my cry.

"Oww." Aiden splayed a hand on the floor to steady himself, his other clutching his head.

"Sorry," I whimpered, nursing my own throbbing lump that would inevitably form a bruise. I mentally prepared myself for a shocked answer of indignation or an unpleasant retort. Something an entitled celebrity would say. *Watch it* or *I'll sue you.*

He said neither. A soft breath of laughter escaped his lips instead, startling me into looking up. His hazel eyes crinkled in amusement, flecks of green shining. "Why does this remind me of the first time we met?"

My stomach swooped low at the deep tone of his husky voice. He remembered me? Had he come looking for me? Haha, as if. No way. Scratch that. What in the world was he doing here then? In my bakery? It must've been a coincidence. Something easily explainable. But what?

If I confided in seventeen-year-old me right now, she would've been squealing non-stop. Teenage-me had dreamt of this very moment. Meeting him again. Except it had gone a little differently in my younger, naive head—him popping into the sports centre again. Or bumping into him at the Australian Open. Not right here, in the safe haven of my family's bakery.

Distracted by my runaway thoughts, I could only gawk at him as he blinked at me with a disarming smile on his face. In one fluid motion, he picked up the tongs from off the floor and lifted himself up.

"We finally meet again, eh?" he said, extending a hand out in the space between us.

I stared blankly at him until the ache in my feet reminded me I was still crouched on the floor. Unable to withstand the uncomfortable position any longer, I gave in, placing my hand in his. A radiating heat consumed me at the contact, like I was sticking my hand in front of an open oven. I tried to ignore it, pushing off the floor at the same time he pulled me up.

Now this was where things went oh-so wrong. Rather than my legs straightening out and finding balance like a normal person, I stumbled forward—and slammed straight into Aiden's chest.

I gasped, the strong earthy scent of his cologne filling my nostrils. My lips parted, preparing to apologise, but my tongue remained glued to the roof of my mouth.

It was all his body's fault. If touching his hand alone felt like being in front of an open oven, being pressed flush against him was one step further. It felt like being shoved right inside of that oven. Way too hot and dangerous. I was going to burn myself. Sweat had already begun to dampen my skin, despite turning the aircon on an hour ago in anticipation of the thirty-five degree Celsius weather forecast. I should've been cold, not hot. What was wrong with me?

A sudden pressure on my shoulder pulled me out of my stupor—Aiden's hand was pushing me back. My skin grew even hotter. Oh my gosh, he probably thought I was acting like a silly fangirl, oblivious to personal space.

Using the momentum of his push, I quickly took a huge step away from him. A fraction of the fiery heat dissipated, leaving me blinking down at the worn floorboards. "S-sorry!" I stuttered, slowly lifting my gaze upward.

Big mistake. No, correction—*huge* mistake. The instant my eyes met his, I was caught in the grip of the mesmerising hazel colour of them all over again. Honestly, they effectively short-circuited my ability to form sentences. "Um..."

"Here." He held out the tongs.

"Thanks," I muttered, grabbing them. I studied his face, but his expression was indiscernible. He could've been totally getting the wrong idea about my weird stumble, for all I knew. But oh gosh, I hoped he wasn't. I wracked my mushy brain for something else I could say, but his attention had already drifted elsewhere.

"Woah. Did you make these?" He closed in on the front counter and pointed to the tennis ball cake pops. "They look like the real thing."

I nodded, cheeks flaming at his praise.

"What's the green stuff?"

"Sanding sugar," I said. The question spurred me to life, and although he didn't ask, I added, "The inside is made of crumbled cake mixed with buttercream and then dipped in melted chocolate. It's an easy recipe."

He leaned closer to the counter, his focus still on the cake pops. "That doesn't sound easy at all," he said with a chuckle, straightening up and turning back to face me. One side of his mouth lifted. "Why does it feel like you downplay everything you do, Not-Serena?"

"Not...Serena?" I repeated slowly, fiddling with the tongs in my hands. Now that was a name I hadn't used in a long time. "But how do you know—"

The bell on the front door jangled, cutting off the rest of my sentence.

"Miss Tsang!" a cheery voice sang out in Cantonese. "Nice weather today."

I pasted on a smile that probably looked overdone. Time to put my rusty Cantonese skills to the test. "Good morning, Aunty." It was just like Mum's most gossipy friend and customer, Mrs Wong, to pop in at this time.

She paused to look around. "Where's Ming?"

I dropped the smile. "Uhh, Ming already left for the day. She's not feeling well."

Mrs Wong frowned. "Poor thing." She patted down the unruly black wisps of hair beneath her sunhat. "She's always working so hard."

No disagreeing with that, even though Mrs Wong was Ming's biggest supporter and therefore completely biased in her favour. She'd often stay and chat with Ming when she dropped by. No surprise there. Ming's angel-like personality charmed just about everyone, and unlike my occasionally off-tone and mediocre Cantonese, she was near fluent. Mrs Wong could've gone toe to toe with Max on how much they loved her.

Probably the only things Mrs Wong loved just as much were gossip and red bean buns. The former was sadly missing without Mum here to chit-chat with, but as for the latter... It explained why she currently glanced forlornly at the right side of the shop where some of the cabinets were empty.

I bit my bottom lip, feeling like I'd personally failed her today. "Sorry, Aunty. No red bean buns."

She gave my shoulder a gentle squeeze. "Don't worry. One person can only do so much by themselves. But do you have my favourite tarts?"

Oh my gosh, the tarts! Thank goodness I'd made them last night, or I wouldn't have had time this morning. "Of course," I said quickly to reassure her, accidentally reverting back to English. That was when I noticed Aiden's gaze lingering on us from a corner of the room with the buns we had in stock. He must've been clueless about what we'd been talking about. Not wanting to seem rude, I continued speaking in English. "They're in the kitchen fridge. I'll go get them now."

I scrambled around the counter, almost tripping over my feet in my haste to get to the tarts. Why was I even rushing? The combination of stress, no breakfast, and no coffee this morning was getting to me. Oh, and how could I forget—an unexpected visit from a pro tennis player to top it off. It was like the universe had decided to throw me down the deep end today.

When I reached the kitchen, I chucked the dirty tongs I was holding into the sink, my heart pounding like a heavy drum.

Breathe, Sere. The bakery wouldn't disintegrate into dust if I stopped for a bit. I inhaled through my nose, basking in the relaxing smell of all the freshly baked goods still cooling on racks. For a moment, with my eyes closed, it felt like a normal day. I could almost imagine Ming working nearby, whistling along to a Disney song.

But then a distant chortle trickled in through the gap in the kitchen door. Aiden Andale was in my family bakery. Aiden. Andale. And he remembered me.

Just like that, my vision of a normal day was thrown out the window.

Nope, this was reality now. Me, deadbeat tired, and a pro tennis player in the next room over. He was here. Really here. It didn't make any sense. How was he here?

Why was he here? And why did his mere presence have such a weird effect on me? It was almost like—

No. I quashed the thought before it fully formed in my head. My exhaustion was starting to affect my brain.

I switched on the tap at the sink and doused my hands with cold water, splashing my face with it. I scrubbed my hands clean with soap, then snatched a paper towel to dry them and sponge the droplets off my face, leaving me feeling cool and refreshed. Ready to tackle the world. Or, well, maybe start with the situation outside.

Aiden's sudden appearance had simply taken me by surprise. I'd been starstruck. That was all. End of story.

I had to get myself together. Mum and the bakery were counting on me.

Okay. Here was what I would do—go back there and be nice. Act as if he and I were good old friends having a long awaited reunion. Pretend he was like anyone else I knew. I could do that, right?

With that settled, I pulled out Mrs Wong's order from the fridge and ambled back, careful not to jostle the box cocooned in the safety of my shaking hands. I elbowed my way through the door, just in time to hear the end of Mrs Wong's answer to a question I hadn't heard. It was surprising to know her English was as good as Mum's, only with a minor accent to it.

"Yes, yes, exactly. The first time I came here..."

I tuned out the rest of her words automatically—thanks to my inability to multitask—and slipped open the box of tarts on the counter. Paranoia always had me double-checking that everything was still in the same condition I'd left them in. Sometimes I had nightmares of coming back to nothing but crumbs and mice scuttling everywhere in the kitchen. Totally not a realistic scenario, but still a very real fear. Losing goods meant losing customers which meant losing profit. Losing all around.

I sighed in relief at the sight of the tarts inside the box. Not a strawberry out of place. No crumbs. No losing today.

"Are you Sere's friend?"

My head snapped up at Mrs Wong's use of my name, all thoughts of tarts, crumbs, and losing forgotten.

Aiden pulled on the strings of his hoodie. "Friend? I guess you can say that. She and I go way back."

Him? Friends with me? I'd been joking about the whole old friends reunion thing. Though I liked how he wasn't lying. In the strangest way possible, we did go way back. Back to a time when I'd accidentally whacked him with a tennis ball.

Mrs Wong hummed, and she got that look in her sharp brown eyes that I'd learned meant she was fishing for gossip. She tapped a finger on her chin. "Were you on TV before?"

Aiden froze. "No," he said, dragging out the one syllable. "But people do say that I look a lot like a young

Tom Cruise."

I cupped a hand over my mouth, holding in my laughter. Yeah right. A young Tom Cruise? Might as well have said Colin Firth was his distant cousin. That would've been more believable.

Mrs Wong's forehead creased. "Who is Tom Cruise?"

"He's a famous actor. You know *Mission Impossible*? I look like him in that, but with slightly longer hair."

This time I couldn't stop a bubble of laughter from bursting out of my mouth.

She totally didn't buy it. Mrs Wong was the shrewdest woman around. It was how she collected all her gossip. No lie passed through people's lips undetected by her. Max had once tried telling her that he didn't have a problem with Ming when she'd first started working at the bakery. Mrs Wong had shot him down for his lie pretty quickly. Luckily for Aiden, Mrs Wong had no idea who Tom Cruise was, and must not have been an avid tennis fan, or she would've asked for an autograph by now.

He shot me a pleading look that begged for me to save him. Who knew Aiden Andale could do puppy-dog eyes?

"Aunty," I called, taking pity on him. "Your order is ready. Six strawberry-choc custard tarts." I pushed the box toward her.

"Oh, good, good." Seemed like Aiden's presence had made her politely switch to English. Or maybe it was because I'd given up speaking full Cantonese.

She opened the box, adjusting her tortoiseshell-framed glasses on her nose bridge to inspect the tarts. "Beautiful. Very beautiful." She smiled brightly like a moon on a starless night, and my heart swelled with pride.

This. This was the reason why I loved baking. Seeing people appreciate what I made. Putting smiles on their faces.

Aiden hovered behind her. "Wow, they look delicious."

Mrs Wong nodded, her smile still beaming wide on her face. "My mahjong friends and I will be enjoying these today. Thank you."

"You're welcome, Aunty."

As soon as she was out the door, I turned to Aiden. "Really? Tom Cruise?"

His lips twitched into a half smile. "Hey, it works sometimes."

"Uh-huh. Maybe you should look in the mirror again."

He laughed. A loud, chortling laugh that left his mouth wide open. It was so unlike his sensible confidence in the media that it took me off guard. When he finally composed himself again, he smirked. "So, have you hit anyone in the head with a tennis ball lately?"

"Of course not." I grimaced at his reference to our fateful first meeting, the memory branded in my mind forever like a tattoo. "That's never happening again. Never ever. It was like a once in a lifetime thing." I wasn't sure if I was trying to convince him or myself.

His smirk only widened at my defensiveness. "And here I thought I was just one of the many unfortunate victims of your tennis skills, Not-Serena." He tugged on the collar of his dark grey hoodie, exposing the smooth column of his collarbone, his arms flexing at the movement.

I dragged my prying eyes away, trying to steady my accelerating heartbeat. "How did you find out that isn't my name? Actually, how did you even find me?"

"Good questions. Maybe I'll tell you the answers if you go out with me for coffee."

Go out with him? Had I heard him right?

I stole a glance at him. That smirk of his hadn't disappeared. Might as well have been etched in permanent marker on his lips. Did that mean he was joking, or was he serious? What would it be like, sitting opposite him for an extended period of time? Disastrously embarrassing for me, most likely.

"Um, I'm working right now."

"Not right now, then. When are you free?"

"Uh, I don't know." Technically, Saturday was my day off—the one day Max offered to manage the bakery during Mum's absence—and the bakery was closed on Sundays. So why was I giving myself excuses? I mean, this was Aiden Andale. A pro tennis player in the flesh. If Dad were here, he'd be hitting my head for passing up this once in a lifetime opportunity. But...

What were his motivations for asking me out for a drink? Purely friendly? Or was he a player like a lot of other famous athletes? I didn't see him as that sort of person, from what I'd gleaned of his personality in public. But going out with him for coffee sounded too much like a date. And that was one thing I was certain about—I didn't do dating anymore.

Not to mention, I had no time to think about anything else but the bakery with Ming's absence. An image of her dimpled face filled my mind. This wasn't the day to risk going out and wasting precious time. Not when I had the bakery to worry about tomorrow or the possibility that she wouldn't be in again. All those buns I had to make weren't going to make themselves.

Oh crap. The buns! I still had a few trays of them to bring out.

"Surely you can't be busy twenty-four seven?" Aiden said, but I was already breezing past him to get to the kitchen. "Hey, where are you going?"

"Give me a second," I said over my shoulder, pulling the kitchen door open.

The smell of baked buns still clung to the air, and I tried not to salivate as I breathed it in. Snatching a clean pair of tongs, I started heaping pineapple buns onto a plastic tray.

By the time I made my way back to the storefront, my eyelids felt unusually heavy. I rubbed them with the heel of my hand, ignoring Aiden's expectant stare following me as I deposited the buns in their display cabinet. With that done, I spun around in the direction of the kitchen for the next round.

But out of nowhere, a rush of dizziness overcame me. One of my feet tripped over the other and I lost my balance. All of a sudden, the floor rose up toward me.

CHAPTER 14

I reflexively flung my hands out in time to break my fall. That worked for a few seconds. Then my limbs felt so heavy that I gave up. My head slumped to the ground like a dumped sack of flour, the cold floorboards pressing into my skin.

In the back of my mind, a voice told me, *Not appropriate. Get up!* But it was like all the energy inside me had been zapped away clean.

"Holy crap." The vibration of footsteps pounded close. "Are you okay?"

A rough shake of my shoulder forced my eyes open. It took a moment for my blurry vision to adjust. Aiden's head swam into focus. "Sorry. I just feel tired." Understatement of the century, but I wouldn't be a complainer. "Just give me a second."

"You should at least sit down for a bit."

"I'm fine. I can—" His glare made me swallow down the rest of my words. "Okay."

His expression eased into something that looked like pity. I didn't need pity. Didn't want it. "Let's get you up first." He looped an arm around me—why were his hands still so damn hot?—and helped me manoeuvre myself into a more appropriate sitting position. "Got a chair somewhere?"

"Yeah. In the kitchen."

"I'll go get it."

"Wait," I said, but he didn't listen. I watched as he disappeared into the kitchen. Not a minute later, he came back with a small wooden chair.

"Thanks," I said, settling into it.

He knelt down to my eye level and fixed me with a penetrating stare. I tried not to look away from those piercing hazel eyes. Even if they seemed all-seeing, it obviously wasn't possible. "Are you sure you're okay looking after the bakery by yourself?"

"Yeah. There's usually another person working with me, but she went home sick." His eyes widened in disbelief. "But I'll be fine," I added quickly. I wasn't some damsel in distress. People like him probably worked a lot harder at their jobs. Who was I to complain about one day of working by myself?

A crinkle formed between his eyebrows. "I don't think you can call yourself fine after falling over like that. Either you rest, or I'm calling for an ambulance." He stood back up and fished a sleek phone out of his shorts pocket, waving it at me threateningly.

He wasn't serious, was he?

His phone screen lit up and he tapped on it, emitting *doot doot* noises.

Dead serious, apparently.

"Oh my gosh. Don't!" I reached up and latched onto his arm without thinking.

He jerked his head down at me, lips parted in surprise.

I let go and found myself clutching onto the ends of my apron instead. "I'm—I'm not feeling *that* bad." Not enough to go to a hospital. I was just utterly embarrassed, that was all. There was no cure for that. Unless hiding under my bed covers for the rest of my life was an option. But I was pretty sure that after a coffee and some food, I'd be fine.

Aiden heaved an exasperated sigh, staring down at me with his hooded eyes. "Give me one good reason why you can't rest."

His unwavering gaze sent weird sensations shooting through my stomach. "I—you wouldn't understand."

He folded his arms and puffed out his chest. "Try me." If I didn't know any better, I'd say he was possibly offended by what I'd said.

I fumbled for words that could explain how I felt. "This bakery is my family's pride." My chest ached. I might not have promised Dad to take care of the bakery like Max had, but that didn't mean I loved the bakery any less. And besides… "My mum put a lot of faith in me by leaving me in charge while she's on holiday. I can't—I don't want to disappoint her. This is her everything." I swallowed down the lump in my throat, willing him to be more understanding.

"It's your mum's everything?" he repeated. "That's why?"

"Mm-hmm," I mumbled with pursed lips. The overwhelming ache in my chest constricted, squeezing tighter and tighter. More than anything, I wished Dad were here to help. Unlike me, he could man the shop easily. I was mentally crumbling under the pressure of working on my own. The next thing I knew, tears welled in the corners of my eyes. I held my breath, lips still pressed together, trying not to blink. But a single tear slipped down my cheek, betraying my inner turmoil.

Aiden stared at me unblinkingly for so long that I wondered if he was going to physically shove me into a bed and force me to sleep. I wouldn't have put it past him to try.

After what felt like an eternity, he sighed and pocketed his phone again. "If that's the case, you leave me no choice. Consider me yours for the day. Hire me."

His words struck me numb. *Consider me yours.* "What?" I croaked out. More tears had escaped from my eyes, and I rubbed my face furiously to get rid of them. "I can't do that."

"Why not?"

I shook my head slowly. "You'd have to sign a contract and I don't have the authority to—"

"Forget about all that. It's just for today so you don't overwork yourself."

"I don't know…"

"Pretend I'm on a trial run. Unpaid." Aiden smiled like it was no big deal. As if he did charity work every day. I doubted it. "If it makes you feel any better, you can repay the favour by having dinner with me."

I chewed on the inside of my cheek, considering his offer. I'd be a fool if I rejected his help. "Okay, if you really don't mind." Some part of me felt like I should've been thanking him profusely for being so nice, but another part of me felt like this was happening too quickly. Like it was all a dream I could wake up from at any moment. Even if this was a dream, I wouldn't let him have his way so easily. I wouldn't be charmed by someone's supposedly kind nature ever again, even if he had been nothing but nice to me so far.

If he wanted to have dinner with me, he'd have to earn it. And the best way to do that?

"Why don't we make it a challenge?" It was something Max and I used to do a lot when we wanted to have something our way, and we couldn't come to an agreement. "If you win, I'll have dinner with you." If not, then more time for me to take a nap and prepare for tomorrow.

Aiden regarded me warily. "What kind of challenge?"

"If you're going to help, you need to know your stuff. Learn the names of everything we sell, the main ingredients, and their prices before the end of the workday."

His brows drew together, then he spun around and scanned the shop. "That's all?"

He asked the question like it was easy, but I didn't issue challenges I couldn't win. "Yep, that includes two of the items that aren't in stock today."

"And how many is that in total?"

"We sell eight different food products." That was more than twenty-four different things he'd have to remember.

I expected him to back out now, to say he forgot he was actually busy or some other well-constructed lie. But nope. "It's a deal then." He raised his hand and I shook it, marvelling at the eternal warmth radiating from his skin. "May as well pick out where you want to eat dinner now."

I bit the inside of my cheek. Cocky much? "Just dinner, right?" I looked up at the cuckoo clock. It was fifteen minutes past nine. "We close at six. Are you sure you want to stay the whole day? Don't you have things to do?"

He shrugged as if he wasn't offering anything important. "I have no other plans for the day." He glanced around the shop. "Unless you're secretly working for the media."

"Why would it matter if I was working for the media?"

The smile fell from his face. "Never mind."

But I did mind. I minded for the next few hours while I allowed him to observe how I served customers and replenished batches of sold buns.

At one point, a customer gave us an odd look and asked him, "Are you that tennis player?"

Before he could blurt out more nonsense about looking like a young Tom Cruise, I said, "He's a new casual at the bakery."

Straight after that close call, I ushered Aiden into the kitchen and handed him an apron from one of the hooks by the wall. As an extra precaution, I made him wear one of those white baker's caps. It wasn't the most cleverly put together disguise, but people wouldn't *really* dare to believe that a tennis star worked in a small local bakery, would they?

The getup also looked absolutely ridiculous on him. His tousled hair flattened out beneath the cap, seeming messier than ever. But he took it in stride. He didn't complain about it anyway. Maybe he would once he saw himself in a mirror.

During rare intervals of quiet time when no customers were around, I tested him.

"What's this called?" I asked, lifting up the new tray of buns I'd brought in from the kitchen.

His eyes narrowed as he peered at them. "Barbecue pork bun?"

I nodded. "Price?"

"Two dollars eighty," he said without hesitation.

And on it went until we'd covered all the items we had in stock today. The only thing he'd gotten wrong was the fact that pineapple buns, contrary to their name, did not actually contain pineapple. Otherwise, he pretty much aced the challenge so far. And that made a ripple of uncertainty weave its way through me.

Crap. I think I might actually lose this challenge. "Do you have a photographic memory?" I asked him, but he only laughed.

"I'm just good with memorisation. Numbers, dates, that sort of stuff. If you said your mobile number right now, I bet I could remember it."

I could barely recall Mum's, yet he was telling me he could remember mine after saying it aloud? "No way."

"Wanna bet?"

So I told him my number—quickly, and only once. Not likely he would remember it without writing it down. That was what I kept telling myself. I really didn't want to think I'd made another mistake on top of giving him an easy challenge.

Close to lunchtime, my stomach growled while serving a customer. I laughed it off, but quietly cursed not being able to take a break until it got quieter.

People flocked here during lunch breaks, wanting a snack for later or, strangely enough, a bun for their meal. I guess I couldn't really judge them, not when I'd eaten a bun for my substitute breakfast earlier. Aiden had also generously manned the store while I'd made us coffee in the kitchen. That coffee had worked wonders. I might not have been standing right now without the strong caffeine fix.

"Mind if I take a break?" Aiden asked not long after my stomach growled.

I waved him off. "Go ahead." Maybe he finally got sick of sticking around and wanted out. I didn't blame him. It was probably boring for him to watch me work. *And* he wasn't being paid for it.

Two customers currently wandered around, but seeing as they didn't require serving right now—a surprising moment of reprieve—I snuck a quick peek at my phone. Just in case Mum called. She loved to randomly call and ask how I was doing, being the worrywart she was.

But no missed calls or messages from Mum appeared on my lock screen. Instead, I came across a message on my notifications from the person I least expected.

Liz: OMG! Did you see this?...

I almost dropped my phone. What the heck? Why was she messaging me?

I'd never bothered to block her, simply because that felt so below me. It would have made me feel like I'd been in the wrong—which I hadn't been. But it had all been okay. She hadn't messaged me in a long time. Until now.

Would she send me spam? I mean, I was the one ignoring her while she was still trying to mend our broken friendship. Even her profile pic was still the one of us at the Sydney International finals from two years ago. If she truly hated me, she would've changed it.

Sighing, I gave in to my curiosity and pressed on the notification and read the preview title of the link underneath her message. But as soon as I did, it was like I'd splashed myself again in the face with cold water.

I read the title again to make sure I was seeing things right. Then a third time.

Andale Announces Shocking Split and Early Retirement.

CHAPTER 15

My mind lurched to a standstill. *Early retirement? Is this for real?* I tapped on the link to the article, my insides squirming in apprehension while the internet browser loaded.

Just as rows of text popped up on screen, someone cleared their throat. "Excuse me?"

My head whipped up. A man slid his plastic tray across the counter toward me and took out his wallet. Oops. I had work to do. How could I have forgotten?

"Hi, how are you?" I smiled, pretending I hadn't just been preoccupied with my phone. I powered off the screen and slipped the device on the shelf underneath the counter.

After quickly serving him, more people lined up to pay. Normally I'd be happy seeing so many customers, but right now all I could think about was that article's title. What did it mean? Would he really be quitting tennis at the ripe young age of twenty-three? It had to be a clickbait title. Or Liz had purposely found fake news to mess with me. Either one of those possibilities were better over the title being the truth.

When the bakery emptied out at last, I didn't waste any time. I nabbed my phone, unlocked it, and immediately started reading at lightning speed.

Australian professional tennis player, Aiden Andale, has recently drawn headlines after his alarming second-round exit in the US Open a few months ago. Despite his full recovery from his knee injury last year, his recent performances consisted of a string of first-round exits and withdrawals. This eventually led him to end his tennis season prematurely for the year.

The young tennis star is notorious for keeping a tight lid on his private life. However, yesterday marked the end of his month-long social media silence. An official post confirmed his split from his coach and father, Morris Andale—a huge shock to many. The two have stood together as a united front from the very beginning of Andale's professional tennis career. Many interviews and statements in the past have acknowledged his father as the most important figurehead in his life.

Andale's latest Twitter update suggested more alarming news with the following words: "Aus Open. Great beginnings for me. Great endings in Jan?"

Fans went wild with their speculations on social media, arguing what his meaning was behind this. Some fans believe the post to be a joke, or made on bad impulses. However, the update has yet to be deleted if this is the case. Unfortunately, Andale has not addressed any of these theories thus far, and his manager has declined to comment at this time.

Bells chimed as soon as I finished reading the last sentence of the article. I stashed my phone in its hiding spot under the counter again, ready to greet another customer.

Only there was no customer. It was Aiden. He lifted a large, brown takeaway bag in greeting. "Hey, I'm back with some lunch," he said, placing the bag on the counter.

"Cool," I said, ignoring my stomach's roiling protests. Yeah, it was so *not* cool that he'd brought food out in front of my face, but I couldn't really diss him for it. I owed him for staying and helping today. But I had to admit, it was hard to ignore the mouthwatering smell coming from the paper bag. Mmmm. "You can take it in the kitchen to eat." Far from my nose, please.

He didn't heed my advice. Instead, he dug out a few paper-wrapped items and handed me one. "I wasn't sure what you liked, so I just got you the classic cheeseburger."

I ogled the paper-wrapped package, its heat warming my hands. "Wait. You got me lunch?"

"Yeah, I was craving some good old grease and thought I should feed you too. Can't have you dropping like an overworked bee again." He rubbed his temple with his arm, shifting the baker's cap slightly off his head in the process. "Here." He pulled out a small pack of fries from the paper bag and passed it to me.

"Thanks. You didn't have to. Aren't you meant to be eating healthy though?" I asked, despite knowing that it didn't really matter if he was retiring.

Retiring. I hadn't even had time to comprehend everything I'd just read. Before his injuries, he'd been one of my favourite tennis players to watch. It felt wrong for him to retire at such a young age without a good reason, so I wanted to know *why*. Had he lost his spark? Here was the most reliable source to ask in front of me. But how could I ask him for the truth without being a snoop?

"Don't you, uh, have a strict diet or something?" I asked, thinking he might admit that wouldn't matter if he was retiring.

"Not really. Go on, eat up."

Huh. I guess asking in a pathetic, roundabout way wouldn't work. Well, since he insisted, I unwrapped the paper package. My stomach gurgled at the delicious sight of beef and grilled cheese clamped between two soft halves of a brioche bun. I took a bite and moaned in appreciation. As Ming liked to say about delicious food, it tasted like heaven. Funny, now that I thought about it. Ming, our secret guardian angel, referring to yummy food as pieces of heaven.

"Do you like it?" Aiden asked.

I nodded enthusiastically and took another bite, the combination of flavours melting in my mouth as I chewed. This burger was something else. Moist and tender beef, flavourful cheddar cheese, crunchy lettuce... though it could also be because I hadn't eaten a proper breakfast. Either way, my stomach rejoiced.

Aiden braced his elbows on the counter and leaned forward, drawing my attention to him. He grinned widely, causing flutters to erupt inside me. Sirens went off in my head at my reaction.

No, no. Do not go there! He was just a nice guy. I wouldn't get the wrong idea. He wasn't interested in me in that way. I'd seen the girls he'd dated before—blonde, beautiful, or a model. Or all three. Geez, I was the exact opposite. Black hair, not super pretty, and definitely not a model. I mean, I wasn't miserable with the way I looked, but it was hard not to feel insecure when I compared myself to those kinds of people.

"You look like you're deep in thought. What are you thinking about?"

I almost choked on the piece of burger I was swallowing. No way was I answering him with the truth. Could I melt into a puddle of embarrassment? My gaze trailed upward to the baker's cap still sitting off-tilt on his head. Could he fix that up?

I wiped my greasy fingers on a serviette and then reached for the cap. He tensed, his hazel eyes tracking my movement like a hawk as I straightened the cap and pulled my hand back. Noticing his eyes were still on me, I decided to answer his question—with a different thought I'd been stewing over. "I was just wondering why you're being so nice to me."

His eyebrows furrowed. "Is that a bad thing?"

"No, but it's unexpected."

And he continued being unexpectedly nice as the day went on; offering to serve customers while I observed, bagging the goods while I was serving, and volunteering to wash a few of the dirty dishes piling up in the sink.

It still didn't make sense to me why he was being so nice. Dad's favourite saying used to be, *There's no such thing as free lunch.* Ironic, because my parents jumped at anything legitimately free. But in this case, I couldn't see any immediate repercussions from accepting Aiden's help.

With the knowledge of today's available stock under his belt, Aiden spent most of his time helping me bag items for customers. I even let him try the cash register a few times for the easier orders. His confidence grew to the point where I would have recommended him to Mum as a permanent employee if he also had the baking skills. So it came as no surprise that at closing time, he successfully passed the challenge.

"Okay, I admit defeat. You win," I announced. He hadn't made a single mistake when I quizzed him.

His answering smile made my heart skip a beat. You would've thought he'd won the lottery from how wide he was beaming.

"So what's for dinner, Not-Serena?"

CHAPTER 16

A shrill tune blared from my phone, and the screen lit up with a new message.

Your order is being prepared. Expected wait time is approx. 20 minutes.

Yes! I couldn't wait. Char siu—Chinese barbecue pork—was my favourite dish of all time. Yum for my tum. After today's struggles, I wanted to treat myself. Except ordering for home delivery also meant the addition of something else in my home.

I glanced at the *something else* sitting opposite me. Aiden propped his arms on my dining room table, his steady gaze trained on me. Disbelief warred with tingles of amazement as I questioned myself and my current state of mind.

Was I deeply tired, and in need of a good nap? Yes.

Was I sleeping though? No.

Was I crazy to invite an almost stranger, fame status notwithstanding, into my home? Maybe.

But I figured I was safe from...what exactly? Theft? Flirting?

I doubted a millionaire would find anything in my home worth stealing. And he hadn't flirted with me today at all, which meant—as I repeatedly told myself before—that he wasn't interested. Not romantically. Besides, it wasn't like I was doing relationships. Nope, nope. Been there, done that. No plans to go and do it again. Ever.

"So, let me get this straight," Aiden said, bringing me back to our present conversation. "You called yourself 'Serena' back then because you hated your real name?"

"Uh-huh." I'd explained it all after ordering the food. But when he reaffirmed it like that, it made my teenage-self sound rather immature.

"Why did you hate being named Serendipity?"

Oh, I could launch into a whole essay about *why*. But I gave him the truncated version instead, counting off each point with my fingers. "One—it's way too long for a name. Two—it's hard to spell. Three—it's super weird and unheard of. And four..." I trailed off. Should I really tell him everything?

"Four?" he prompted.

"Four." I raised another finger. Would it hurt to tell him? He didn't seem like he would judge me. "When I was younger, a bunch of kids used to make fun of me for it." I dropped my hand into my lap as the hurtful memories flooded into my mind. "These boys in my class..." I didn't even remember their faces now, just their jeering, prepubescent voices. "They used to call me names. Seren-dip-in-pee or Dip-in-pee for short."

Aiden's face scrunched as he sank back in his chair. "Geez, kids are horrible." He ran a hand through his hair, messing it up. "Please tell me they got in trouble for it." The tone in his voice made it sound like if I said no, he'd personally punish them. I didn't really know what to make of that.

"Hmm, they didn't ever officially get in trouble for it, but my brother threatened to bash them after I told him." Back then, Max had been more than a head taller than everyone my age, and overprotective of me. "The boys stopped after that." But the damage had been done.

Why hadn't I been named something more normal? That thought had circulated through my still-developing kid brain, and my solution had been simple—convince everyone my name was something normal, like Serena.

"Lucky you have a brother who's there for you." Aiden smiled in satisfaction. "Do you have any other siblings?"

"Nope." My face scrunched up at the idea of another Max. Imagine two annoying brothers calling me Dippy. Actually, the second brother would probably come up with another annoying nickname, like Dipster or Ditzy Dipity. Yeah, no thanks. I'd accepted Max's silly nickname as an odd endearment—he'd been calling me Dippy for as long as I remembered—but that didn't mean I wanted any other nicknames added to the list. "One brother is enough for me. He already annoys me like ninety percent of the time." The remaining ten percent he didn't was the only reason I still called him Gor Gor.

Aiden chuckled. "That must be nice. I'm an only child, so no annoying siblings for me. But I was lucky I didn't have to put up with bratty classmates."

Now that he mentioned it, I recalled once reading about him having a busy childhood. "Were you homeschooled?"

"Yeah. Since I was eight." He stared past me, seemingly lost in his thoughts. "Sometimes I think about what it would've been like to have a normal school life."

"School is overrated." At least, it felt that way to me. What I did back in school hardly mattered now.

"Maybe it is," he said, but the wistful look in his eyes gave away his true feelings.

For the first time, I wondered if he wasn't happy with how his life had turned out. Although his private life stayed shrouded in mystery, I was beginning to see a hidden side to him from the rare glimpses he'd shown today. And from what I'd seen so far, he was different than how he portrayed himself in public. Sure, he carried himself with the same confidence, but I also sensed an underlying uncertainty and sadness to him. Though it wasn't my place to uncover those secrets, I'd be lying if I said I wasn't the least bit curious.

"What was it like being homeschooled then?" I asked.

"Let's see..." Aiden said.

We continued chatting while waiting for the food to arrive. It was surprisingly easy banter, like how I used to talk with Liz. As much as I didn't want to think about her, it was hard not to when she'd spent many years teasing me about Aiden Andale. I could imagine her eating up this current interaction between us.

But no. I was still supposed to be angry at her. Strangely, all I could muster up right now was disappointment when I thought about Liz, so I tried not to think about her at all. It helped that most of my conversation with Aiden involved him asking me more questions.

"How old are you, by the way?" he asked.

"Twenty-three."

"Nice. Same as me." He drummed his fingers on the table. "Do you still play tennis?"

"Nope, not anymore. No time."

And on it went. Normally with those types of questions, I would have been as stiff and hard as an overcooked bun with my responses. But somehow, the conversation flowed so easily with him, like we could talk for hours without getting bored—until he hit a sore spot.

"So what do you do when you aren't working at the bakery?"

"Um…" I bit my lip. "The thing is…I don't normally work at the bakery."

The look Aiden gave me would've been comical if it wasn't aimed at me—mouth slightly agape, eyes rounded, and brows arched high. "Really? But you look like you were born to run the place."

I laughed, the sound hollow to my ears. "I've been helping my parents since I was little, so I should hope that I'm good at it by now." That was all it really was though. Helping. And not even much of that, until these last two weeks. "I've been working part-time at a law firm this year, but next month I'll start working there full-time."

"That's… I wouldn't have guessed that." He almost sounded disappointed. Why? It wasn't that bad. I might not love my job, but it paid well. I could support Mum this way. Give her more holidays, contribute to the renovations, or help hire a new casual employee for days when she deserved a break.

When Aiden asked more about my work, I gave him non-specific *hmms* and *yeahs* in response. My heart just wasn't into the conversation after his reaction. Perhaps he finally got the point, because he said, "Okay. You're probably tired of all the questions now. Your turn. Ask away."

Free rein to ask him *anything*? I already knew what questions occupied my mind. *Is it true you're really retiring from tennis when you're only twenty-three years old? Why did you ditch your coach dad?* Yeah, those didn't sound very nice. As I contemplated how to better phrase them, my phone vibrated in my hand. "Oh, the delivery person's here. I'll get it."

A few minutes later, only the noise of eating filled the air as I enjoyed every bite of my meal. But every now and then, I couldn't help sneaking a peek at Aiden. Could this be a dream? A really vivid dream? Because if someone had told me yesterday, *You're going to have dinner with Aiden Andale,* I would have called them crazy.

I was so immersed in my own thoughts, I didn't realise I was still staring at Aiden until his eyes met mine. "What's up?" he said.

I averted my gaze to my takeaway container. Slices of char siu dripped with a generous coating of the brown-red barbecue sauce. I should've been continuing to gobble it all up, but my mind was elsewhere. *Are you retiring because of your dad? Did your dad do something to make you want to quit tennis?* Nope, both still sounded too abrupt and rude. "Do you like the food?" I asked instead.

"Yeah. It's nice." He bit into his piece of sauce-slathered char siu, chewed, and gave me a thumbs up. "It doesn't really taste like usual barbecue sauce though."

"It's a Cantonese-style dish, so the barbecue sauce is made from hoisin sauce and—" I huffed out a laugh, stopping myself before I went into a full explanation of how to make char siu sauce. "I'm glad you like it. I wasn't sure whether you would." He'd told me to surprise him by ordering the same thing as whatever I chose.

"Hmm." He poked at another slice of char siu with his plastic fork. "You mean you think I'm a rich snob who only eats from high-end restaurants?

That was actually along the lines of what I'd been thinking originally, but I wouldn't admit that to him. "Well, you are rich."

"That's subjective. A lot of money was also spent for me to get to where I am." He frowned. "But more importantly, do you think I'm a snob?"

"No," I said immediately. He hadn't once shown off his wealth. He was more down-to-earth than I would've imagined. I suddenly felt bad for presuming I knew anything about him. "Sorry if it sounded like I was judging. I'm sure the media does enough of that for you."

He blinked slowly, gauging my words. "It's okay. I'm used to it."

"I can tell you still dislike it, though. You joke about it, but sometimes people use jokes to hide what they're actually feeling." I'd cracked a fair few jokes myself after the bitter breakup with you-know-who. Sometimes you had to fake it to make it.

Aiden lifted a shoulder in a half-hearted shrug. "I joke all the time. That's just me."

"You don't joke on the court." Whenever I saw him play, he never made any attempts at trick shots. He also never went easy or relaxed, even when he was up two sets or several breaks.

Setting his fork onto a napkin, Aiden folded his arms. "Playing on the court isn't a joke. Not unless I want to pay the price for it after." He let out an exasperated huff. "Well, maybe that won't even matter anymore."

I held my breath. Was he implying what I thought he was? Retirement? This was it. The opening I'd been waiting for to ask him the big bad question.

I cleared my throat. "Are you—are you really retiring?"

He exhaled sharply, shaking his head. "You already heard about that? Stupid news travels too fast."

"So it's true then? About your dad and—"

He lifted a hand to cut me off. "Can you just—I don't want to talk about it."

I blanched at his sudden, harsh tone, lowering my gaze to the food in front of me. "I'm sorry." Minutes ago, I'd been gobbling up my meal without a care in the world. Now? My appetite was gone, replaced with a painful sensation building in my chest. Why did I have to be such a busybody? I just had to go and mess things up and—

"Hey. Serendipity?"

A thrill passed through me at the whisper of my name, but my eyes remained fixed on the char siu I still didn't feel like eating. "Yes?"

"I'm sorry. I was being an idiot." The sincerity in his soft tone drew my eyes back to him again. He stared at me with a pained expression that seemed to plead with me to believe him. "It's just—I was happy not thinking about tennis today for once in my life. You mentioning it brought me back to reality."

"It's okay. I get it." I got it more than I'd admit. And because I was the biggest hypocrite, I had to say exactly how much I understood. "You were running away."

Aiden closed his eyes, scrubbing a hand over his face. "Ugh, yep. Running away. You got me there." He stayed quiet for a beat—then broke the silence by thumping a fisted hand to his chest. "You know what? We should have another challenge."

Uh-oh. "What kind of challenge?"

"An easy one." The corners of his mouth pulled up into a smile. "You can ask me a personal question, but in return you'll let me ask you one too."

A question for a question. That sounded like a fair trade. Most of my curiosity would be sated without any lingering guilt. But then... "What will you ask me?"

"I don't know yet." He cocked his head, his eyes glinting. "It's all part of the surprise. So what do you say? Are you up for the challenge?"

I chewed on my bottom lip. What was the worst question he could ask? He'd pretty much already interrogated me. "Sure, why not. This is more of a deal than a challenge." Real challenges usually involved Max and I daring each other, with high rewards and even higher penalties. Once, I had to clean his room for six months straight after losing to him. This was child's play in comparison.

"Call it whatever you want, but you only get one question." He grinned cheekily, and I could tell he was having a lot of fun thinking this up. "Better make it specific so I don't give you a one word answer."

"Okay." Mr Smarty Pants. I massaged my temple, begging my brains to think of one question that would resolve most of the questions floating around my head. *Why are you retiring? Why did you split up with your dad as a coach?* Although they were worthy questions, they were insensitive. If I was going to be personal, I'd at least have the decency not to be rude again. "Why were you happy not thinking about tennis today?"

Aiden's eyebrows rose. "That's your question? I could just say, 'Because I'm not happy with tennis,' and be done with it."

I'd thought of that possibility, but he didn't seem like the type of person to do that. Was I arrogant or naive? Guess I was about to find out. "Is that your answer then?"

"No." He blew out a breath. "I'm an idiot, not a jerk." I waited for him to continue. "I guess you can say I'm in a love-hate relationship with tennis, and lately, it's been leaning heavily on the hate side. It's just been causing me such a big headache that I was happy doing something different today, just so I didn't have to think about it."

"So you hate playing tennis now?" Oops, that was more than one question.

But to my surprise, he answered me. "No, actually. Sometimes I miss playing. It's more the other things associated with it that make me hate it."

I digested this new information, relief settling over me. He didn't hate playing tennis. He also didn't outright admit he was retiring. Maybe he would change his mind if he was. Maybe I could convince him to overlook the things associated with tennis that made him hate it. But who was I kidding? He had barely let me ask him one question.

Trampling footsteps echoed up the stairs, putting a stop to my overly hopeful thoughts. By the sound of the footfalls, I recognised who it was before I saw him—Max.

I stood and walked over to intercept him before he recognised Aiden and embarrassed me somehow. That was when I noticed the phone held to his ear. "I'm home now. Yes, we've got lots to eat. Don't worry," he said in Cantonese as he slipped off his sneakers. "Yes, I know. Ma, have fun in Hong Kong." He paused. "Huh? Wait a moment." He lifted the phone from his ear and glanced behind me. "Who's that?"

"My friend," I replied, defaulting to Cantonese too. I didn't need Aiden to know he was being talked about. "I'm telling you now—don't you dare ask him anything."

He rolled his eyes and passed me the phone. "Ma wants to talk to you."

I cupped the phone to my ear. "Hello?"

"Sere!" Mum yelled enthusiastically. "How is everything going at the bakery? Have you been remembering to order more eggs and checking how much flour we have left?"

"Yes, Mum. Stop worrying."

"Okay, okay. You know how Aunty owns a grocery shop?"

"Yeah." What did that have to do with anything? I'd expected a full ambush with her asking me the specifics of what I'd done and hadn't done. And why wasn't she worrying about Ming too? Hadn't Max told her? I eyed him warily. He stood next to Aiden, at the dining table, talking to him. I strained my ears to hear their conversation. I caught the words *if I had known* and *thanks,* but I couldn't multitask as Mum prattled on.

"Aunty says she has some spare bok choy not suitable for selling anymore, but still good for eating. She'll bring them over soon. You can use them for dinner tomorrow."

"Sounds good." Mrs Wong's small grocery shop was only a few blocks down from us, which meant we often got our Chinese vegetables and other food from her.

Aiden's signature chortling laughter usurped my attention back to him and my brother.

"Who's that laughing?" Mum asked.

"My friend," I said, feeding her the same line I'd given Max.

"Oh yes! Aunty told me. She said your boyfriend was in the bakery. When did you get a boyfriend?"

Of course Mrs Wong had told her that. The gossipy woman. "He's not my boyfriend. He's my friend." I specifically said this in Cantonese so Aiden wouldn't overhear.

"But he's a boy," Mum said gleefully. I pictured her smug smile as she said it—one side of her mouth wrinkled. "Aunty told me he's not Chinese. Do I know him?"

I cringed. Thank goodness Mrs Wong hadn't known who he was, or she would have dished the dirt to the whole world by now. "You've never met him." Seeing him once on TV didn't count, right? I imagined how much she would freak out if I told her he was a famous tennis player. Probably more freaked out than she'd been when Max had told her he'd asked Ming to be his girlfriend.

Mum tried asking more about the mystery boy friend, but I managed to dodge her attempts until she changed the topic.

Once she hung up, I handed Max back his phone, shooting him the evil eye. "Did you tell Mum about Ming being sick?"

"No. Did you want her getting worried? Ming's still not feeling much better. She said she'll be taking tomorrow off too."

"Nooo," I moaned. Just great. My body felt ready to collapse at the mere thought of the upcoming workload.

"Then I'll have to get up super early tomorrow to start prepping."

"About that." Max slapped me on the back. "I have some good news."

"Good news?" My shoulders went taut. I wasn't sure if my head could handle another bombshell surprise today.

"Yep. My team finished all the urgent client work today, so my boss approved my annual leave. I'm off for the rest of this month. You'll need all the help you can get since Ming is still sick."

"Thanks, Gor Gor!" No more worrying about the bakery's workload alone. Thank goodness.

Aiden exchanged a smile with me. "That's great, Sere."

Yeah. Who would've known Max would be my new guardian angel in disguise?

CHAPTER 17

Ten minutes later, I opened the front door to the bakery, staring in confusion at the sight before me. When Mum said Mrs Wong was dropping by, I had actually expected to see...well, Mrs Wong. That was a mistake. I scrutinised the tall guy, with raven black hair, wearing a basketball jersey. From the translucent plastic bag with the hint of green dangling from his arm, I guessed he was here to deliver the bok choy in Mrs Wong's place. I totally hadn't seen this one coming.

Mum: 1. Me: 0.

"You're Mrs Wong's son, right? Ben?" All I remembered about him was that awkward time when he came to the bakery years ago. Seemed like we were about to have a belated round two full of awkwardness.

Ben nodded. "Yep. Are you ready to go?"

"Go? Go where?"

"Uh." He gave me an isn't-it-obvious look. "Dessert?"

I shook my head. "I have no idea what you're talking about."

"Your mum said you'd be interested in having dessert with my family tonight, so..."

It was like his words switched on a light in my head. Everything became brilliantly clear—and embarrassing. "Oh my gosh, I never said that! She must be setting me up again!" I baulked at the curious looks a couple gave us as they passed by on the sidewalk.

When I shifted my attention back to Ben, his head was bowed in shame. Probably a shame that came naturally with having a matchmaking, gossipy mum. "Sorry, I had no idea. Mum is...urgh." He threw up his hands, the bag of veggies swinging.

Urgh was right. Clearly I'd underestimated Mum's and Mrs Wong's scheming skills.

"What's going on?" I looked over my shoulder to see Aiden behind me. He'd somehow snuck up without me noticing.

Ben's eyes went as round as saucers. "Woah, are you— you're Aiden Andale."

Aiden took a step closer to me. "Um, yeah. That's me." He placed a hand on my shoulder. "Is everything okay, Serendipity?"

The way he said my name made it sound more like a melody than a terribly long name. I barely heard my own words over the galloping of my heart. "Yeah. There was just a misunderstanding." *Calm down. He only said your name and touched your shoulder. Two perfectly normal things.* But my heart failed to slow its beating at my logical reasoning.

Ben continued gawking at Aiden like he couldn't quite believe what he was seeing. I couldn't blame him. I'd acted pretty much the exact same way this morning. "Can I have a selfie with you?"

Okay, I was taking it back. I hadn't acted like *that*; I wouldn't have had the gall to ask for something so embarrassing as a selfie.

Aiden's hand fell from my shoulder, allowing me to breathe a little easier. "Sorry, man. Now's not a good time." He didn't sound sorry at all. More like annoyed.

"Oh, a-all right. Th-that's okay," Ben stammered. He disentangled the plastic bag full of veggies from his arm and shoved it into Aiden's hands. "Here. This is for you. I mean"—his eyes darted to me—"for her." He ducked his head. "I better go now. It was nice to meet you. Bye." He took off down the street at neck-breaking speed. I peered outside just as he disappeared around the corner. Well, that was awkward.

"Aren't you super popular, Mr Andale," I teased, closing the door and turning to face him.

"I don't mind the fans when I'm in a match or something, but when I'm out minding my own business, it's different." He set the plastic bag on the counter. "It's just..."

"Just a reason why you hate tennis?" I guessed. He certainly hadn't looked comfortable this morning when Mrs Wong thought he'd seemed familiar, but he'd looked obviously annoyed when her son had actually recognised him.

Aiden winced. "Yeah. Sometimes I wish I was a normal person with a normal job."

Poor guy wouldn't be saying that if he knew what a normal job was like. "It's not always a good thing when things are normal."

"Yeah, that's true." He shot me an amused glance. "So, is it normal for your mum to set you up on a date?"

Damn, I'd hoped he hadn't overheard that. "It's not what you think," I said, feeling the flush of embarrassment on my cheeks. He flashed me a look of disbelief, and I mentally crumbled. "Okay, it was for a date." Ben had called it dessert with his family, but I wasn't stupid. It was definitely a setup for a date. "That's how my mum is. She's always trying to set me up with guys. Nothing I say or do changes her mind. I've managed to avoid all that since I stopped working at the bakery, but this time she pulled a sneaky one on me."

Aiden laughed. "Your mum is hilarious. But why didn't you want to go out with that guy?"

"Because I don't date," I said.

"Why not?"

"It's...complicated."

He squinted at me. "Messy breakup? Pining over a guy?"

I glared at him, refusing to respond. He had things he didn't want to talk about, and I had mine.

He raised his hands in surrender. "Okay. Sorry. Not my business."

No, it really wasn't. So why did it take all my willpower not to divulge all the details to him? He had some magnetic pull on me that rendered him irresistible to talk to.

And that was when he decided to pull a sneaky one on me that would've made Mum proud.

"Can I use this as my personal question?"

Oh boy had I been wrong to assume nothing could be worse than what he'd already asked me during dinner. "Do you *really* want to ask? It's more sad than interesting."

"I happen to be invested in your sad story. So yes, I really want to. If you want to answer. Not going to force you if you want it to stay buried. I know the feeling."

I sighed, folding my arms in a poor attempt to hold my emotions together. "You've had a girlfriend before, right?"

"Right..."

"Did you ever really love her? So much that your whole world revolved around her? That you'd do anything for her? That you planned a whole future with her?"

Aiden pursed his lips, twisting them. "No. No to all of that."

"Really?" I thought back to a magazine I'd bought with him in it. Him and that blonde model. Hadn't he loved her? "It wasn't true love?"

"Maybe I thought I loved her at the time, but now I know it was just the idea of love." He looked me directly in the eye. "Real love shouldn't demand that your life revolves entirely around theirs." His gaze cut me deep, his next words a mere whisper. "What happened, Sere? Did someone break your heart?"

I gulped. "Let's just say...the last time I had a boyfriend, I ended up losing him and my best friend too."

"Woah, what? He left you for your best friend?"

"No!" Just like that, my frail composure broke. "Oh my gosh, no. If that had happened..." I shook my head, not knowing what I would've done.

"What happened then?"

Oh, we were so *not* going there. "Sorry, but you already used up your personal question ticket." Thank goodness he'd only had one question and not more. "Anyway, thanks for helping me out today. You're a real lifesaver."

Aiden's lips puckered up in a pout, looking like he wanted to launch into a full-on interrogation with me. But then he smiled, tugging his hoodie up over his head. "No problem. I better get going."

"Right." I opened the front door for him and we both slipped outside. "You should drop by the bakery sometime. I'll let you try as much stuff as you want."

"As nice as that sounds, I don't think your customers would be happy with me raiding your stock," he said. "But I had fun, uh..." He rubbed the back of his head. "I never asked what you preferred to be called. Serendipity? Sere?"

Serendipity, I wanted to say. But because I couldn't stomach the rush of flutters I felt whenever he said it, I just told him, "Sere is fine." Anything was better than Not-Serena.

"Sere," he said. "Thanks for today. I'll see you when I see you. Good luck with the bakery." He waved a hand in farewell and started walking down the same path Ben took.

All I could think was, *That's it*? After all these years and coming back into my life for one day, he was going to leave again? Just like that?

"Wait!" I shouted. Against my better judgement, I ran after him, arm outstretched. My fingers managed to grasp the back of his hoodie and pulled.

He jolted backward, coming to a complete stop. Releasing my hold on him, he righted himself and whirled around. The look of surprise written on his face was probably equal to the amount causing my heart to hammer against my chest.

I urged myself to think of something—anything—I could say. "You..." I faltered. *You can't just leave like that. You don't really know how much your help meant to me today.* "You never explained how you knew my name wasn't Serena," I finished lamely.

The surprised look on his face morphed into a mischievous smirk. "No need to explain. I think you'll find out pretty soon. See ya."

And with those enigmatic parting words, he walked off again, leaving me more confused than before.

CHAPTER 18

I rang the Miller's doorbell, and it punctuated the air with a loud *ding dong*. With my hand now free, I bent down to pick up the large containers I'd left on the ground, hugging them to my chest.

A thick beam of sunlight warmed my back like my own personal heater. Ah, this was nice. Not too hot to be out, but warm enough to ditch my cardigan in the car. Fortunately, I'd dressed accordingly in my favourite sleeveless floral dress, the hem billowing just above my kneecaps as I shifted restlessly on my feet.

Worried thoughts gnawed away at me after a minute passed and nobody had answered the door. Did I come too early? Had I gotten the address wrong? Surely not. I eyed the right side of the house where blue balloons decorated the front porch, attached by ribbons to the bushes bordering it. Highly unlikely I'd accidentally gone to the wrong house with another birthday party going on.

A faint rattling from inside, followed by a muffled shout of, "Wait a sec!" finally eased my concerns. I took a careful step back as the door creaked open on its hinges. Rose appeared from behind it, a smile lighting up her face. "Ah, Sere! Sorry for the wait. I was in the middle of getting food ready for the barbecue. Come in, come in." She pushed the door open wider to let me through.

"No worries. Can you take these in for me first?" I jerked my chin at the two stacked containers I held.

She lowered her head to peer inside them. "Ooh, the cake pops! Isaac will love these!" She clasped her hands together, then promptly hoisted the containers off me.

I shook my hands a few times, wriggling my cramped fingers. "Thanks. I've got a few more things to bring in." I hadn't wanted to risk piling up too many and dropping them by accident. It had taken a few hours of solid work yesterday and this morning to prepare everything. "I'll go grab them now."

Without waiting for her reply, I jogged back to my car. I already had the car door open when she said, "Do you need some help?" I was about to answer no when she added, "Oh, Aiden. Good timing. Can you be a dear and help her?"

My hand froze on a container on the floor of the passenger seat.

Aiden? Was it a coincidence? Aiden was a common Australian name after all. It might not even be spelled

Aiden. It could be an Aidan or an Ayden, or even an—

"Hey, Sere," a familiar voice said, instantly grounding my theory into dust.

I slowly turned around. Lo and behold, as if the universe wanted to prove me wrong, there he was. Aiden Andale.

"Wh-what are you doing here?" I whispered. I hadn't seen or heard from him since he'd helped me out at the bakery days ago. "Did you know I was coming here?"

"Maybe."

Seriously? "Did Isaac invite you?" That sounded impossible. But then again, other things I'd once called impossible had already gone and happened; Ming had fallen sick, and a pro tennis player had worked for my family bakery. It really couldn't get much more impossible than that.

"Yeah, Isaac invited me." I waited for him to elaborate, but he changed the topic. "Woah, you sure brought a lot of stuff. Let me grab some of that for you."

"Uh, thanks." I passed him two containers and carried the remaining two, following him back to the front porch. He opened the door for me and I stepped into the main entrance. The first thing that caught my eye was a bright silver *Happy Birthday!* banner sparkling over the front archway. Aiden led me straight down the hallway, passing by multiple closed doors on both sides.

At the end of the narrow hallway, the house opened up to a spacious area. The left side resembled a dining room, occupied by a long table and chairs. What looked like a doorway to the kitchen was off to the side of it. Across the dining room to the right was a living room area, with a cosy sofa and a large, flat-screen TV. Beyond that, curtains parted to reveal a window into a backyard.

I spotted Isaac outside. A net was set up across a mowed lawn. He and another boy stood on one side of the net, with two other children on the opposing side, hitting the ball over to each other. It was like a mini tennis court, minus the proper markings.

I chuckled. It was *so* Isaac to live and breathe tennis on his birthday. I'd go say hi to him later when he wasn't so busy.

"Is it okay if I leave your stuff here?" Aiden asked, drawing my attention back to him.

He pointed at the containers sitting on the dining table. The cake pop containers I'd given to Rose were also there.

"Yeah, that's fine," I said, making my way over to him. I deposited the containers I carried beside the others and motioned for him to step aside. As I pulled the lids off one by one, the scent of the cookies wafted out, followed by the freshly baked smell of the cake pops and cupcakes.

"Holy cow." Aiden stepped forward to take a closer look. His T-shirt grazed my bare shoulder, eliciting a shiver from me. "They look so good."

I glanced at the round sugar cookies topped with green sanding sugar and white chocolate, then at the cupcakes and cake pops fashioned in a similar style. I'd made everything resemble tennis balls. Because I hadn't known what to get a boy turning eleven, I had decided to bring more baked goods in the theme of his favourite thing. My insides did a little happy dance at how perfect they'd all turned out.

"How did you make these?" Aiden asked, the awe unmistakable in his voice.

"It's ea—"

"Don't say it's easy."

I bit back a laugh at his ability to read my mind. "It's not too hard," I amended, launching into a step by step explanation of the recipes I'd half thought up, half followed online. "...and you finish it off by piping the white chocolate on, and voilà, they're done."

Aiden studied me with the same rapt attention a baker would give to their finished masterpiece. I tugged at the ends of my dress, suddenly self-conscious. "What is it?"

He smiled. "It's just... You do make it sound easy, but I know it can't be."

I resisted the urge to roll my eyes. He was giving me way more credit than was necessary. "Honestly, it's not that hard. If you practice, it'll become easy."

"I'll take your word for it then," he conceded. "But you'll have to prove it to me sometime."

His statement confused me. Less than an hour ago, I thought I'd never see him again. Now he was suggesting we should see more of each other? Or was he just making polite conversation? I honestly didn't know anymore.

Before I could mull over it any further, the glass door to the backyard slid open. A man came inside, carrying a distinct, mouthwatering aroma of barbecued sausages with him—which made sense when he placed a plate full of them onto the table. Mmm.

The man grinned when he caught sight of us. "What's up?" He slung an arm around Aiden. "Who are you charming here, Aiden?" He fixed his gaze on me, scanning me up and down. "Hey, you're the peace girl!"

Peace girl? What the heck did that mean?

He scratched his scruffy chin. "Oh. Am I wrong?" His question earned a glare from the pro tennis star that he ignored. "She is the girl, right? The one from that photo in your wallet?"

The one from that photo in his—what?

"Ehhh." Aiden's mouth twisted into a grimace.

The man elbowed him, either completely oblivious or purposely disregarding Aiden's look of personal torment. "Go on. Show her."

Yeah, show me, I would've said if my mouth had been working. But I'd completely blanked out. The idea of him having a photo of me was super weird. Was this some deranged dream I was going to wake up to tomorrow morning and laugh at?

Aiden sighed in resignation and shoved a hand into his shorts pocket, digging out his wallet. Opening it up, he withdrew a palm-sized photo and held it out to me.

I blinked, taking a moment to steady my shaking hand before I took it. My pulse raced full speed ahead as I stared at the photo. And stared some more.

It was *the* photo. The one from seven years ago that Liz had taken of us. The one I'd never seen.

"I did promise to show you the next time I saw you. I just didn't realise how far off next time would be," Aiden murmured huskily.

"Me either," I whispered, still staring at the small rectangular slip.

"It's still mine, you know." He tried swiping the photo off me, but I dodged his hand.

Not yet. I needed to sear the image of this photo into my memory. It was perfect. Like I'd guessed all those years ago, I smiled naturally in the photo, with my signature peace sign that explained the man's nickname for me. Aiden was grinning too, but his eyes were focused on me instead of on the camera.

"You kept it in your wallet this whole time?" The knowledge struck me numb. "Why?"

In my daze, Aiden snatched the photo from me. He gave it a cursory glance before stuffing it inside his wallet again. "I lose things pretty easily. It just made sense to keep it there."

I supposed that sort of made sense. I personally hoarded all my receipts in my wallet until it overflowed and I was forced to clean it out. But as I took in Aiden's sheepish smile, I couldn't help but wonder if that was really the case.

"You forget that you lose your wallet too," the man remarked, looking smug. "It's how I always see that photo." He flashed me a grin. "This boy loses his things so often, I'm surprised he hasn't lost himself." He guffawed at his own dad joke, but I was too stuck on everything I'd just learned to laugh with him.

"I'm Mike, by the way. Rose tells me you make a mean custard tart. Any chance you brought some today?"

"I—uh," I stammered, my mind finally coming back down to reality. "Sorry, I only made cookies, cupcakes, and cake pops for today." Had Rose ever mentioned a Mike to me before? Mike, Mike... "Oh, you're Rose's husband!"

Mike showed off his impressive grin again, full set of neat white teeth glinting. "The one and only."

Rose had once told me her husband travelled internationally and was hardly ever home. I put two and two together. He travelled the world *and* seemed chummy with Aiden. That couldn't be a coincidence. "Do you work with Aiden?"

"Yep. I'm his personal trainer. But lately you can say I'm more like his personal babysitter. These days, I'm buying his groceries and feeding him more often than training him."

This time when he laughed, I joined in.

Aiden groaned loudly. "Stop embarrassing me, Mike!"

Mike playfully shoved him in the side, nearly knocking him into the table. "Where's the fun in that?"

Aiden glared at him again while my brain struggled to find clarity, flailing to piece together the various bits of new information with what I already knew. It was such an unbelievable it's-a-small-world scenario.

Aiden's personal trainer was this man, Mike Miller. A guy who happened to be the husband of a woman who frequented my family bakery. A woman who I'd met by chance because...I'd once happened to randomly help her sister out at a supermarket checkout.

Oh no. There was a word for this. The same word Mum had decided to name me when she unexpectedly fell pregnant with me against all odds.

A good thing that happened by chance.

Serendipity.

"Mike!" Rose's voice boomed, jarring me from my revelation.

Mike looked in the direction of the kitchen. "Well, duty calls. See you lovebirds later."

Before I had time to dwell on the fact that he'd called us lovebirds, the glass door slid open again. I turned to see Isaac coming toward us.

"Hey, man, did you win?" Aiden asked.

Isaac nodded excitedly. "Paul and I are undefeated." His huge smile left no trace of his usual shyness to be seen. I'd noticed long ago that this happened whenever he talked about tennis.

"Nice." Their hands smacked together in a loud high-five.

Isaac was still smiling when his gaze met mine. "Serry! You came."

"Happy birthday, Isaac. I baked some things for you." I gestured at the containers on the table.

He made his way closer to them, his eyes widening. "Nice. Thanks, Serry. Can I try one now?"

"Go ahead. Take as many as you want. It's your birthday."

He grabbed one of the sugar cookies and bit into it, nodding in approval. "Yum. This is the best cookie ever." He took a few more bites and licked his fingers clean. "Oh yeah! Are you going to play tennis with us too?"

I was so pleased by his compliment that it took me a few seconds to take in his question. "Uhhh..." Embarrassing myself in front of kids who were half my age wasn't exactly what I had planned for my weekend, but Isaac's pleading eyes didn't make it easy for me to refuse him. "I don't know..."

Isaac's smile turned into a pout.

"Geez, *Serry*, you wouldn't want to disappoint the birthday boy, would you?" Aiden teased.

Oh great, did they both have to guilt-trip me like that? Playing with me would only result in a big blunder, like me accidentally hitting someone. Really. You'd think Aiden of all people would know what I was capable of. "I think I'm better off just watching."

Apparently that wasn't a good enough answer for Aiden. "Come on, Sere. Don't be like that." He snaked an arm over my shoulders, pulling me closer to him. I almost jumped at the warmth of his breath on my ear. "What if I challenge you?"

I stiffened, my heart suddenly accelerating to twice its usual speed. I worked my jaw, but the words in my head wouldn't come out of my mouth. With barely any space between us, it was a miracle I could think at all. So I did the only thing I could—I extracted myself from his hold.

As soon as I was safely outside of his grasp, I frowned. "You really like your challenges, don't you?"

One side of his mouth quirked up. "What can I say? They're addictive. And don't forget that *you*"—he nudged my arm playfully— "started it all off by challenging me."

Goosebumps sprouted on my skin where he'd touched me. "Uh-huh." I was beginning to regret starting that challenge now. Though my childhood was filled with memories of Max and I challenging each other, we barely did it nowadays. He usually only issued one whenever he saw the opportunity to see me fail and wanted to get something out of it as an added bonus.

For Aiden, these felt more like ways for him to get me to do what he wanted, while I got something out of it too. Almost like a strange, forced compromise. I shouldn't have been falling into the trap of taking them, but in the end, my curiosity got the better of me. "What's this challenge then?"

"It's simple. We play Isaac's tennis game," he said. "You get one personal question ticket from me if we win."

Now that got my attention. "Really?" Normally I would say winner bribes didn't work on me, but Aiden sure knew how to play his cards right.

I turned to the birthday boy who'd been watching us with a confused crinkle between his eyebrows. "Okay, Isaac. Count me in."

"She'll be on my team," Aiden added.

"Yes! Awesome!" Isaac pumped his fist and took off running to the backyard, no doubt to spread the good news to all his tennis buddies.

As for me, I'd count it as good news if I made it through this without thoroughly embarrassing myself.

CHAPTER 19

A few minutes later, we were outside with the blinding sunlight bearing down on us. I adjusted my sunglasses. Good thing the bright glare wouldn't factor into any mistakes I made. Or was that a bad thing? I no longer had anything to point the blame at for any slip ups I made, except my own lack of skill. Oh well, too late.

"The rules are like normal tennis, but we added in two extra. Rule one is that all of this grass counts as the court. So any ball that lands on the grass is fine, as long as it goes over the net first," Isaac explained to us. Made sense since we didn't have a proper court with painted lines.

"Rule two is everyone has to participate and take turns hitting the ball. You can't take your partner's hit when it's their turn. We'll continue in whatever order we hit in first, and no changes." Uh-oh. That was not good for me. I couldn't rely on Aiden to carry the game. "First team who can't hit the ball before it bounces twice or doesn't hit in the right order, loses."

"Sounds good," Aiden said. "Let's play."

After quickly slapping on some sunscreen and borrowing a spare racket from Isaac, Aiden and I stood on one side of the mini net. Isaac and one of his friends, Paul, were on the other end, legs spread wide and squatting in receiving positions. Ready and raring to thrash my unskilled butt. My only saving grace was that the pro tennis player was on my side. Thank goodness.

And that was all I had time to be thankful for, because Aiden took his serve then. Clearly he didn't have the same reservations as I did about losing to a bunch of eleven-year-olds.

At the mere thought of losing, my mind suddenly chose to remember something important—Aiden never told me what *his* prize would be if I failed this challenge. What if he got another personal-question ticket? My stomach churned in dismay at the possibility, but it was too late to ask now. The game had already started.

Right after Aiden served, Isaac caught the ball cleanly on his racket and sent it flying over to me.

I rushed to the ball, swinging my racket with no real aim other than to get it across the net—which I barely did. Isaac's friend effortlessly returned the ball.

Yep, I was definitely the only tennis noob in this makeshift grass court.

I watched as the ball went back and forth between players, steeling myself for my next turn. It happened faster than I could blink. With a squelch of sneakers on artificial grass, I pivoted at the incoming ball, letting it rebound off my racket strings at the right angle. A shudder reverberated through my arm, and I silently cheered at my success. Yes, a good shot!

This went on for some time, and we settled into a smooth rhythm. Aiden, Isaac, me, Paul, then back to Aiden. I wasn't lulled into a false pretence of it being easy —because it definitely wasn't, despite the three of them making it look effortless—but I did relax a bit whenever I knew the ball wasn't coming for me next. Which was a big mistake on my next turn.

I reacted too slowly with my shot, resulting in a lame, giant lob. It sailed up in the shape of a rainbow at a snail-like speed, giving Paul enough time to get into a prime position to counterattack. He tilted his head up, racket pulled back, ready to smash the ball over.

This was it. Game over. But then he squinted against the sunlight, and when he swung, the ball made contact with his racket frame—and flew straight at Aiden.

Aiden didn't even flinch. Like the pro he was, he shuffled back and shifted his racket behind him, catching the ball between his legs.

A *tweener*? I'd never seen him do something like that in a real match.

Isaac yelped, lunging for the ball as it clipped the top of the net. He got it just before it made its second bounce. I watched as the ball soared high, toward the veranda behind us.

Wait. Was that going in or out? Crap.

I broke off into a run. All that existed in that moment was me and that ball.

It had already reached the peak of its arc and was now falling. Fast.

The ball hit the grass, bouncing up again.

I pumped my inactive legs for all they were worth. The soft grass beneath my feet transitioned into much harder concrete, pounding against the soles of my sneakers.

As the ball made its quick descent back to the ground, I dove for it, arm outstretched. The ball rebounded off my racket with a satisfying *twang*. I flung my arm up overhead, directing it back toward the net.

And then I crashed onto the concrete like the complete noob I was.

Lungs heaving, I breathed in and out in raspy gasps. Luckily, my arms had broken the fall. Though my hands ached, I moved to push myself off the ground. But that was when I felt it—a throbbing pain in my knee. My legs buckled, refusing to allow me to stand back up. What in the—?

Releasing my hold on my racket, I clamped my hands over the sharp stinging. Something wet soaked my fingers. I already guessed what it was before I pulled my hand away. Blood.

I hissed through my teeth.

"Crap. Are you okay?" Aiden called. He ran the short distance much faster than I had and dropped down beside me.

"Yeah, I'm okay. I just scraped my knee."

"Let me see."

Slowly, I repositioned myself so that I sat on the concrete with my hurt leg facing up. I squeezed my eyes shut, teeth clenched in a bid to suppress the biting pain. Damn, that hurt.

"Is Serry okay?" Isaac asked anxiously.

A feather-light touch brushed my skin near the injury. "Yeah. She should be okay. But we should get you fixed up inside."

"Okay." I cracked my eyes open to find him staring at me intensely. Hopefully the dumbfounded look on my face was partially covered by my sunglasses. "Just—let me get up."

"No, stay still. I've got you." He wound an arm under my legs and his other around my back, scooping me up and slowly rising to his feet.

"Wh-what are you doing?" I squeaked out, squirming against his chest. "It's okay! I can walk!" My embarrassment seeped into my voice, making me sound too high-pitched. Too flustered.

Aiden's arms tightened around me. "Don't worry. It'll be easier this way. You can't walk properly in that condition."

Yeah, okay, he had a point. But I couldn't ignore the fact that he was carrying me across the porch and into the house, bridal style.

Bridal. Style. My brain fizzled out until only those two words occupied it. Every part of my body tingled at his touch, my heart hammering like it was furiously pounding dough. I closed my eyes again, unable to take it anymore, my mind threatening to drown within these overwhelming feelings.

I heard the glass door sliding, followed by Aiden mumbling, "Thanks."

At the sound of a feminine gasp, I wrenched my eyes open again.

We were inside now. Rose stood beside us. Her eyes zoned in on my injured knee. "Oh no. I'll get the first aid kit."

"Thanks, Rose." Aiden's chest rumbled against me as he spoke. "Can you get a clean cloth and some bottled water too?"

"Sure thing, dear." She hurried off in a flutter of skirts.

Aiden crossed the living room and eased me down onto the sofa. Feeling like everything was too dim inside with my sunglasses, I took them off, folding them over the neckline of my dress. From here, I had an unhindered view of the backyard.

Isaac stared in our direction. The poor guy looked like he'd accidentally kicked a puppy. He didn't deserve to feel bad on his birthday for my own misfortune. Fuelled by my guilt, I gave him two thumbs up and yelled out, "Go win your next game."

I wasn't sure if he heard me, but his face morphed into that of surprise, and he curled his arms up around his head to form an O for okay. Turning his attention back to his group of friends, they got into positions to play again.

Good. That was one problem I could fix at least.

The sofa dipped, jostling me and evoking a twinge of pain from my knee—a stark reminder of the other problem I couldn't fix myself. I swivelled my head to see Aiden now sitting beside me.

"Nice work out there," he said. "I mean, if you don't include the injury, I think we did a good job."

"It *was* fun," I admitted, because I honestly hadn't expected it to be. Why would I, when I was so out of shape and not a natural at tennis? "But is it sad that we were super competitive against eleven-year-olds?"

"No," he answered easily. "Those kids were good. Real good. They had the potential to beat us."

Well if a pro tennis player thought that, it made me feel better. "Imagine the headlines," I said. "*Eleven-Year-Olds Beat Aiden Andale in a Backyard Match.*"

He threw his head back and let out a loud chortle.

Seeing his carefree laugh, and knowing I was the one who caused it... An indescribable ache burrowed its way through me, one that wasn't coming from my knee. All I knew was that I needed to see him laugh more like that.

"It's a good thing we won that one," he wheezed out, "or that would've ruined my image."

No way. "We won? How?"

"Your ball made it just over the net, and Isaac didn't expect it. But everyone was more shocked at you on the ground to care about the game anyway."

"Okay, then. Scratch that headline out. You can keep your good public image."

Aiden chuckled. "Thank goodness. In that case, the headline will have to be much more clickbaity." His eyebrows drew together in a moment of silent thoughtfulness. "*Girl Who Once Hit Aiden Andale in the Head Bleeds Her Way to Victory.*"

We both cracked up in a fit of laughter as Rose returned.

"What's so funny?" She placed all the items he'd asked for onto the sofa next to him.

"Nothing," we said in chorus, like it was a scripted line we'd practiced together.

She glanced between the two of us, looking sceptical.

Aiden cleared his throat and straightened himself up. "Thanks, Rose. I'll take it from here."

"What a gentleman." She beamed. "You better patch up Sere so she's in tip-top shape to work at the bakery, or the whole suburb will be screaming for lack of buns."

"You got it," he said and, with that assurance, Rose left us on our own.

After inspecting the items Rose had gathered and finding them acceptable, Aiden unscrewed the drink bottle and drenched the towel with water. "This may sting a bit."

"Well, it's already stinging." I flashed him a reassuring smile, but it was gone the instant I felt the damp towel on my wound.

Ouch. I bit back a groan. Before might have stung, but this stung *more.*

I sucked it up, watching Aiden expertly set about thoroughly washing the wound. "All done," he declared when he'd finished taping gauze over it.

"Thanks. I'll live another day." I bent my leg experimentally up and down. Not bad, so long as it didn't prevent me from working tomorrow. "Guess I can't play anymore, though." Not that I was too sad about that.

Aiden batted his hand in dismissal. "You had your glory. Now we can watch the birthday boy have his."

And so we did. Isaac was, no joke, quick on his feet. Winning one off him had definitely been a big fluke. "Do you think he has the potential to play professionally?" I asked Aiden.

"He could," he said. "But it might've been better if he'd started training professionally a bit earlier. I'm not sure if he would want that anyway."

That was a weird thing to say. Why wouldn't Isaac want it, if given the chance? He was crazy about tennis. Unless... "Did you not want that?" Because I got the distinct sense he wasn't talking about Isaac anymore.

He turned to face me, his eyes searching mine. "Are you using that as your personal question?"

"No!" I wasn't going to waste my precious question on something I'd already guessed. "I take the question back!" I waved my hands frantically at him.

He chuckled. "What did you want to ask then?"

I sucked on my bottom lip in contemplation. "I haven't had much time to think of a question yet." It still hadn't sunk into my head that we'd actually won. "Give me a minute."

While I continued watching Isaac play with various tennis friends, I pondered. What did I want to know about Aiden? Or more specifically, what did I want to know so I could help him change his mind about quitting tennis? Because, after everything I'd learned about him today and the other day, that was all it came down to.

I didn't want Aiden Andale to quit tennis.

It was like some instinctive part of me insisted I stop this from happening. He might come to regret it if he quit. If not, then I wanted to at least know *why* he would even think of retiring so early in his career.

"You said before that you have a love-hate relationship with tennis. Does it count as my question if I ask you to name all the reasons why you hate it?"

He eyed me warily. "Why do you want to know?"

I wet my lips, drawing upon all the courage I had within me. I didn't know if he would get annoyed like last time, but if there was a chance in convincing him, I would take it. "I was curious about it, that's all. You're so secretive to the public." *And I don't want you to be secretive to me too.*

His throat bobbed. Once. Twice. "Fair enough," he finally said, nodding. His eyes bored into mine, swimming with unsaid emotions. Curiosity. Doubt. A hint of fear? "Yeah. That can count as your question." He let out a loud, ragged breath. "This may sound weird, but I feel like I'm having a mid-life crisis at the age of twenty-three. Just..." He opened his palms and stared at them, as if they could provide him with a solution to all his problems.

"Just?" I urged him.

"It's just...tennis took away any opportunity for me to have a normal life. And I know you said it's not always a good thing when things are normal, but for me, that's not the case. It isn't always a good thing when things aren't normal either. If that makes any sense."

"I kind of get it." Being constantly in the public eye, he probably didn't get much peace if people recognised who he was. Being a professional also meant all his time and energy went into the sport. "But my personal question was asking you to list each reason why, not give me a general summary."

"Hah, you're not making this question easy for me, are you?" His lips pressed together in a thin line. "First reason, I guess, is that tennis is all I'm good at."

"That's definitely not true." Uh, how about his memorisation skills and ability to learn quickly? "But go on. That's one." I raised a finger to count.

His face scrunched up. "I'm paid well," he started, "but... don't take this the wrong way. I'm grateful for it, but I feel like money can't buy happiness."

He never flaunted having money during the time we'd spent together, so this wasn't surprising. I simply raised a second finger and let him continue.

"And..." He paused again, folding his arms. Thinking. Perhaps wondering if he wanted to share this with me. Finally, he said, "And I feel like it's ruined my relationship with my dad."

"Three." I tried not to think too deeply about this statement. If I did, my brain would get bombarded with more questions which I'd inevitably voice aloud. And that would really get him pissed at me for not minding my own business. "Are those all your reasons?"

He raised his eyebrows. "Do you really want more?"

Good point. "Nope. Three is plenty enough."

"Plenty enough for what?"

"To prove that you're wrong." This was it. Step one of my grand plan. "I challenge you, Aiden Andale."

He stared at me blankly for a few seconds, then buried his head in his hands and groaned. "We're just going to keep challenging each other to get what we want now, aren't we?"

"It *is* an effective strategy."

He lifted his face from his hands and gave me a sad smile. "True that. So what's the challenge?"

I gulped, swallowing down the dread sluicing around in my stomach. I had to phrase this in a way that would entice him, or he'd definitely say no. "I have until the end of December to change your mind on these three reasons for why you hate tennis. If I can't, then you get a personal favour *and* a personal question ticket from me."

There. Hopefully that was appealing enough for him.

"What do you get if *you* win?"

Of course that hadn't slipped past him. "I get the same as you."

"Hmm." He raked a hand through his hair, his face deep in concentration. Was he weighing the pros and cons in his head? Or thinking of a polite way to refuse the challenge?

"Okay, challenge accepted," he said at last, and I released a breath I hadn't realised I'd been keeping in. "I should warn you though—it's not easy to change my mind. I can be really stubborn."

I planted my hands on my hips. "We'll see about that. By the end of this challenge, you'll be living life with no regrets." Like the other day, I had a sense of being a hypocrite. *Living life with no regrets.* Yeah, I wasn't exactly a role model for that.

But when Aiden held out his hand for me to shake, I took it.

This is it, I thought as his larger hand encompassed mine. By the New Year, I'd make sure Aiden Andale would have decided not to quit tennis. Hypocrite or not, this was one thing I could live my life not regretting.

CHAPTER 20

"Sere!" Ming yelled out. "Your boyfriend is here."

I glanced up from my phone, glaring at her choice of words. Scrambling off the sofa, I stalked across the living room toward her. "He's not my boyfriend!" Not in a million years.

Ming's eyes went wide and, sensing what was coming, she backpedalled.

I cut her off from her path to the stairs, stuck my hands out, and tickled her.

"Oof—no! Please stop!" she gasped out in between bouts of uncontrollable squealing. "I take...it ba-ack!"

I withdrew my fingers, letting her breath catch up to her. When she finally calmed down, she shot me one of her dimpled smiles. "But you do like him, right?"

"Like shmike," I muttered. Clearly I hadn't tickled some sense into her. "I told you before—never getting into another relationship."

Ming frowned, her dimples disappearing. "I thought you'd finally moved on. Isn't it time you dated a new cute guy?"

Mum must've been rubbing off on her. Ming didn't usually play wingman for me. I gave her a cold, hard stare, hoping she would get the picture and stop asking me silly questions.

It didn't work.

"Max told me he's a famous tennis player," she went on, her dimpled smile returning. "That's so cool. You two meeting is like a fairytale. Just imagine the scene when he —"

"No!" Ming's imagination tended to get the better of her. A true romantic at heart, she'd forced Max to watch all the Disney films. As sweet as she was, I didn't need her dreamy thoughts taking a weird turn. Aiden was not some charming prince, and I was not a princess that needed saving. "No, Ming. Don't even think about it. It's never going to happen."

Ming pouted, looking like a berated puppy dog. "Why?"

My shoulders sagged in defeat. She wasn't going to drop this, was she? I would have to lay it on her straight. "We're too different from each other, that's why. He's famous, travelling the world and living a busy life, and I'm, well..." I waved my hand around aimlessly, the words failing to form.

Her lips puckered up, a sure sign that she wasn't convinced with my argument. "You know, Max and I didn't get along when we first met."

"Yeah, I remember." I'd shown her the ropes when Mum had employed her two years ago. But during an occasion I hadn't been around for, she and Max had met and clashed over something. I never got to know the full details about it. If I had to wager a guess, it had probably been my brother's fault. He'd always been a moody bum back then.

"Max misunderstood something I did and judged me. Those first few weeks I worked here, I was pretty sure he hated my guts."

Hard to believe, considering how he was so lovey-dovey with her now. How had their first meeting gone so wrong? Had Ming accidentally messed up the baking? She'd been flawless on her trial runs with me, so I doubted that'd been the case.

"Maybe you're misunderstanding that guy too," Ming continued, interrupting my train of thought. "Maybe he's your perfect match, but you're just too blinded by your past to see it."

Nope. That was where she was wrong. My past was what allowed me to understand the situation perfectly, rather than act like a naive, love-struck girl. Aiden might be down-to-earth and funny, but he lived in a completely different world than me. If I took the fall and liked him, I knew how it would all end. Badly. The exact same way my last relationship had ended.

Someone like Aiden would inevitably tire of me and find another girl who was more beautiful, more everything that I wasn't. This was all assuming there was even a chance of him liking me.

No point explaining this to Ming, though. So instead of trying, I clambered down the stairs to the kitchen. Incoherent voices rumbled from the storefront, becoming clearer once I shoved open the door.

"—more it'll be obvious. She's always been like that," Max said. He manned the counter while Aiden stood in front of it, twirling a wrapped cake pop in his hand.

"Who's always been like that?" I asked, drawing their gazes to me.

"Hey, Serendipity." Aiden lifted his chin in greeting and placed the cake pop back in the cardboard stand. "Your brother was just telling me about the tart recipe you made."

"Really?" That better have been all he'd told Aiden about. I would sooner give up the challenge than let something embarrassing slip out, like my teenage crush on him.

"Yeah, guess what?" Max said. "Your tarts already sold out for the day."

"Nice. Try to convince people to donate for the cake pops too," I reminded him.

"I know, I know. Don't worry. We've almost reached our goal."

"Thanks, Gor Gor. We'll be upstairs if you need me." I held open the door to the kitchen, gesturing for Aiden to follow me.

Even a week and a half after our first meeting, it was still surreal to see him. To take in how it had all transpired. The crazier thing to acknowledge? That I'd invited him over today on my Saturday off, five days after Isaac's birthday party.

During this week, I'd brainstormed ways to address his three problems with tennis.

1) He is only good at tennis

2) Money can't buy happiness

3) It's ruined his relationship with his dad

Yeah, that third one would be the trickiest thing to tackle. But today I was setting out to prove him wrong for the first one.

"How's your leg doing?" Aiden asked.

"Good. Great, actually." I straightened my leg out to point at the scab. "Doesn't bother me at all now. Thanks again for helping me out." The memory of him carrying me still sent a warm flush through my body every time my brain decided to randomly replay the moment in my head. Like right now. I hoped my face wasn't beet red.

Get it together, Sere.

I snuck a look at Aiden, but he only smiled at me like normal. "No problem. Glad I could help." He followed me as I led us up the stairs. "So what's this great task you have for me today?"

"Remember when you said I'd have to prove to you that the food I brought to Isaac's party was easy to make?"

"Yeah?"

We reached the top of the stairs. "That's what we'll be doing." I slipped my thongs off my feet.

"And you'll prove me wrong about only being good at tennis while we're at it," Aiden guessed. He paused midway through pulling his sneaker off his foot. "I think you should know that I have no baking experience whatsoever."

"You'll be fine." I'd specifically chosen a simple recipe. It was foolproof.

"I mean it. I've never baked anything in my life."

"That's okay. You can learn." Pretty certain that serving a tennis ball required more skill than cracking an egg. "And cake pops are pretty straightforward to make."

He continued to shimmy out of his sneakers, then set them down next to the neat row of shoes we kept by the stairs. "Those lollipop things?"

"Yeah." I walked to the kitchen bench and snatched a paper I'd printed out earlier, giving it to him. "Just follow the instructions on here."

He scanned over the sheet, his face scrunched in extreme concentration. "That's all there is to it?"

"Yep. It's—"

"Easy," he finished with a smile. "If I fail big time, I'm going to make you eat your words—and whatever disaster I create."

"Deal." Unless he burnt the cake to a crisp, which I'd make sure he didn't do, I was safe. "But if they turn out good, they're going in the bakery."

"Oh, so that's your real motivation. I'm your free labour."

His playful smirk showed he was joking, but I decided to play along. Playing along meant that I could pretend hanging out with him was the norm. It meant I wouldn't think too deeply about what we were doing. "You already volunteered as free labour last week, so you've only got yourself to blame."

"True. Well, as long as I have the privilege of learning under you, I won't complain."

"Okay, if you say so." I let out a nervous laugh, unsure of what to make of his statement. *He's just being nice,* I told myself. *Don't take it the wrong way.*

Luckily it was easy to distract myself as we got to work. Or rather, as he got to work and I stayed on the sidelines, content to sit at the dining table and yell out my advice whenever he needed it.

For someone who claimed to have never done any baking before, he managed to do everything without too much trouble. Granted, I'd bought premade cake mix to simplify the process, so he only had to measure out the butter and milk and crack three eggs to bake the cake. But it still impressed me. He was a natural compared to Liz.

As hard as I tried, I could never forget the one time she tried to make her own egg tarts and accidentally tipped over a kilogram bag of flour. Yeah...it was safe to say he was doing well in comparison.

"What are you smiling about?"

I shoved the memory aside to see the curious look Aiden threw my way. "Nothing. Just thinking that you're doing much better than my friend did when she tried to make egg tarts. My mum banned her from our kitchen after she doused half of the room in flour."

"Woah. That must've been annoying to clean up. Is that the same friend who was with you that time at the sports centre?"

"Yeah."

"The best friend who isn't your friend anymore?"

"Mm-hmm."

He nodded thoughtfully. "Do you miss her?"

I blinked at him, repeating his question in my head. "Sometimes," I admitted, because it was the truth. Like now, when I could imagine her between us, giving me suggestive looks whenever Aiden wasn't paying attention.

Or saying something subtle like, *Aiden, did you know Sere is your biggest fan? She even has a collection of photos of you.* That sounded exactly like something she'd say. Something I'd want to smack her for, but at the same time laugh at because of how much more daring she was than me.

A surge of longing hit me all at once. I took in a deep breath, mentally pushing it aside. "How are you doing with the cake?" I asked, eager to steer the topic away from Liz. Away from things that couldn't be changed. I jumped up from my seat and approached Aiden.

He opened his mouth, looking like he wanted to question me some more, but then showed me his finished cake mix.

"Looks good. Let's put it in the oven."

While the cake was baking, Aiden worked on making the buttercream and melting the chocolate for the cake pop coating.

"Did I do this right?" he asked.

He raised the glass bowl to show me. I examined the melted chocolate inside, then glanced up at his face. Wait, was that...? I smothered a laugh with my hand.

"What's so funny?" He scrutinised the bowl. "Did I do something wrong?"

I pointed at a dark brown spot on his cheek. "You've got some chocolate there."

"I do?" He wiped his hand on the apron I'd lent him and patted his face blindly, smudging the chocolate around even more.

"Stop! You're making it worse." I laughed. "Here. Let me do it." I grabbed a tissue and stood on my tiptoes to dab it gently against his cheek. A strange sensation rattled my stomach at his proximity, as though it was trying to separate huge clumps of flour stuck together in a sifter.

"Is it gone?" he asked, his voice cracking.

My gaze trailed up to meet his eyes. "Yeah, it's gone."

His answering smile had me pulling my hand back and looking away, breaking all forms of contact.

You don't like him. I kept repeating the words in my mind. I repeated it when I demonstrated how to assemble the cake pops. I repeated it again when we were finished and he gave me a high-five that sent shockwaves shooting down my arm.

You don't like him. I repeated it over and over until it sounded like a broken record in my head. Until I was no longer certain if it was even the truth.

"Thanks, Serendipity. I had fun today," Aiden said when it was time for him to leave. He shot me that one-sided, quirked-up smile of his. "I think I might have to say I'm good at something besides tennis after all."

And then he swept me up in a hug without warning. I clutched feebly to the back of his shirt, breathing in his heady scent. My heart did somersaults, a feeling akin to falling from somewhere way up high. An endless falling.

You. Don't. Like. Him.

Maybe if I said it enough times to myself, it would come true.

CHAPTER 21

Oh crap. I was late.

The sweltering heat hit me full force the instant I exited my car. I slammed the door, fumbling with my keys and pressing firmly on the fob. The car doors locked with a resounding clack. I hopped onto the footpath and power-walked across the car park, my heels click-clicking on the pavement.

The back of Aiden's head popped into view as soon as I rounded the corner, his ruffled, dark brown hair in disarray.

It'd been five days since we'd completed part one of my challenge, yet seeing him again made it feel like it was only yesterday.

"Sorry I'm late," I huffed out, feeling like I was dying in this heat. Sweat dampened my face and underarms. Ugh. This was what happened when I got spoiled with air conditioning every day.

Aiden whirled around to face me. "Oh, hey." He blinked, taking in my appearance. "You look different. Professional."

I self-consciously dusted my black pencil skirt and straightened the white blouse tucked under it. "Sorry. I didn't have time to change out of my work clothes." Or shower. I ran my fingers through my hair, hoping I still looked somewhat presentable after rushing off the train in thirty-degree heat and hightailing it here.

"Yeah, work. What happened there? I thought you weren't starting full-time until January."

"That was the original plan." I rolled my neck in a semi-circle motion, stiff from the hours of sitting in front of a computer monitor. "Too many people called in sick this week, and the boss needed someone to help finalise some things before Christmas." What a great early Christmas present that had been, waking up to an urgent call from my boss this morning. I'd been tempted to ignore it, but logic had won in the end. If it helped give a better impression to my boss about my work ethic, then maybe I'd get a pay raise. And more work I'd hate doing, but I wouldn't think about that just yet.

There were more important things to think about. Like how my master plan was coming along. "Ready for part two of the challenge?"

"Hah, yeah. I guess I don't have much of a choice." Aiden ran a hand through his hair, causing it to stick up even more. Somehow he made it look cute instead of sloppy. Wait—cute? No, no, no. What was I thinking?

I tore my eyes away from him, trying to find something else to focus on. Anything else. The fenced-off tennis courts in the distance would do. My eyes traced over the lines of wired fencing as he carried on, thankfully unaware of my inappropriate thoughts.

"I can't believe I let you talk me into doing this challenge. What was I thinking?"

No clue, but as long as he couldn't tell what *I* was thinking, I was okay with that. "Were you practicing tennis earlier?" I asked, eager to steer my mind away from more inappropriate thoughts.

"Yeah, just a bit with Mike."

I looked around the empty car park. "Mike was here? Actually, why is this place so deserted?" Nothing else besides these out-for-hire tennis courts were around this area, but I would've expected more people to have hired them.

"Yep, Mike was here," Aiden confirmed. "We booked out all the courts for half the day, so that's why it's so deserted. I have Mike to thank for that idea."

That was nice of him, but wasn't Mike only his fitness trainer? "You two seem pretty close." More like friends than employer and employee.

Aiden shrugged. "I guess we are. He's been with me through thick and thin. Anyway, what's part two of your great challenge?"

"Oh, right." During my lunch break today, I'd texted him, asking to take him to our next destination when I was done with work. He'd told me to meet him here. I stuffed my hand into the front pocket of my handbag, palming a piece of paper. "Part two is a surprise until we get there."

His eyes zoned in on my half-hidden hand. He moved closer to me, angling his head over my handbag. "What are you hiding?"

I staggered backward, warding him away with my free hand. "Hey, this is a sweat-free zone," I said, totally ignoring the fact that my own perspiration already broke that rule. "And no peeking, or I win the next part of the challenge by default."

"You're joking," he said, but didn't take another step toward me. "How's that fair?"

"Who says I'm playing fair? I'm playing to win. Besides, all's fair in love and challenges."

"I think the right phrase is love and *war*."

"War, challenge. Same thing."

He shot me an amused look. "Are you declaring war on me, then?"

"Ha ha. No, thanks. I'm not sure I want to go up against you and your sweat in a war."

He frowned. "Geez, man. I'm pretty sure I don't smell that bad." He pulled the collar of his shirt to his nose and sniffed. "Yeah. I do *not* smell bad."

I pinched my nose for show and pretended to gag. "Are you kidding? Your sweat could be bottled up and used as a stink bomb."

His eyes slid to the smile I couldn't quite hide. "Oh, now you're getting it." He made a grab for me, and I yelped, leaping aside.

But he was faster, banding his arms around me in a strong grip that lifted me off the ground.

"Truce! I...call...truce!" I rasped out. The hot weather, coupled with his body heat, didn't bode well for me at all. I may as well have had a pile of goo in place of my brain, because that's what I felt like mine had melted into.

Thankfully, he loosened his grip, allowing me to wriggle out of his arms. "All right, truce accepted on one condition," he said as my feet hit the ground again. "No more comments about my sweat, and at least give me a hint about what we're doing so I'm not going in blind."

I smoothed out my hair, and nodded slowly. On one hand, I wished he hadn't let go of me so quickly, but on the other, I was having a difficult time ignoring the crazy emotions swarming inside of me as it was.

"So it's a deal?" he asked.

"Okay. Deal." I smiled at the brilliant plan I'd already formulated, excitement simmering inside me. "We're going to go Christmas present shopping."

He thought money couldn't buy happiness, but I would prove him wrong.

"'Scuse me, coming through." A woman barged past me, ramming me in the process.

I massaged my shoulder, glaring at the woman as she continued to bulldoze her way through the crowd.

Maybe this isn't such a good idea. I scanned over the rest of the customers congregating around the entrance of the store. Why had this been my bright idea again? I should've taken into account all the late Christmas shoppers, which was apparently enough of the local population to fill out every square metre within my line of sight. Three days before Christmas. Ten days left, including this one, for me to win our challenge.

Refusing to resort to the barging woman's brutal tactics, I sidestepped and squeezed my way through the clusters of people instead. "Maybe we should try another store," I muttered.

Aiden's voice came from behind me. "They'd probably be just as packed."

"True." We pushed past the throng of customers queuing for the checkouts and eventually arrived at my intended destination further back in the store.

The shelves were crammed with toys, and a steady stream of families occupied each aisle. Children squealed loudly as they raced past us, each holding a different toy in hand.

Aiden cocked his head. He'd worn a sleeveless hoodie with the hood up. Precautions, he'd said. So tennis fans wouldn't recognise him. "The kids' section? Who are we buying Christmas presents for exactly?"

I smiled secretively. "Here's the shopping list." I withdrew the piece of paper I'd hidden from him before, shoving it into his hands.

"Colouring book? Barbie doll?" He recited the whole list written on the sheet until he came to the last item and squinted. "Dog?" He glanced up from the paper and fixed those inquisitive hazel eyes on me. "Did you grab a kid's ultimate wish list from Santa or something?"

That wasn't far from the truth, but I kept my lips sealed, wanting it to stay a surprise for now. He'd know soon enough. "Let's just go down the list and mark everything off as we get it."

Instead of arguing about the ambiguity of what we were doing, he surprisingly went along with my request.

"I have to know," he said while we searched through a section of children's books. "Does 'dog' mean a real dog or a toy dog?"

"Probably a real dog." My eyes roved over the vast selection of colouring books I'd found. "But we're obviously not getting a real one. We can just grab a robotic dog or plush."

"That's cruel, Sere." He clutched his heart dramatically, giving me a beseeching look. "Think of the poor child waiting for their dog."

I rolled my eyes. "It's reality. We're not getting a real dog." I ran my finger along a children's book coincidentally featuring a puppy with its tongue lolling out. "Look, this is perfect. Why don't we get this instead?"

Aiden barely gave the book a glance. "Haven't you ever wanted a dog before? Or any pet?"

I turned to give him my full attention. "Yeah, sure, but as a kid you always want things." Things that had seemed so important to a young child's brain, but now, looking back, felt stupid. "Just because a child wants things, doesn't mean it's a good idea for them to get what they want."

"I guess that's true." He picked a colouring book off the shelf and started flicking through the black-and-white pages. "When I was a kid, I wanted to be the world's number one tennis player." Reaching the end of the book, he slapped it shut. "It was all I ever dreamed about."

"Is—" The rest of my words broke off at the sound of a commotion in our aisle. Two screaming children charged past us, one whacking the other with a foam sword.

"Hah. Kids." Aiden laughed, placing the colouring book back onto the shelf. "What about you, Sere?"

My eyes focused on him again. "What about me?"

He flashed me an easygoing smile that made my stomach feel like pancakes flipping in a frying pan. "What was your childhood dream?"

"Um…" It wouldn't hurt to tell him, would it? He'd told me his, after all. "It's silly, really. When I was little, I wanted to be a successful baker with my own shop, catering to parties and events. I wanted to make up all my own original recipes and thought all I had to do was bake the goods and people would flock to buy them. Every time one of my cousins had a birthday party, I would bake all the snacks. Cookies, tarts, cake—you name it, I baked it." I chuckled at how naive I'd been. As if starting a business would've been that easy. When Aiden didn't laugh along with me, I stole a glance at him.

His face was sombre and thoughtful, eyes unwavering. "I don't think that was a silly dream to have. Isn't that basically what you did for Isaac's birthday? Didn't you enjoy that?"

"Yeah, of course." It had taken me hours of work to bake it all, but it'd been worth it. In fact, I'd go as far as to say it was the most fun I'd had in ages.

"Why not do it for a living then? I think you'd be great at it."

A flicker of uncertainty passed through me. "I don't know. There are too many risks in starting my own business." Too many what-ifs. What if people didn't like what I made? What if I couldn't earn enough money to keep the business running? What if, after everything I did, I failed spectacularly? It was better to play it safe. "Besides,

I'm already starting full-time next year at the law firm I work at."

Aiden raised an eyebrow. "Is that what you really want to do? Do you actually like working there?"

What was with all his questions? "Does it really matter? Life's not all about doing what you like."

His eyes darkened. "It should be. We only have one life, so why spend it doing something you don't like? I'd rather do what I like to make it worthwhile."

Why was he getting all philosophical with me? I was meant to be the one resolving his problems about his career, not the other way around. "Keeping a business running is difficult work," I said, mainly so he would stop pestering me about it. "My parents had to work really hard for our bakery to stay in business. There's a chance that I'd just be wasting my time and money if I try."

Thinking back on my childhood, there were years when Dad wanted to watch the Australian Open, but we struggled to have the money to go. Even when we could, Dad would take the long drive there instead of the short flight because we couldn't afford the plane tickets. I didn't know if I'd have the same struggles with money, but it wasn't like I had that leap of faith to find out.

"You don't really know until you try," Aiden said.

"It doesn't matter. We're here for you today. It's my challenge to prove you wrong, remember?"

He folded his arms. "And why is that?"

The words were out of my mouth before I could think. "Because I don't want you to quit tennis."

His nose crinkled. "What..." He shook his head, our silence filled by the store speakers playing *Jingle Bells*. The merry song didn't go well with the anticipation swirling inside me.

Was he going to tell me that it was no good? That nothing I did was going to change his mind? That couldn't be true. I'd seen the way he'd had fun playing at Isaac's party, and he'd admitted that he didn't hate tennis itself, just the troubles and doubts that came with it. Would he really have practiced tennis today if he hated it that much?

If I could convince him to overlook all the bad things, then maybe he would happily go back to playing tennis. Was I in way over my head to assume I had the power to do that? Maybe.

But when my gaze met his again, he said, "It won't be easy for you to change my mind."

I laughed in relief. Like that would stop me. "It's called a challenge for a reason, Aiden." And I was going to win it.

CHAPTER 22

"Last stop for the day," I announced. I indicated left into a small parking lot and reversed my car into the first free space I found.

After hefting out the multiple bags of Christmas presents, I led us along the footpath bordering the parking lot to a small place between a second-hand clothes store and a fruit shop.

"'Gifts of Gold,'" Aiden said, reading the plaque beside the door. "'Give More Than You Get.' Is this a charity?"

"Yep. These"—I lifted up the bags I held—"are things that children from families-in-need requested for Christmas."

Understanding reflected in his eyes as he glanced at the bags in his hands and then me. "So *that's* how you're proving me wrong." I could see the internal cogs turning in his head. Money couldn't buy happiness, but using it to help others could give someone else theirs, and therefore your own. That was my logic anyway. "You're really something else, Sere."

"Nah. It was Max's idea to use the money we raised from selling the cake pops."

"That's what he meant the other day when he said you guys had nearly reached your goal?"

"Yep. But Gifts of Gold does all the hard work. I don't really get to help as much as I'd like." Definitely not as much as they'd helped us. We'd struggled financially the year Dad had been in and out of the hospital. We hadn't been able to run the bakery full-time and had almost been unable to pay for some of the bills. That was when Gifts of Gold had stepped in and offered to cover the cost for paid TV so Dad could watch Aus Open from his hospital bed. Then they'd brought him better meals than the hospital ones.

I shook my head, clearing my thoughts. "Let's go." The summer heat had died down, but it was still too humid for my liking. My blouse stuck to me like a second skin and my feet felt clammy in my heels. Ugh.

I pulled down on the door handle and pushed through. Immediately, a relieving gust of cool air blew in my face. Ahh, glorious. I walked in, taking in the festive decorations. Red and green tinsel hung on the walls, and a miniature Christmas tree took up a corner of the small room. A woman sitting behind the counter looked up upon our arrival. "Good evening. How can I help you today?"

"Hi." I plopped one of my tote bags onto the counter and took out a piece of paper from my handbag, handing it to her. "I'm here to deliver some Christmas presents."

"Oh yes. Thank you." She squinted at the top of the paper. "Serendipity. That's a pretty name."

"Thanks." Though I hadn't been so fond of it before, I was beginning to feel like my name wasn't too bad—especially with the way Aiden said it.

The woman proceeded to sort through the bags and mark off each item on my list. "Did you want to wrap the gifts? We've got all the supplies set up in a room at the back there." She motioned at the hallway on our right.

"Uhhh." I turned to Aiden. "Do you want to?" It wasn't really part of the challenge, and I didn't know how much time he had to waste.

He smiled. "Sure. May as well since we're here."

And that was how we ended up, for the next hour, wrangling wrapping paper with scissors and sticky tape. Or more accurately speaking, Aiden was the one wrangling; I was trying to salvage his attempts at wrapping a colouring book.

"I thought you had good hand-eye coordination." I carefully retaped the edge of the wrapping paper so that it was no longer sticking out at an odd angle.

"Yeah, at tennis. Not wrapping presents. I've never had to wrap a present in my life."

"*Never*?" I plucked off another piece of the sticky tape. "How about for birthdays?"

"Not for birthdays or Christmas. I don't really celebrate them."

"That's a shame." It wasn't like my family was big on those events either, but I did get Mum and Max a birthday present each year. We didn't really celebrate Christmas nowadays though—which was why I'd insisted on Mum staying in Hong Kong until after New Years—but as children, we got gifts and Dad cooked lots of food. How could someone go through their entire life without celebrating birthdays or Christmas? I couldn't imagine it. "You've been missing out."

"Yeah, that's why I said I wanted a normal life."

I immediately wanted to stuff my words back into my mouth. Oh no. This wouldn't do. I couldn't have him reverting back to his old reasonings for hating tennis when I was so close to convincing him otherwise. "Here, cut these in one-metre lengths," I suggested, sliding a tape of festive red ribbon on the table to him. "You should do it this year then. Give people presents, I mean. You could give something to your mum or dad."

"Mum's out of the state." He unwound the ribbon and snipped it with a pair of scissors. "I came here to visit her, actually, but all the hassling from my dad and attention from the media was too much for her."

"Hassling?" Much of Aiden's personal life stayed private, so I didn't know anything about his mum.

"Yeah, when I stopped answering his messages, he started pestering my mum instead. I'm so sick of his behaviour." His fingers tightened on the length of ribbon he'd cut. "He's why there's no way you can win this challenge."

"Because you think I can't help you mend your relationship with your dad?"

"Because I *know* you can't," he corrected. "It'll be impossible to convince him to change his ways enough for me to let him into my life again."

A deafening silence followed his statement. It was true that I'd known his third reason would be the hardest to change his mind on, but what exactly had happened between them to cause such a rift in the first place? From what little I remembered about his dad, that one time I'd seen him, he'd seemed like a strict, no-nonsense father. But he'd also worried when I'd hit his son on the head with the tennis ball. So he wasn't a complete tiger parent. There had to be some sort of hope for their relationship to mend, right? "At least you have a chance to talk it out with him."

His head lowered in shame. "I'm sorry. I've been dissing my dad, and I just realised you..."

"It's fine," I said quickly. "Everyone has a different situation." I knew Ming used to have a rocky relationship with her mum too when she'd chosen to pursue a different career than the one she'd expected her to take. Despite that, she'd told me now it wasn't as bad. Her mum had eventually come around. Maybe all Aiden had to do with his dad was have a heart to heart too.

"Have you ever tried talking to your dad about how you feel? Maybe talk about your problems with him?"

Aiden's eyes narrowed. "What's the point? He's so stubborn in his ways that he won't accept anything else but his own version of what's right."

"Why don't you just try anyway? I can't say you've won the challenge until you've tried," I said. "Unless you're happy giving me a free win."

"You play a hard challenge to beat, Serendipity." He exhaled loudly. "Fine. What do I have to do to count as 'trying'?"

I hummed thoughtfully. "First of all, you have to tell me *why* you're mad at him."

He bit his bottom lip. Then, letting go of the ribbon in his hand, he fished his phone out from his pocket. He unlocked the screen and tapped it a few times. "This is why."

He passed me the phone. It was open on a messenger app in a conversation with "Dad." The first few messages on the screen dated back two weeks ago.

Dad: Where are you right now? Have you come to your senses yet?

Ignoring me won't make the problem go away. You can't just quit now.

Tell your mum she's a bad liar. I know you're with her.

Aiden: I can and I will ignore you until you admit you were wrong. Leave Mum out of this.

Dad: You know I did the right thing with Mike. He was a bad influence on you. Keep your eyes on the prize. You've lost sight of your goals.

You better be keeping up with your training. Everything is sorted for January. I'll see you then.

I took a moment to analyse the texts, surprise overtaking me, slowly morphing into anger by the end. "Your dad is a jerk. What did he do with Mike?"

Aiden's nostrils flared. "Mike's contract with me was going to end last month. Obviously I was going to extend it, and up his pay too, but my dad had other ideas. So I fired my dad before he could let Mike go."

That was why he'd split with his dad? "Why did he say Mike was a bad influence on you?"

He crossed his arms, his posture rigid. "My dad—he's always been strict. Intense with my training. I guess I was used to that because he gave me a bit of freedom whenever I was doing well, which was most of the time—until I got injured in the US Open last year. I had a tough time recovering after that. When I was finally ready to play again, I couldn't play at my best either.

"My dad thought I just needed more training, but honestly? I felt like I was suffocating every day practicing non-stop. I didn't find it fun anymore. Every time my dad said, 'Think of the end goal' and 'You need to be stronger,' I kept wishing that I'd get some life-altering injury so I had no chance and he would shut up about it.

"Mike suggested I needed a bit of a break from tennis. Maybe go home to Sydney and see my mum for a few months. He said a nice holiday like that would lift my spirits. My dad shot down the idea as soon as he heard it. When I tried to go anyway, he thought it was all Mike's doing. Told me he was a bad influence and that I was better off without him."

"That's so...stupid." So unbelievably stupid. His own son had burned out and he probably hadn't realised it. For Aiden to have wished for a horrible injury just to get out of playing? How much training had he endured to reach that point? "He shouldn't have done that. If you need a break, you should take one."

"No kidding. So tell me—after knowing all that, do you really think I can forgive him and pretend to go back to being the obedient son?" Aiden held a piece of ribbon, looking about ready to strangle someone with it. "It feels dumb to say that I'm twenty-three, but that my dad's dictated most of my life. To the point where I was so used to it that I didn't fight against him until he finally did something to make me snap."

I gently extracted the ribbon from his tight grip and used it to tie a bow on the present I'd already wrapped. "Your dad really is something else." And that was putting it mildly. "But I don't think you should be embarrassed that you followed him for most of your life. I mean, he's your dad. Who else are you meant to look up to?" By the sounds of it, his mum wasn't as much of a constant in his life. "I wouldn't blame you if you wanted to stop talking to him, but did you ever tell him how you felt? That he was pushing you too hard?"

"I don't think there's any point."

Maybe not, but he'd never get past this hole in his life if he avoided his dad forever. I could see it was eating him alive to live with all that hurt. To suffer because of someone who was supposed to love and support you. Now more than ever, I was intent on helping him mend this wound. And for that to happen, his dad needed to hear just what he thought.

"You can email him if that's easier. I can help you write it," I offered. "You don't have to do it alone." And because he looked so vulnerable and uncertain in that moment, I shifted closer to place my hand on his.

The instant I did, the heat of his touch spread through me. *This is such a nice feeling. I should never let go,* some silly part of me thought. I tried to ignore it as he stared at our hands.

I gave him what I hoped looked like a reassuring smile. "What do you say?"

He rubbed the back of his head with his free hand, pinning me with his sharp gaze. As if he was searching through the depths of my soul. For my sincerity? Any hidden agendas? Too bad for him, my only ulterior motive wasn't a secret now that he knew about it.

"Okay," he finally agreed. "It's worth a try." His hand slipped out from under mine, and I mourned the loss of its warmth. But then he moved it to pat my shoulder, making me lose my breath all over again.

A smile shone on his face, bright like a beacon. "I look forward to winning this challenge."

Wow. If he was that happy at the prospect of winning, maybe it wouldn't be such a bad idea to let him win. Now that I knew he'd suffered a mental burnout from tennis, it made sense he wanted to quit.

But then I remembered what was at stake. If he won, he got to ask me a personal favour and a personal question.

Oh no. I had no idea about the favour, but I had a bad feeling about what he would ask for the question. He'd shown a bit too much interest in knowing the details about my last relationship.

Nope. I couldn't afford to lose this challenge and let him ask me anything about *that*. Besides, winning didn't automatically mean I was forcing him back into tennis. It was about showing him that there was more to tennis than just the bad points he'd singled out. Maybe his dad had made him hate it, and maybe I couldn't mend their broken relationship. But I would do everything in my power to help Aiden see how much he still loved tennis.

Determination hardened my resolve.

There was no other choice. I had to win this challenge.

CHAPTER 23

This was by far the most luxurious restaurant I'd ever been in. I picked at the fancy slice of red velvet cake in front of me with my fork, cutting smoothly through the creamy frosting. Mmm, could I replicate this? They probably used the most expensive brand of everything, so even if I repeated the recipe perfectly in terms of technique, it most likely wouldn't taste as nice.

"Don't like the cake?"

My gaze swung upward at the sound of Aiden's voice. I drank in the sight of him sitting across the table from me, butterflies whooshing in my stomach.

His hair was combed more neatly than its typical dishevelled state, and rather than donning his usual sports clothing, a close-fitting collared shirt hugged his body, accentuating his muscled figure beneath. Yeah, it was hard not to stare.

I set down my fork and clasped my hands together on my lap, dragging my gaze away from his too-fit body to meet his eyes. "It looks too good to eat."

During the past hour of our dinner, I'd purposely avoided maintaining eye contact in a vain attempt to subdue this annoying feeling in my stomach. That obviously wasn't working too well, so I tried another tactic —small talk.

"Can you believe it's your last day in Sydney already?"

"Yep, I know. It's crazy." The flutters multiplied at the appearance of his unreserved smile. "Time flies when you're having fun."

Time did fly, and weirdly enough, our challenge had actually been fun. Was it only a week ago when I'd had the fleeting thought I wouldn't mind losing to him? Past-me would never have thought that if she'd seen me sitting right here, already suffering the consequences of my loss.

My eyes swept over our surroundings. The glass railing beside me showed off our shimmery, faded reflections. Mine was an expression of barely contained awe. Aiden's was a look of amusement as he glanced my way. The Sydney Harbour Bridge loomed over us, a gigantic bridge of arched steel spanning across the water, countless tiny lights winking both along and behind it from all of the city buildings.

Okay, I could hardly call it suffering when all Aiden had asked of me for his personal favour was to spend dinner on

New Year's Eve with him. He'd insisted on paying too. Free food? Heck yes. At the type of restaurant I'd once wrongly assumed he would only ever dine at, no less. But that raised another question.

Why? Was he trying to impress me with his money? That couldn't have been it. He'd never rubbed it in my face during the weeks we'd spent together. What then? Winner's guilt?

"Are you still sad you lost the challenge?" Aiden asked. "Seriously, Sere. It was just a bet. No hard feelings."

What he meant was no hard feelings for being a loser. A huge L-O-S-E-R. Because my brilliant last plan had failed big time. We'd drafted a meaningful email to his dad, full of heartfelt words and a plea for them to have a good talk. I'd been so sure his dad would've at least agreed to meet and talk over their problems. Yet here we were, more than a week later, with no response from the old grouch.

So with great reluctance, I had finally admitted defeat and declared Aiden the winner of the challenge yesterday.

Meeting his hazel-eyed stare now, I tried and failed to ignore the frantic palpitations of my heart. And the darn butterflies. Over these last few weeks, they hadn't ceased at all whenever I'd been in his presence. I had even considered bailing tonight just to avoid the emotional flutter-fest, but then thought better of it. What kind of person would I be if I promised a prize for winning the challenge, but then refused to deliver it? Not a very good one.

"You're really hung up about it, hey?" Aiden said when I didn't respond.

I mentally shook off my wayward thoughts, giving him my full attention. "Nope, I'm over it. How about you?"

He cut off a sliver of his strawberry cake and bit into it. "What about me?"

"Are you doing okay? I know you said you had no hope for patching things up with your dad, but it still sucks that he didn't reply." If his dad only cared about him tennis-wise, he totally deserved the Worst Dad of the Year trophy.

"I'm fine. Let's not talk about him." His dismissive tone suggested otherwise, but if he didn't want to discuss it, I would let him be. After all, I wouldn't be seeing him again for a long time after tonight, if at all. It was better to fill this night with happier memories.

"Why don't we dance instead?" he asked, as if he'd read my mind. His eyes flickered to the space on the opposite end to us, right next to the balcony. Couples were swaying to the slow beat of the music. Together. Closely.

A flush of heat surged through me at the thought of us doing the same. "I can't dance," I warned him, but I was already sliding out of my seat. Stupid body doing what it wanted.

His laugh carried easily over the music, making me shiver. "What makes you think I can dance?"

I shot him an incredulous look. "Why'd you ask then?" He wasn't standing up. Had he been joking? I moved to sit back down, but he jumped out of his seat, grabbing me by the hand.

"Come on." His thumb brushed over my wrist, igniting another myriad of flutters within me. At this rate, my whole stomach was going to drown from the sensory overload. "It'll be fun. Something normal."

I let him pull me along. "You still want to be normal." It was a statement, not a question. Because without a doubt, it was true.

"Do you think I'm stupid for wanting that?" he asked as he guided me to the dancefloor.

It was hard to organise my thoughts properly with his hand around mine, but him, stupid? No. He was human. He wanted things the same as anyone else did. It just so happened that what he wanted was probably what everyone else didn't want.

By the time I'd thought this all through, we were already on the dance floor. I had no idea how to do this, so I glanced at other people for guidance. The couple closest to us—the man had both hands around the lady's waist, and hers were draped over his shoulders. They swayed to the rhythm, oblivious to the world around them.

I gulped. Did Aiden want us to dance the same way?

A sudden touch on my waist jarred me. My breath hitched as I looked down to see his hands resting there, giving me my answer.

My attention drew back to him, our gazes locking. The fairy lights strung above us reflected the flecks of green in his eyes, a mischievous glint in them. He took a step back, pulling me with him. Not wanting to lose my balance, my hands automatically moved to hold onto his shoulders. Following Aiden's lead, I glided along to the music with slow, measured steps.

I let myself relax in the calming rhythm and his hold. The scent of his cologne teased my nose, a smell I'd now familiarised myself with over the last few weeks. I closed my eyes and breathed it in deeply, relishing his closeness, wishing this perfect moment could last forever.

Eventually, my eyes fluttered open to find him staring down at me.

"Hey," he said.

"Hey." There was a beat of silence, and then I decided to fill it by saying, "So what have you been up to today?"

He shrugged, the movement almost jostling my hands off his shoulders. "Nothing much. Just tennis practice for most of the day."

"You're still practicing?"

"Yeah. I've still got to train before the Australian Open."

"Right." Duh. It wasn't like he would just stop practicing altogether before the big event. "That's good."

His lips lifted into a smirk. "Are you trying to do small talk to distract me? Don't think I've forgotten about my personal question ticket."

Just like that, my bubble of comfort broke with a *pop*.

Of course I knew he hadn't forgotten—not with his memory. I'd just been waiting for him to ask. Stalling for time.

"What did you want to ask?" I said, pretending that I was totally fine with whatever he would throw my way. *Fake it until you make it.*

His hold on my waist shifted slightly. "Your best friend. What happened between the two of you?"

Unease stirred in the pit of my stomach. I'd had a feeling he would ask about this. "It's...complicated." That was an understatement. But it was more than that. I didn't want him to think badly of me.

My teeth clenched together, remembering the venomous words I'd spat out to Liz a year ago. Words that I could never take back.

No. He didn't need to know *that*.

"It's okay. You don't have to share," he said, perhaps sensing my reluctance. "Let's try something else."

"Sure." Anything else was better.

"Your ex-boyfriend," he started.

My feet that had been dancing seconds ago suddenly grounded to a halt. Aiden's grip on my waist tightened as he quickly steadied himself to avoid ramming into me.

I forced myself to speak. "What about him?" My voice came out unusually high-pitched and defensive, instead of casual and nonchalant like I wanted.

Aiden's hands slid off my waist and he took a step back, my arms falling off his shoulders in the process. He regarded me with those sharp eyes of his. Quiet. Assessing.

I averted my gaze to look at the Harbour Bridge, unsure of what he was searching for. Afraid that he would somehow find it.

"I thought maybe you still liked your ex and had feelings for him."

My head snapped back to him. He ran a hand through his hair, a pained expression overtaking his face.

"No!" Why would he think something like that? Did I look like some sad, sobby girl? I didn't think so. "I don't feel anything for him anymore. I'd be stupid to still be holding onto feelings for someone after that long." As stupid as I'd be to have feelings for the guy I was looking at right now in front of me.

"Good," Aiden said, his voice barely audible above the sound of the music playing.

Good? What did that mean? Was he suggesting...?

My eyes darted to his mouth as his lips parted. "I thought you were still hung up on someone else. But if you're not—"

Fizzling noises filled the air, interrupting him. Trails of multi-coloured fireworks burst out in circular patterns around us, painting the night sky bright pink, blue, then green, and so on. Until the entire sky was lit by bright colours. We wandered closer to the railing along with the rest of the people on the dance floor.

"It isn't even midnight yet!" Aiden shouted over the noise.

"They have nine o'clock fireworks, too!" I yelled back. For kids who had early bedtimes. It had completely slipped my mind until now.

It seemed like other people had forgotten as well, because they all started getting up from their seats and rushing to the railing where we stood. A young couple, ignorant to their surroundings, already had their selfie stick raised, ready to take photos. Realising I was next to them in the photo, I scrambled away to get out of their shot. In my haste, I slipped on what felt like someone's shoe, stumbling backward.

Hands grasped my arms at the last second, preventing me from making a huge fool of myself. I twisted around, coming face-to-face with Aiden.

"Maybe we should take a selfie too," he suggested loudly, eyeing the same couple I'd gotten away from.

"Really?"

"You don't want to?"

"I don't mind." I didn't look completely terrible since I'd bothered to dress up for tonight. After he'd revealed we would be dining at a super fancy restaurant, I'd pulled out my nicest clothes—a dark blue, off-the-shoulder midi dress—and painstakingly done a bit of makeup. Nothing too extravagant, because I wasn't very skilled at it. Just the basics. Foundation. Blush. A bit of mascara. Shimmery lipstick that had probably already faded after eating and drinking.

I was just shocked because I'd thought *he* wouldn't want to take a photo. Not after he'd blatantly refused to take one with Ben Wong the other week. Apparently I was wrong about that.

Taking out his phone, Aiden switched the camera to selfie mode. I smiled nervously at our close-up faces and put my hand up in my signature peace sign.

He wrapped an arm around me, squeezing my shoulder. "Lighten up, Sere. You look like you're about to be eaten."

I rolled my eyes, but his silly words worked and I was smiling without the previous tension wracking me.

"One, two, three."

After he snapped a few shots, we settled by the railing, watching the fireworks.

As the last of the crowd dispersed, Aiden slung his arm around my back. Nerves immediately invaded my stomach like a full-force torpedo. "Let's go to the other side."

In my daze, he easily led me to the opposite end of the dance floor, the corner furthest away from the crowd. My full-length dress swished around my legs, mimicked by the reflection of the glass railing as I approached it. I tilted my head over the edge. The Harbour Bridge lights gave off a stunning glittery view of the dark ocean below.

"It's beautiful."

Aiden rested his back against the railing. "You know what's also beautiful?" He flicked on his phone screen and showed it to me. It was a photo he'd taken. Both of us beamed at the camera, a large blue and yellow firework behind us.

"Yeah. The fireworks look nice in that one."

"Who said I was talking about the fireworks?"

My thrumming pulse overtook my ears as my brain took in what he said.

What did he mean? Was he actually flirting with me?

No. No way. Sure, he had said some things lately that could be interpreted as flirting, but this?

I laughed nervously, turning away to look at the now-empty sky. "Haha. Good one."

Aiden sidled up closer to me until his shoulder pressed against mine. "I'm not joking."

I held my breath at his soft admission, not knowing how to answer him. The next thing I knew, he was holding my shoulders and pivoting me around to face him.

"Serendipity, have I just been annoying you these last few weeks?"

"I—" His question caught me off guard, and coupled with his mesmerising hazel eyes? I was a goner. I had to work my mouth a few times before I could speak. "No. You haven't been annoying me at all."

His mouth parted in surprise, then he rubbed his nose with his knuckles. "That's a relief." His eyes darted over my face, down to my lips. "The thing is, I've been thinking about you..."

My face heated up at his proclamation.

Without warning, Aiden leaned closer. Closer and closer, until all I could focus on were his eyes.

I drifted toward him, pulled in by the magnetism of those eyes. My gaze dropped to his slightly parted lips just as he pulled me toward him, closing that last bit of distance left between us.

I closed my eyes, savouring the feel of his hands running up and down my bare arms. I knew what was coming next. I knew it, but didn't dare stop to think about it. So when his breath fanned over my mouth, I didn't move. I simply let his lips capture mine. I gasped at the gentle pressure of them, at the strawberry taste from the cake he'd eaten.

All the emotions that had built up inside me these last two weeks fought to break free. *You like him*, they said to me. *You really like him, and he likes you. Nothing else matters. Just keep kissing him.*

I would've listened to that voice, would have never stopped kissing him—if not for the sirens that went off in my head.

Stop, stop, stop! This won't end well if you like him. Remember what happened last time? Last time, when you thought it was true love?

Heeding that tiny bit of resolve inside me, I twisted, breaking away from him. My lips were left tingling with an indescribable sensation. Wanting more.

No, I didn't want more. I *couldn't* want more.

I pressed a hand over my mouth. "I'm sorry. I don't..." *Don't want to risk my heart again. Don't think you really would like someone like me. Don't want my heart to break into too many pieces when you realise I'm not actually what you want.*

But I knew if I said any of those words to him, he'd easily refute them. He was just as stubborn as me, if not more. It was better to let him think I didn't want him.

Aiden studied me carefully, and he must've seen the uncertainty I tried so desperately to exert because his jaw clenched. The sparkle died from his eyes, and his expression hardened. "Sorry. I thought you..." He couldn't finish the rest of his sentence, but the look of sheer rejection on his face told me enough.

I had broken the hope of something more, and all I knew was this—I didn't deserve his feelings, misplaced or not.

"Aiden... I'm sorry. You've got the wrong idea." The uttering of that one sentence hollowed out my entire being with it. I decided to put the nail in the coffin. Go for the kill. "This. *Us.* I don't think of you that way."

It was the biggest lie I'd ever told. Bigger than the one I told Dad when I promised him I would be happy. Bigger than the one I told myself when I said I would live my life with no regrets. It left a horrible taste on my tongue that made me want to clean my mouth.

Aiden stuffed his hands in his pants pockets and ducked his head. "You don't have to be sorry for anything. I get it."

It took me a moment to register that he'd so quickly dismissed our awkward exchange. But this was good, right? It was for the better. It was good that he understood. That I didn't have to come up with more lies to cover the lie.

I was about to thank him like an idiot when he pulled something from his pocket and held it out toward me. "Here. This is for you. A late Christmas present."

I stood there, dumbfounded by the sudden change in topic, staring at the white envelope in his outstretched hand.

He took my limp hand and placed his present there. The envelope was small, crisp and unmarred by any writing, with no indication to its contents.

"It's a ground ticket for the Australian Open. If you decide to go, you're welcome to watch any of my matches from my players' box."

At the mention of a place that held so many memories of Dad, my emotions threatened to overwhelm me. "I don't think that's a good idea."

"Why not?"

"You know why." I wrapped my arms around myself, tremors wracking my body. "I can't go back there. It holds too many memories for me."

Aiden's eyes flashed with an emotion I couldn't identify. "I didn't realise you were such a coward, Serendipity."

My stomach dropped to the floor, but he didn't give me the opportunity to question him as he went on.

"You know what I think? I think you're running away from your problems, just like me. Except you're not owning up to it. You told me you loved the place because of your dad. How do you think he'd feel if he knew you weren't planning on ever going back?"

Grief wedged itself deep in my throat, preventing me from speaking. It was true. I did love the place because of Dad.

An old memory at the Australian Open came to me. Me, holding onto Dad's hand as we walked toward a giant arena. The feeling of my hat constantly sliding over my eyes while Dad animatedly voiced his excitement. *This will be a great match to watch. Wouldn't want to miss it for all the world.*

"No," I croaked out, swiping the memory from my mind. "I don't want to talk about this." The envelope scrunched under the force of my fisted hand. I hugged myself tighter, trying to squeeze away the pain.

Sure, it was easy for Aiden to say. For him, going to the Australian Open didn't hold the same meaning. For me, going back without Dad would hurt too much. He'd loved the event more than anything else, yet he would never see another match ever again. How could I go without him and see something he never would? How could I justify doing that when I'd always only ever gone with him?

My stomach knotted up at the idea of it, an all-too-familiar stab of pain prickling my chest. "I don't feel so good. I think I should go home."

The silent tension between us was so palpable that it might as well have been physically strangling me. Aiden looked like he wanted to say a lot more, but he nodded. "Okay, fine."

Fine? I didn't feel fine. Not with the cold look he gave me. Not with the knowledge that in a few days, I'd be going to work again. Life would go on, back to normal, without Aiden. Wasn't that the funny thing? The normal that Aiden Andale wanted so desperately was the normal I'd been struggling to escape from.

But fine? It wasn't fine. Not as we parted ways at the train station with stiff goodbyes, and I was left wondering if this was the last time I'd see him.

Nothing was fine at all.

CHAPTER 24

Time heals all wounds. That's how the old phrase went. It might have held true for some people, but not for me. My slowly healing wounds reopened as soon as I laid eyes on my latest phone notification.

Liz: What's going on? Something you want to tell me?

A link to an article was attached underneath. She really liked sharing those with me lately, didn't she? But unlike the previous titles, this one was totally different.

Andale Moves on from Mystery Girl, New Romance with Tennis Star Dunham.

Pain dug into me like a cut from a sharp kitchen knife.

In Liz's previous messages—ones I'd also never replied to—I'd been featured in some blurry photos with Aiden. All from the night when everything had gone wrong. Apparently someone had recognised Aiden and sneakily taken photos without us realising. I'd sucked it up and dealt with it as best as I could in the aftermath. It helped that nobody was able to name me in those articles. I'd simply been referred to as Aiden's "Asian Mystery Girl."

Who in the world was Dunham though? My finger hovered over the link. The logical side of me said I shouldn't click it. Let things be. What good would it serve me to know this information? Only misery and self-loathing awaited me. The emotional side of me rebelled. I had to know. Eventually, I'd find out through something I saw by accident. It was better to choose now to find out all the details.

My mind made up, I opened the article and skimmed through the first paragraph.

Isabelle Dunham, one of America's rising tennis stars, was spotted with popular Australian tennis player Aiden Andale on Thursday afternoon at one of Melbourne's top cafes. The 20 year-old is well known for her part-time job as a model for various brand names, including—

I scrolled down to read the rest, only for a photo of the two together to usurp my attention. An attractive blonde girl sat opposite Aiden at a small round table sheltered by a large umbrella. Both of them were laughing together like old friends. Or lovers.

My throat dried up. I quickly snatched up the remainder of my lukewarm cup of coffee and downed it in a few gulps, stewing over this new knowledge.

He'd moved on quickly with his life. Like our dinner two weeks ago had never happened. Like the time we'd spent together last month was all ancient history.

Isn't this what you wanted, Sere? You have no right to regret it now.

I backed out from the article to return to Liz's message.

What did she think of all this? She'd always teased me for my teenage crush on Aiden, so I wouldn't be surprised if she told me off for not giving him a chance. Though, knowing her snarky attitude, she would also be badmouthing Aiden for moving on so quickly.

A sad smile touched my lips at imagining her telling him off. If only things were normal between us. If only I had my best friend to support me. My fingers itched to type a response, but I thought twice about it. What could I possibly say?

It's a long story. He came to my bakery one day, and we became friends. But then I went and messed that up.

I hadn't spoken to Liz for over a year now. Wouldn't it be weird to write to her without addressing our fallout? Although she was the one starting the conversation, I wouldn't feel comfortable carrying on like everything was normal. My poor attempt to explain the situation with Aiden all in one short paragraph wouldn't do me any justice either.

Before I could mull it over more, my phone vibrated with an incoming call, giving me a reprieve from my sad thoughts.

Or not. I eyed the name on the screen.

Crap. It was my boss. I inhaled in a deep, composing breath, then swiped to accept the call.

"Hi, Albert."

"Have you sent off those invoices yet?" Albert's voice boomed.

I winced, extending the phone away from my ear and rubbing the heel of my hand on the top of my head. Another migraine was coming, and I already dreaded its impending arrival. It started at the back of my neck and ended at my forehead, a continuous and unrelenting pulsing.

"Are you there?" my boss demanded.

I pressed the phone back to my ear. "Yes, sir. I'm here. And yes, I sent off those invoices before lunch." This wasn't the reason for him calling me during his holiday though. He could've just checked his email to confirm, so what did he want now?

"Perfect. I'm forwarding you another lot I need done before tomorrow."

Another lot of invoices? No, no, no. "What about John?" I gave a cursory glance to the desk beside me where the intern usually sat. Empty. Probably off somewhere on an extended lunch break when he was meant to be attending to the mounting pile of work I'd left on his desk at the beginning of the week.

The boss let out a grunt. "John's still in training, so I've got him doing part of another lot. I trust you to get the job done much faster, so you've got the bigger portion."

Oh, yay. I clicked to open the new email from him, and downloaded the attachments. "Aren't these all your direct clients?"

"Yes. Is that a problem?"

Yes. I hate work. Let me get an early mark on Friday, for once in my tired life. "No. Not a problem, sir."

"Good. I've got two more weeks of my holiday left. Let me enjoy it in peace. Especially for the Australian Open next week."

"The Australian Open?" He was going *there*? Right where Aiden Andale would be. Just when I thought I'd finally stopped thinking about him, he wriggled his way back into my mind.

"Yep. You've been doing some good work, Sere. Keep it up." If he'd said this to me a few months earlier, I would've been over the moon. Right now, however, I could barely muster anything that sounded semi-enthusiastic at best.

"Mmm, thanks, sir. Anything else?"

"No. That's all for now. I'll leave you to it then."

He ended the call, and I peeked at the time. Well, it looked like I would be staying late today. Again. The last stack of invoices had taken almost half a day to do, and this was a bigger lot.

I fired off a text to Mum, letting her know I'd be late. After I sent the message, my finger lingered over the message overview screen, my eyes inevitably locking onto the last message Aiden had sent me. I must've been a glutton for punishment today, because instead of finally going through and deleting the whole thread of our messages, I tapped to view our conversation again.

Me: Thanks for tonight. Good luck in the Aus Open!
Aiden: It's cool. Thanks.

The problem with texting was that I had no idea if what he said was really a genuine response or not. The short sentences marked by full stops just seemed...cold. I guess it didn't really matter. He was back to his own life, in his own separate world. But, as if my body still couldn't help itself, I automatically started scrolling all the way back up to the very first message from him.

Hey, just messaging you to prove I can remember your number :) Aiden

I stifled a laugh. It didn't matter how many times I read that first message, I could still imagine his cockiness as he wrote it.

A pinging noise came from my computer, jarring me from my procrastinations. I looked up to see a notification for another email from Albert pop up. Bleh.

Stowing away my phone, I turned my attention to the new email.

Time to get started.

Approximately six hours later, I finished the last of the invoices. Time to call it a day.

No sooner had I thought this than a new email notification popped up. I sighed and clicked on it, only to sigh even louder after reading the message.

S, this is incomplete. Fix it.

Oh, you have got to be kidding me.

But he wasn't. I looked through the rest of the email trail. Totally unreliable intern John had done it again. He'd forgotten or ignored some details that needed to be added to the invoices. I was beginning to suspect the latter the more often he did it. No one could forget more than once, and this was probably his third or fourth time.

Ugh. Kill me now. Which was sadly appropriate for me to say because when I finally finished fixing everything up, I felt like death. Using the last dregs of my energy, I switched off my computer, powered off the aircon, and flicked off the office lights.

I could finally leave. The thought should've made me relieved, but my mind wandered back to the article from earlier today. Aiden laughing with another girl, moving on with his life as though I'd never been part of it.

Once again, my heart was assaulted by a sharp, cutting pain, and I pressed a hand against my chest.

Time might heal all wounds, but it would be a long while before this one patched over.

CHAPTER 25

Mum and Max had never fussed over me so much in my whole life. Mum had even momentarily left the bakery in Ming's hands—something she'd never usually do on a busy Saturday morning.

"You rest today, sweetie," she insisted. She tucked the edges of my blanket tightly around me, snuggling me up like a burrito. She hadn't done that since... I couldn't even remember when. Other people might have found it nice to be coddled, but in my case, it was an overreaction.

"Mum, I'm fine."

Max leaned over my bedside, scrutinising me with narrowed eyes. "Don't believe her, Ma. She'll go back to work on Monday and do the same thing."

I glared at him at the same time Mum looked over me in disapproval, as if I'd already gone and done exactly what he suggested.

"I'm okay!"

"Sure, if your definition of 'okay' is tripping down the stairs first thing in the morning," Max retorted. "It's a miracle you didn't injure yourself."

Ugh, it was just my luck that he witnessed my fumbling fall. "Whatever," I said, unable to think of a better comeback.

He rolled his eyes and lowered himself onto the edge of my bed. "You should stop overworking yourself. You're not even being paid for overtime. Couldn't you have finished your tasks next week?"

Nope. I couldn't have. The deadline had been crystal clear.

"You've got your priorities all wrong," he went on. I pinched my arm to make sure I wasn't dreaming. Was my big brother actually lecturing me? He normally sat back and let Mum do the reprimanding while he nodded and agreed.

To make matters weirder, Mum didn't say anything. She only looked between us like an uninterested third-party spectator. Then, the next thing I knew, she stepped out of my room without another word, leaving him to carry on without further interruptions.

"Do you care about your own wellbeing at all? It's not like you love what you're doing at work. What do you think..." He trailed off, squeezing his eyes shut. After a few seconds, he opened them again and stared me down to deliver the striking blow. "What do you think Ba would say about all this?"

I opened my mouth to reply, but nothing came out. He was right, of course. Here I was, slaving away full-time at a job I didn't truly feel passionate about. All in the name of... what exactly? Money? Happiness?

Happiness... I'd promised that to Dad once before, hadn't I? I recalled the exact moment I'd looked into his drooping eyes and assured him, *Yes, Dad. I promise I'll study hard and be happy.*

I choked on a sob. A soft wailing noise escaped my mouth.

It had been a lie. Sure, I'd made the effort to do things I thought would make Dad happy, but had I ever been happy myself?

The reality hit me hard in the chest all at once.

No. I hadn't been happy. I wasn't now either. All the years spent studying hard to uphold a promise I hadn't truly understood. But how could I change that? How could I be happy now?

"I don't know what to do." It was the first time I admitted it aloud. All this time, I'd been miserable on the inside. I thought all I'd needed to be happy was a small break. But the break had come and gone, and things were still the same. Nothing had changed.

Max patted my head. The awkwardly endearing action set off an avalanche on my bottled-up emotions. Tears cascaded down my cheeks. Before I knew it, I was bawling like a baby.

He heaved a loud sigh and wrapped his arms around me. "Come on, Dippy. Did you forget what you told me? 'Live your life with no regrets.'" His soft voice vibrated against my shoulder.

"Mm-hmm," I mumbled back. After Dad had passed away, Max had withdrawn into a shell of himself. Unlike Mum and I, he never openly cried. Until one night, on the way to a late-night toilet trip, I'd heard some muffled noises coming from his room. It turned out my brother did cry, just not in front of us.

At the time, it had taken all the self-control I instilled within myself not to cry along with him. Wanting to cheer him up, I told him my own mantra to stick by—live your life with no regrets. The very same mantra I'd said to Aiden.

I was such a hypocrite. When was the last time I'd followed that mantra? How had I forgotten why I'd made such a mantra in the first place? Dad had lost his life too early. When it came down to it, I didn't want to leave this world knowing I wasn't fully satisfied with what I'd done.

"It's not too late to start living your life with no regrets," Max said.

Was that true? Look at the huge mess I'd gotten myself into. And not just with my job. With my whole life in general.

"What do you think Dad would say now if I told him I've messed things up?" I asked Max.

"He'd probably tell you you're overthinking it like Ma does. That you should take it one step at a time, or just throw the bad buns out and start over again with a clean kitchen bench."

I gaped at him, completely stunned. That did sound exactly like something Dad would've said.

Max scratched his chin. "What? I spent a lot of time thinking about things he'd say to me after I failed classes in uni. Sometimes I even imagined the advice in his voice."

I could relate to that. "I used to spend a lot of time thinking about what he would say to me too. Every time I did though, it just made me remember what he made me promise him." I hiccupped, suppressing my urge to cry some more.

"Didn't you promise him you'd study hard? Pretty sure you passed that without a problem."

"It wasn't just that." I clamped my eyes shut, forcing myself to recall those words that held so much power over me. "'Study hard, be happy.' That's what he asked me to promise him."

"So," Max said, "you're finally admitting that your crazy overtime at work isn't making you happy."

"Of course I'm not happy about it, but it's part of my job. What else can I do?"

"To be happy? I think I know what Ba would've said to that."

"What would he have said?" I wanted his advice now more than ever.

Max patted my blanket-padded body. "It's better if I show you."

I stood beside Max, crinkling my nose at the usual clutter littering his bedroom desk. A notepad full of scribbles, used tissues, and a whole lot of I-didn't-even-want-to-know. I resisted the impulse to clean it all up for him and focused on the culprit of the mess.

My brother slouched forward in his chair, click-clicking away with his computer mouse. "Found it!" He double-clicked a video file icon with a series of numbers as the title. I caught a glimpse of the tiny thumbnail—our bakery kitchen?—before a new window materialised on the screen.

Background noise came out of the computer speakers, followed by a familiar voice that made my body freeze.

"Ah, look at you. Already helping Baba," Dad said in Cantonese.

Mini-me, perhaps five or six years old, leaned over a bench in the downstairs bakery kitchen. I stood on top of a wooden stool, waving a cooking brush in the air, the bristles soaked in egg wash. "When I grow up, I'm going to sell all the bao," I declared, referring to the Cantonese name for buns, my cheeks puffing out in pride.

"Then I can retire earlier." Dad laughed, lifting me off the stool and spinning me around in a circle. I let out a loud squeal of delight.

When he set me down, I lifted my gaze up to look at him.

Although I didn't remember this moment, I could almost feel everything I would've felt in that instant. Love. Admiration. A desire to please. "I want to be as good as you, Daddy."

Dad ruffled mini-me's hair. "You will be. All you need to do is practice. You're so smart, you could be anything you want to be." He swiped the cooking brush from my hand and dabbed at a tray of pineapple buns on the bench, possessing the same baking grace and poise as in my memories.

A familiar ache weighed heavily on my chest.

Max hit pause on the video. "And there you have it."

"I remember recording that." I turned around to see Mum lingering in the doorway, her eyes glistening with unshed tears. "I took it the day your baba finally let you help out in the kitchen. You impressed him by how quickly you learned everything. But most of all, he loved how it made you happy. Your happiness was his happiness."

My happiness was his happiness.

What Mum said was true. I'd been too blindsided by my promise to Dad to realise that.

Study hard, be happy.

I had taken his promise at face value, falsely believing I had to achieve academic greatness to make Dad proud. Then I'd never achieved the second, more important part of my promise to him.

Be happy.

"Is it too late to do things the right way?"

"It's never too late," Mum said. "Nothing is ever too late, so long as you're living."

"That's right." Max swivelled around in his chair to face us, his eyes shining bright. He took off his glasses and rubbed his eyes. "Ba would want you to live your life to the fullest. To do what you want."

I looked at Mum. "I thought you wanted me to study law. I didn't want to disappoint you or make you stressed."

Her reddened eyes turned sorrowful. "Oh, sweetie. I never would've pushed you so hard if I knew this was how you'd feel. I just wanted you to have a good, stable job so you wouldn't have such a hard life like your baba and I did. If there's something else you really want to do, then you should do it. You're a smart girl. You can do anything you put your mind to."

Part of my worries thawed away at her declaration, but uncertainty still lingered. "What if something I want turns out to be a big mistake?"

Mum folded her arms, and her eyes sharpened. "It's called creating chances for yourself, Serendipity Tsang. I didn't raise you to be such a scaredy-cat." She closed in on me, brushing off a flyaway hair from my face. Tracing her fingers along my cheek, she stopped to tap my nose. "It's half the reason why I chose your name. Good things happen by chance, but sometimes those chances don't happen unless you're willing to take risks."

I let her admission sink in. "That's how you met Dad, isn't it?" By pure chance. A pang of longing shot through me, and I clutched my chest. "Can we go through his scrapbook?"

Mum pursed her lips in contemplation. She'd put together a scrapbook of specially selected photos after Dad passed away. A sort of physical commemoration of his life. Of who he'd been. Of what he'd achieved. Whenever one of us had a hard day, we'd take the album out to reminisce.

"Okay," Mum said at last.

We followed her to the living room where she rummaged through the cupboard and retrieved the scrapbook. Settling onto the sofa next to her, with Max on her other side, she flipped through each page, telling us the story behind each photo. "This is when he first came to Australia from Hong Kong. He was twelve." The photo featured a smiling boy wearing a school uniform. She recalled everything Dad had told her of his childhood. How it was hard for him to learn English, but he befriended several kids at school over a game of tennis during sports class. How he kept up that same passion for tennis for the rest of his life, becoming an avid tennis fan and taking us to see the Australian Open almost every year.

Many photos later, we reached a page with a photo of him in a chef's hat. It was my favourite story—how Dad met Mum while working at a Chinese restaurant. "He was so friendly. Too friendly. I thought he was too good to be true at first," Mum said.

We'd heard the story before, but we still loved to hear it anyway. About how Dad had asked her out after a week of knowing her as one of the waitresses at a small restaurant.

"I said no since I didn't really know him, but he didn't give up. He asked me again a month later." From the smile on her face, she didn't need to clarify that she'd said yes that time. "He said he liked me because I was funny. I acted very 'Aussie' but at the same time I acted very Chinese." Mum had moved to Australia from Hong Kong when she'd been five years old, so she'd grown up more fluent in English than Dad.

The most interesting part though centred on the fact that it all happened based on several chances. Or as Mum loved to call it—serendipity. "He was only there to temporarily cover for another chef who'd been badly burned the week before. I almost wasn't going to work there either. I had a bad experience with my manager at the restaurant I worked at, so my friend offered me a job at her family restaurant instead. And that's how I met your baba."

The story reminded me of her words from earlier.

It's called creating chances for yourself... Sometimes those chances don't happen unless you're willing to take risks.

That night in bed, my thumb hovered hesitantly over my phone, one sentence typed out and ready to be sent.

Can we talk?

Short and simple.

If I was to overcome all my regrets and live a life Dad could be proud of, I had to tackle the biggest regret in my life first. It was time to risk it all and create a chance for myself. A chance to right my wrongs.

With a huge gulp, I pressed the send button before I could change my mind.

CHAPTER 26

You can do this. You're not walking to your death. My stomach roiled non-stop as if to convince me otherwise. It felt like someone was whisking egg whites at maximum speed inside me. I didn't usually get so easily nauseous, but the mere thought of what I was about to do made an acidic taste rise in my throat.

I swallowed it down and inhaled deeply through my nose. *Take it easy, Sere. Breathe in. Breathe out. In. Out.*

I continued the calming routine as I pushed open the door to the cafe. On my next inhalation, the scent of coffee hit my nostrils full force. I salivated over the smell saturating the air, grateful for a distraction while I mentally braced myself. Finally, when I felt confident that I wouldn't run away, I took a tentative step forward and let the door swing shut behind me.

My gaze scanned over the area. The cafe had a very nature-esque theme to it. Potted plants sat on the small window ledges, and fake vines climbed the wooden beams and poles. But it also seemed modern with its round, white tables and matching chairs. Most of the seats were unoccupied, which naturally drew my attention to the only person sitting alone at a table.

I slowly made my way over, repeating the same chant as before in my head.

You can do this, you can do this, you can—

"Sere."

My former best friend leapt up from her seat as soon as she saw me. If we'd still been close, I would've teased her for the worried expression on her face. She looked like she'd been told her favourite tennis player was possibly retiring. Which would probably be true if her favourite player was Aiden Andale.

At that thought, my anxiety increased twofold. *One step at a time, Sere.*

"Hey, Liz." I lifted a hand in greeting. The action made the plastic bag around my arm smack me, reminding me of its existence. I extracted it from my arm and offered it to her. "Here. This is for you."

"Thanks." She opened the bag and peered inside it. "Egg tarts?"

"Yeah. Your favourite." A peace offering. I hadn't been certain what her reaction would be to seeing me, despite her agreeing to meet up. Since she'd tried instigating so many conversations by messaging me, I had high hopes that we could talk this out as two mature people. But honestly, I wasn't sure what to expect from others nowadays. And from the slightly bemused look on Liz's face, I wasn't sure if my offering had worked either.

"So, it's been a while," she said.

"Uh. Yeah. A while." That was putting it mildly. She looked completely different from the last time I'd seen her. Her hair was cropped short in a pixie hairstyle, a far cry from its previous below-the-shoulder state. "How've you been?"

She stared at me, unblinking, and I shrunk under her penetrating gaze. "How have I been?" She placed her hands on her hips in her infamous Judgy Liz look. "You mean, besides you ignoring me for more than a year? Not too bad, I suppose."

I winced. Of course Liz wouldn't beat around the bush. She'd crash headlong into it and stuff the consequences, thorns, scrapes, and all. That was her. "Yeah, about that..." I'd gone through a dozen practice sentences in my head, but they didn't sound appropriate now that I was here. She would only accept something as straight as her own blunt words.

Just as well it was her that ended up breaking the ice for me. "Look, I get it," she said. "I was an idiot. I should've been the first person to tell you when it happened. But I didn't know how to. It wasn't exactly a nice topic. And I know you may disagree, but you were better off without him."

"I know. You always made it perfectly clear you didn't think we were a good couple." A year ago, I would've uttered this with hatred boiling inside me. Now, thinking about what had happened only evoked a small twinge of pain within me instead. I was no longer consumed by it. No longer wishing for karma to hit everyone who I thought deserved it. "How is Jeremy anyway?"

Liz's eyebrows hitched up high. "Do you really want to know?"

I blew out a breath. "Not really." I didn't know when it happened, but I'd stopped thinking about him. My thoughts nowadays were thankfully all Jeremy-free. What a shame it couldn't be free of a certain pro tennis player too.

"Yeah, I gathered you had more important things to talk about." Liz pointed in the direction of the cashier. "Why don't we get something to drink first?"

"Sure. Sounds good." Moreover, it gave me time to think about how to best explain my reason for contacting her.

After ordering an iced coffee, I took it back to the table and slid into the chair opposite Liz.

She took a sip from her cappuccino. "So what did you want to talk about?"

I followed suit, gulping down some of my iced coffee. The heady dose of caffeine eased the trepidation swirling in my stomach, the coolness of the drink waking my senses. Clearing my throat, I finally found my voice. "I want to apologise. It's just that—I, uh…" Though I'd spent hours in bed rehearsing what I would say, all the words tangled on the tip of my tongue, a jumbled mess of nonsense.

Liz rested her elbows on the table, tucking her chin in her hands. "What exactly are you apologising for? For ignoring all my messages?"

"No." I forced myself to look straight at her. "It's just—I don't want us to hate each other anymore. I realised life's too short for us to hold onto hate."

"Wait." A wrinkle formed between her brows. "I get why you would hate me," she said slowly, "but why would you think I hate you?"

"Because of what I said that day." There was no need to clarify when "that day" was. We both knew. "I've had a lot of time to think about it." I didn't add that most of that time had been spent playing the victim. It was only after Max reminded me of my mantra yesterday that it dawned on me—I would never live my life with no regrets unless I got past this.

"I didn't really mean it. What I said to you," I said since Liz had gone uncharacteristically quiet. I knew I sounded vague, but the last thing I wanted to do was repeat the damning words I'd once said to her.

My hands gripped hard on the glass of iced coffee as I recalled "that day." The day Jeremy had broken my heart. It wasn't a day I liked to remember. I made it a point to divert my thoughts any time they came anywhere close to thinking about it. But enough was enough.

Like the snapping of a rubber band, the bad memory flung back into my mind.

The day Jeremy had broken up with me, I'd rushed over to Liz's home after my meltdown to her on the phone.

"It's okay, Sere." Liz rubbed circles on my back as I lay slumped on her bed in a messed heap, surrounded by used tissues. I'd been crying for a whole hour, an overflowing, pathetic waterfall of tears. "He didn't deserve you."

Like a lovesick fool, I didn't listen to what she said. "Why would he do that? Who would he even love? I should ask him, right? I deserve to know at least that much. That girl needs to know she's a boyfriend stealer."

"Sere..." Liz paused in her back-rubbing ministrations. "I don't think that will help you."

"Who said I need help? I just need closure." I pulled back from her, my hands balling into fists. "How can I move on from him if I don't even know who he's moving on with?" Anger burned like a fire within me. Every thought I had of Jeremy, of what he confessed to me, only stoked it.

"You need to let it go," Liz urged me. Even behind the glossiness of my recently shed tears, I saw something like fear shining in the depths of her large brown eyes, which made no

sense. She chewed on a nail, a habit I'd grown up recognising as a nervous tic. Even in my heated anger, something felt off to me. Why would she be nervous? Shouldn't she be angry too? I would've been kicking her boyfriend where it hurt most if the situation had been reversed. I could only think of one possible reason for her nervousness.

"You know something." The thought teetered on the edge of my mind, threatening to spill more fuel to the internal fire. I tamped it down. Surely there was a reasonable answer. Maybe she'd heard something. "What do you know, Lizbeth?" I used her full name to draw her out. Set up the bait.

She took it like a fish on a hook. "I—I don't think you want to know."

That was where she was wrong. There was nothing more I wanted to know. "Tell me."

"Sere," she pleaded, resignation lining her voice. "I wanted to tell you, but if you didn't know—"

If I didn't know? My best friend knew about this all along?

The anger I'd held at bay suddenly built up inside me at warp speed. No, no, no—

I exploded.

"You knew about Jere liking someone else? Why didn't you tell me?" My hands clamped down on both her shoulders, shaking hard. "Who does he love?"

Liz's eyes bulged. Her hands flew up in surrender. "I didn't know! Not at first. But then my parents started inviting him over..." Her face leached of colour. "You have to know, I wanted to tell you. But I didn't know how. She already has everything. I didn't want her to get your boyfriend too. But then she did. She always gets everything she wants in the end."

What was she talking about? My anger waned, and my mind grew sluggish in its attempts to comprehend the ambiguity in her words.

Liz moved to clasp my wrists and drew my hands off her shoulders. As my hands fell limply to my sides, everything else fell into place.

She always gets everything she wants in the end. There was only one person who Liz thought owned the world and more.

"Your sister," I rasped out. "You're saying Jere loves your sister?"

A loud laugh cut off the rest of the nightmarish memory, jolting me back to the present. I focused on Liz, her head tipped back, cackling like she'd lost the plot. "Wait. You think I've hated you all this time just because you called me a—"

I covered my ears. "Don't say it!" I'd sooner wash my mouth with soap than hear her repeat what I had called her.

"Oh, come on. I've been called a lot worse than what you called me that day."

Wait... She hadn't hated me for that?

She continued to laugh. "I know it was a lot coming from you, though. You're like some saint who doesn't swear."

"I'm not a saint." Far from it.

"No, you're not. I wouldn't have expected you to be when you found out." Her expression turned sombre. "What Jerky did was horrible, but he didn't cheat on you, you know. He ended it with you before he started a relationship with Ellie."

"That's not why it hurt."

"Yeah, I know," she whispered, her voice filled with unwanted sympathy. "You loved him." She levelled her heavy gaze on me. It reminded me of Aiden's gaze. All-seeing. Unnerving. "But he left you. Just like that. It's kind of like the same way you just left me."

That was so not the same thing. In retrospect, I saw now how my heartbreak had morphed into a fiery rage. Heartbreak focused on myself. Rage, on the other hand, could be directed at someone else, and I'd found that I liked having someone else to take the blame. To wish horrible things to happen upon. But that was no longer the case. "Liz—"

"Nope, let me finish. You left me, but I deserved it. I deserve your hate." She blinked rapidly, and her throat bobbed. "You're not the only one who thought a lot about things this past year, you know. I've got a lot to apologise for too. I'm sorry I was a crap friend. I should've told you about my sister and Jerky."

"Why didn't you?" That was something I still didn't understand. The betrayal.

Why hadn't my best friend told me about my boyfriend spending so much time with her sister? I'd never gotten the answer—had always convinced myself it was unnecessary—because I'd run away from her that day after my outburst.

"It's stupid, really." Liz palmed her face and let out a long groan. "At first, I didn't tell you because I didn't want to stress you out over nothing. You were dealing with a hard year at uni. I thought, was there any point in telling you? Jerky was just being a goody-two-shoes. You always overthought things too, so you definitely would've had a fit over it if you'd known. And I figured if anyone should've told you, it should've been him."

"He didn't." Although he'd told me he spent time volunteering to help cancer patients, he never mentioned one of those patients was my best friend's sister. Pretty big detail he'd omitted there. "Why didn't you tell me later then?"

"Because I could tell Ellie really liked him." Her face twisted into a grimace. "I wasn't sure if he felt the same, but I thought if I told you then, everything would go downhill from there. You would break up with him and then Ellie would definitely get him. That was the last thing I wanted to happen."

If I'd still held a grudge, I would've cornered Liz. Put her on the spot. *What didn't you want to happen more? Me breaking up with my boyfriend, or Ellie getting what she wanted?* They were two very different motives. Selfless versus selfish. But that wouldn't accomplish anything now. Reopening old wounds wouldn't do anyone good. I would know—I had plenty of them struggling to heal as it was. As for Liz, if she still had a problem with her sister, that wasn't healthy either. "Do you still feel that way about Ellie?"

"I... No. I'm better now. I try not to care so much about her." Her gaze lowered to the table. "But I know that's no excuse for breaking the girl code and hiding something important from you. I really messed things up. I'm sorry, Sere."

I leaned back in my chair, drinking the rest of my iced coffee with shaking hands. The tiny remains of ice clattered as I set the glass back on the table. It was true Liz had betrayed my trust, but I hadn't been much better. I'd never given her a chance to explain herself back then. What was a person meant to do without chances?

My long-forsaken mantra floated into my head. *Live your life with no regrets.*

She was sorry. I was sorry. Was there any point in prolonging the hate? Wouldn't I come to regret it if I never forgave her? Maybe our friendship would never perfectly piece itself back together again, but I'd be lying if I said I wanted to live the rest of my life without her in it.

I sighed. "I think it's fair to say we were both in a bad place that night. We can start from square one or whatever, but I think we should leave all that baggage in the past now. What do you think?"

Liz's wide eyes met mine, as if she couldn't quite believe me. As if she was still waiting for the punchline where I told her to get lost. Maybe if she'd explained it to me back then I would've, but I was past all that now. I didn't love Jeremy anymore, and whoever he loved no longer concerned me either.

Liz trembled as she cupped her mouth and nodded. "I want us to start over. More than anything."

A zing of guilt struck me. I guess I hadn't been the only one affected by our separation. "I forgive you." And because I truly did, I thought it was time to come clean to someone about everything. If anyone could give me blunt and firm advice, it was Liz. "I guess you want to ask me about that article you saw?"

Liz perked up like a dog smelling a treat, straightening in her seat. "Yes! You. And. Aiden. Andale. What's going on there?"

I raised a hand to placate her. "I know, I know. I'll explain everything."

And so I did. I told her everything from the beginning. His sudden appearance at my bakery. Him volunteering to help me. One by one, I recited each moment of my time with him. A tender ache bloomed in my chest. Reliving the memories was like peeling away the measly bandages I'd wrapped on, but I had to see if the wounds had scabbed over. I had to get past this pain.

Liz grinned like the Cheshire cat when I got to the part about New Year's Eve. "I can't believe that was your favour for losing. A romantic dinner by the harbour with him? You totally like him, don't you?"

A hot flush of embarrassment coursed through me. "Yeah," I whispered, because there was no denying the truth anymore. I liked Aiden Andale. Really liked him.

Liz squealed. "I knew it! Are you two together now? I saw that article about him with Isabelle Dunham, but—"

"We're not together." I'd probably messed up the chances of that ever happening. "I told him he was mistaken about my feelings."

The excitement on her face immediately sizzled out, leaving her frowning at me. "Why would you lie and say that?"

I released a shaky breath. "How was I supposed to know if he really liked me? Maybe he did, but how would I ever know if it would last? How would I know it wouldn't end like my last relationship?"

Her frown deepened. "You never know until you try. And you didn't try."

A heavy weight pressed on my chest. What she said echoed Mum's words.

No, I hadn't tried. I hadn't risked the chance to try.

"Hey." Liz's expression lightened. "It's not the end of the world. You can apologise to him and tell him the truth."

"Hmm." If I told Aiden I'd lied, what would he think? Would he hear me out? Get mad at me for lying? Tell me that he was so over me? "Maybe I'll text him." The worst response for a text would be him ignoring it, but at least then I'd know I'd tried.

"Text him? Don't take the easy way out." Liz rolled her eyes. "I know you don't like confrontations, Sere, but if you want the guy, you've got to put in some effort."

"Should I call him then?" I wasn't sure if he'd even answer.

"Why don't you go to the Australian Open and tell him in person?"

My jaw dropped at her suggestion. "I don't know about that..." I had yet to sort out my work problems, but even without that, there were other costs. The airfare from Sydney to Melbourne wouldn't be cheap and the accommodation wouldn't be either. Having the Aus Open ground pass from Aiden was my only advantage. But to actually go there without planning anything? It was so spontaneous. Too spontaneous for someone like me.

My stomach gurgled as if to agree.

Liz laughed, a melodic sound that I'd missed hearing for the past year. "Well, you can't make a decision on an empty stomach." She took out the plastic container of egg tarts I'd given her, removed the lid, and handed me one. "Here." Then she grabbed another and took a huge bite out of it. "Mmm. I've missed this."

"The egg tarts?"

"Not just the egg tarts. I missed *this*." She gestured between us with her half-eaten tart, making crumbs scatter across the table. "Oops."

I chuckled, taking a tentative bite of my own tart. The crust fell apart in my mouth, mixing with the soft, pudding-like texture of egg custard. "I missed this too." Having someone to confide in, to share my thoughts with.

A heavy weight lifted off my chest, and my lips curved into a smile as I realised what emotion I was feeling. An emotion I hadn't genuinely felt since Aiden left Sydney.

Happiness.

CHAPTER 27

It was hard to believe that at the beginning of last year, I'd jumped at the opportunity to take a part-time position at this big law firm. It had been my big goal. The one I'd worked my butt off for the past few years. I'd studied hard for it. Endured a lot to earn it.

And now I was about to throw it all out the window.

My boss released a gruff sigh that was doubly audible over the phone. "I thought it was an April fool's joke from HR when they told me you handed in your resignation. But no, it's only the middle of January. Just when I was going to promote you. Are you sure you won't reconsider?"

I paced around the empty office meeting room, jitters running through my body. I wiped the sweaty palm of my free hand on my dress and cleared my throat. "Yes, I'm sure." As sure as I ever could be. It was funny how unsure I'd been before about taking this huge leap of faith, but the last month and a half had taught me everything I needed to know about how to live my life. "I've thought a lot about it, and this is my final decision."

Sure a promotion and big pay raise were great things I could gain, but there were other more important things I had my heart set on now.

"I understand," he said, though I suspected he didn't really. Who in their right mind would quit just when their boss said they'd promote them? After they'd spent years of studying at uni, completing additional courses and working many hours of compulsory legal training just so they could become a paralegal?

Me, apparently.

My boss let out another sigh. "Well, it's been great having you on the team, Sere. I guess I won't be seeing you since you'll be gone by the time I'm back from my holiday." A loud chorus of cheering and clapping echoed through his phone speakers, reminding me of where that holiday was.

The Australian Open. Lucky him. Not that I was jealous, but I would have given anything to be anywhere but here, stuck in this office. Too bad I couldn't be. I might've been resigning, but I still had to work for a few more weeks before I could be officially done with this job.

Ah well. I'd take a holiday somewhere after all this was over.

Mondays were usually the bane of my existence, when my mind was preoccupied with dreading another four tiring days of work. Today, however, I had something to look forward to, besides soon leaving my stressful job forever.

As soon as I collapsed onto a seat on the train home, I dug out my earphones from my handbag and popped them into my ears. Aus Open match highlights were already up. I made it a habit to watch them every year whenever I couldn't watch the actual matches.

Wicked forehands, surprising drop shots, consecutive aces—the highlights never failed to entertain. I was still riding on the high of watching the end of the last video—a clever lob over the opponent—when the next video suggestion appeared. It took me a few seconds to notice it. Unlike all the previously suggested videos, this one wasn't a match highlights one. My pulse thumped hard in my ears as I stared at the title. And stared some more.

Aiden Andale: "Why don't I let everyone in on a little secret?"—Australian Open On-Court Interview 1R.

A little secret. *What* little secret? Although I knew he'd won his match—I'd viewed the scores on my phone during lunch break—I hadn't seen this. Unable to resist the temptation, my finger pressed on the preview image and the video buffered to life.

Aiden took up the left half of the screen. He held a drink bottle in his hand. His hair was pulled back by a dark blue headband that matched his equally dark blue shirt. A knot formed in my stomach at the sight of him. He looked good. So good. There was no other word for it. It hurt to look at him in his natural element, dressed like he was all ready to win a Grand Slam.

A male interviewer who I recognised as a former professional tennis player stood beside Aiden with a microphone. "Congratulations on your win, Aiden. I think we can all agree that was a really tough match out in the heat today. Back when you were down a break in the second set, it seemed like this match could've easily gotten away from you. How did you manage to recover?"

"Well..." Aiden ran a hand through his already dishevelled hair. "I tried to focus a bit more on each point instead of the bigger picture. I needed to concentrate on hitting my shots better because there was nothing I could do about how well my opponent played."

My throat closed up at the sound of his husky tone. Had it really been more than two weeks since I'd last heard his voice? How had I gone so long without hearing it?

"You showed immense control out there over your emotions. It looked like you wanted to break your racket right after you lost that crucial point, but you didn't. How were you able to stay in control?"

"Yeah, I guess it was easy to tell I was losing my cool." Aiden smiled sheepishly, sending a twinge of pain shooting through me. "Why don't I let everyone in on a little secret?"

The title of the video. My heart thudded faster and harder.

"Oh, do tell. You're always so full of mysteries. I bet we're all eager to know what you have to share."

"It's something someone told me once, and it's stayed with me since." He paused to take a sip of his sports drink. "A racket is like your partner. Your friend. You wouldn't kick your friend in the head. At least I hope not." The interviewer and crowd laughed at the statement. "So yeah. I try to treat my racket with that same respect."

A fluttering filled my stomach like a million dancing butterflies.

"Who gave you such great advice?"

Me. I knew without a doubt he was talking about me.

Aiden pointed at the interviewer with his drink bottle, a mischievous smirk on his face. "That, I'm afraid I can't say."

"Ah, so you're still keeping secrets from your fans in the end."

He laughed that familiar chortling laugh of his. "You know it. How else will I remain mysterious?"

"Let us in on one thing, though. You can't keep your fans hanging like this. Don't you agree, everyone?" The crowd shouted in approval. "Is this person from your family? A former coach? A fellow tennis player?"

Aiden cocked an eyebrow at the interviewer's suggestions. "No, none of those. But I can tell you she's played an important part in my life as someone who helped me become who I am today. Actually, she probably doesn't know the impact she's had on me, since I'm so secretive and all."

He was still grinning as I tried and failed to digest the meaning behind what he said. How in the world had I helped him become who he was today? But then his face grew stern, and his next words changed everything.

"I have one last thing to say, so I hope she's watching." He turned to look directly at the video camera. "I challenge you to come to the Australian Open. Come and watch me play. If you do, you win. I'll give you anything—any one thing that you want and it's yours."

His words short-circuited my brain. Was he seriously challenging me for all the world to hear? With such a ridiculously generous reward? Any one thing I wanted and... What would I even ask him?

The interviewer blinked at him with a confused smile on his face. "Who are you challenging, Aiden, and why are you willing to give them anything they want if they come here?"

Aiden just smiled and lifted a finger to his lips, making a gesture of zipping them shut.

"Okay, then," the interviewer said, scrambling to recover from Aiden's lack of response. "You are a secretive man. I guess that's all the secrets you're willing to spill for us today. Tell us what you think about your potential next round opponent instead? You'll either be facing..."

The rest of the video played on, but it was all lost to my ears.

I challenge you to come to the Australian Open.

Had he really said that? Why was he challenging me? He must've been doing it for the same reason I'd challenged him before. He wanted to prove a point.

I shifted my gaze to the train windows, conflicting thoughts clashing in my head as fast as the landscape whipping by.

I knew exactly what point Aiden was trying to prove. The question was—would I let him prove it? I could just ignore this challenge and pretend I'd never seen it. Go on with my life.

A gnawing deep in my gut protested against that idea. Ignoring this would make me exactly what he'd called me. A coward.

I didn't want to be like that anymore. What if, one year from now, I regretted not going? Or even two weeks from now, when the Aus Open was already over? Even if this was completely uncharacteristic for me to do, I would rather take the chance than leave another trail of regrets formed by my own inaction.

He wanted to prove a point to me? Fine. I would prove a point to him too.

Challenge accepted, Aiden Andale.

CHAPTER 28

This was so not how I imagined spending my Saturday afternoon.

The oppressing heat of the Melbourne sun shone down on me, a heat worse than standing in front of an open oven. I hurried through the steady stream of people, dodging those heading in the opposite direction. Left, right, left, left. Perspiration dripped down the nape of my neck, making my hair stick uncomfortably to it.

Damn Australian summer. It must've been at least thirty degrees today. Why hadn't I brought a hat? Of all the things to forget to bring. At least I'd brought sunscreen, but still. How did tennis players avoid being burned to a charred crisp in this weather? I'd have to ask Aiden how he did it—after I completed the challenge.

My heart hammered against my ribs, the reality dawning on me.

Was I crazy? I was actually completing this absurd challenge. I'd gone and done the exact thing I swore I'd never do.

Go to the Australian Open. Without Dad.

The realisation hit me hard, spurring me onward.

I was already here. I wouldn't disrespect Dad by running away from his favourite place due to my own problems. I had to find Aiden and talk to him. I might have come here for his challenge, but in truth, I had other reasons too. Even if Aiden had moved on with his life, I hadn't. I needed to do this. For myself. For closure. To live my life with no regrets.

Before long, I eyed the Rod Laver Arena in the distance. Sunlight glinted off the slightly curved, off-white structure, the crisscrossing of the triangle-patterned exterior hypnotic. My feet gravitated toward the set of steps that led to its entrance, but I quickly came to my senses.

No. The arena wasn't my destination. I didn't even have tickets to get in. Which was probably for the best. The last time I'd entered the arena had been with Dad, excited to watch a men's semi-finals match. It'd been the last match I'd seen live with him at the Australian Open. Before he passed away.

My lips pressed together as moisture gathered in my eyes. No, no, no. I would not cry. I'd had the whole plane and bus ride to prepare myself for this. No crying. I hadn't even found Aiden yet. Be strong.

I forced my feet forward, my eyes scanning across the Grand Slam Oval next to the arena as I passed by. The grassy area was decked out with tables and chairs covered by blue umbrellas, all of them unsurprisingly occupied.

As a child, I'd often traipsed through this very oval, eating food my parents had bought from the food trucks and lounging on the lawn chairs to watch live matches from the large LCD screens. Every time a player Dad supported scored a point, Max and I had both cheered alongside him. I couldn't help smiling at the fond memory now. Though those fun times had long passed and they would never happen again, I would always treasure them.

I clasped a hand over my heart as if to physically hold those memories there, then set off again.

I was pretty sure I knew the way to my destination, but I double-checked on my phone just in case. According to the scheduled times on the website, Aiden should've started practicing on Court Sixteen less than half an hour ago.

Come and watch me play, he'd said, but he hadn't specified that it had to be a real match. A practice session counted, right? Otherwise, I'd need to reveal myself to him first; all his scheduled matches were in either Rod Laver Arena or Margaret Court Arena, both pay-to-enter arenas that had sold out their tickets before the annual event.

I pored over the map I'd downloaded of Melbourne Park. Court Sixteen wasn't too far from here, but with the heat not letting up, I needed some supplies first.

After buying a cold bottle of water and a cap to protect my head from the sun, I continued to Court Sixteen. The closer I got to the large fenced-off courts, the more I doubted myself. It was a silly idea, after all. Travel all the way from Sydney to Melbourne, get here to the Australian Open, and complete the challenge Aiden had issued. Then what? Apologise to him? Say that he'd been right in calling me a coward? That was the extent of my shabby plan.

I felt too unprepared for this. Like I was going into an exam without studying first. Well, too late now. The courts already loomed up ahead. Blue sheets covered the high fences bordering them, making it impossible to see much from afar. My feet ate up the distance, passing by Court Eighteen and then Court Seventeen. The heat pressed down on me. Or was it my anxiety?

By the time I reached Court Sixteen, huffing like the inactive person I was, I paused at the scene before me. People swarmed the area, both behind the short fence on one side of the court and sitting on the tiered seating on the other side. Even the observation bridge overhead was filled to the brim with people leaning over the railing in rapt attention at the courts below.

Uh-oh. I should've known this would happen. As if the place wouldn't be packed if an Australian player was practicing. Especially if that player was Aiden Andale.

My stomach did somersaults as I squeezed my way through the masses. I spent a solid few minutes trying to get into a promising position in the audience.

In the end, I settled into a small space squished between two teenage girls and an older couple. From here, I could barely see over the heads of the first few rows of people, but this was as good as it would get.

The sound of a ball smacking the ground told me the practice session was still on. Not that I could see much from behind the human wall of the audience. Besides the cheers and claps, which was when I knew Aiden had probably made a good shot, I could hardly tell what was happening.

I craned my neck to and fro, going on tiptoes. Finally, after almost half a minute of annoying head bobbing and tilting, I saw a glimpse of tousled dark brown hair. Just a glimpse, then it was gone again.

As the practice went on, an unbearable pressure pressed in on my head. Ugh, not now. I did *not* need a headache to add to my list of worries. I dug out the bottle of water from my handbag and held it across my forehead. The coldness afforded me some relief, but not much. Not enough to survive sticking around for the whole practice match. But I couldn't leave now. Not until I'd at least snuck a peek at Aiden and took a photo of him for proof of completing the challenge.

Fortunately, groups of people began to leave, allowing me to flit into the gaps that opened up. Either they were getting lunch, had to take a trip to the toilet, or wanted to flee the wrath of the sun. Whatever their reasons, I thanked my lucky stars and quickly manoeuvred into a prime spot in the front row of spectators. My eyes immediately latched onto the right side of the court.

I took in Aiden's appearance, my stomach wobbling like jelly. He looked exactly as he had in the video I'd watched five days ago, dressed in the same sports gear that suited him so well. A dark blue shirt, white shorts, his signature wristbands and a headband that pushed back his mussed hair.

My eyes followed him back and forth as he chased after the ball along the baseline, every movement—from the position of his feet, to the smooth arc of his arm when he hit the ball—seamlessly executed. And those backhands. The way he planted his left foot forward as a base, pulled his left arm toward his chest and then swung it back out to hit the ball cleanly with his racket... I couldn't fully describe it, but it was like he'd casted a spell on me. Watching him almost made me forget about my headache.

Photos. Don't forget to take photos, some logical part of my brain thankfully reminded me. I chucked the now-warm drink bottle I'd been holding into my handbag, grabbed my phone, and opened up the camera app. Sunlight glared off the screen, making it almost impossible to see what I was aiming my camera lens at. Snap, snap, snap. I took as many shots as I could. It didn't matter how bad they were, so long as they proved I'd seen him play.

"Let's take a short break," Aiden yelled out.

All at once, the aggravating pulsing in my head returned.

I lifted the front of my cap to massage my head. My gaze swept over to a blonde man walking over to Aiden. In my entrancement, I hadn't taken the time to look at his practice partner. I observed him as he said something to Aiden. He didn't look familiar. Was he his new coach? A hitting partner? I guess there was time to ponder about it later.

With my head on the verge of imploding, I fled the hot confines of the crowd and rushed to find a cooler sanctuary.

Ah, this was the best.

Large electric fans whirled at high speed, simultaneously spraying water while blowing gusts of wind in my face. I shoved away the loose wisps of my hair tickling my nose, savouring the refreshing coolness. Could I stay here forever so I wouldn't have to feel the heat? Although my headache had lessened to a dull throb, thanks to the pain relief tablets I'd taken, I wasn't in a hurry to be anywhere.

After I'd left the practice match, I'd found these fans nearby and then texted Aiden the photos I'd taken of him as proof of completing the challenge. So far, no response. I almost felt like a kid eager for their Christmas present. Or a teenager waiting for a message from her crush. Not sure which one sounded worse. Probably the teenager, except I couldn't even use the excuse of still being one. I was just a sad, young adult.

So when my phone vibrated in my pocket, I pushed down the hope brimming inside me. For all I knew, it could be an email notification or one of those scam texts that said you won some competition and asked you to click on the link to claim your "prize." I wasn't stupid enough to fall for those. Only stupid when it involved a certain tennis player.

The phone continued rumbling in my hand as I slipped it out of my pocket.

My eyes snagged onto the screen, and I stopped breathing.

Incoming call. Aiden Andale.

In my standstill, water from the fans spritzed onto my phone and face, giving me a well-deserved wake-up call. I spun around, letting the water soak the back of my tank top instead, and swiped through the water droplet splatter on my phone screen to answer the call.

"Hello?"

"Hey, Serendipity." The sound of his voice saying my name raised goosebumps on my arm. Even over the phone, he had that effect on me. "Are you really here?"

A lump formed in my throat. I swallowed a few times, working to remove it. "Yeah."

"Cool." He paused, and a million questions crossed my mind in the span of a few seconds. What was he thinking? Was he happy? Impressed? Totally unaffected?

"Can we meet up?" he asked, cutting off my internal monologue.

"Sure." I could do that. Wasn't that my real reason for coming here? "Uh..."

"Meet me in front of Melbourne Arena in ten minutes. At the entrance opposite the oval. See you there. Bye."

He hung up as abruptly as his words, giving me no chance to refuse him. Not that I would've, but I wondered why he wanted to meet in front of Melbourne Arena, of all places. Didn't he know that he'd be easily swamped by fans there?

After a quick trip to a bathroom to freshen up, I arrived in front of the arena and surveyed the area for any signs of him. People bustled about, many of them filtering in and out of the arena.

Melbourne Arena used to be called Hisense Arena back when Dad and I watched matches there. It'd been his favourite because we didn't have to pay any extra money to watch. Though the arena had undergone some renovations since then, a sad feeling settled in the pit of my stomach at another inevitable reminder of Dad at this event. It was impossible to look in any direction of this place and not find some connection to him.

"Sere."

I let out a small yelp. In my daze, I hadn't noticed someone coming up to stand beside me.

"Hey." Aiden tilted his head down to stare at me. Or at least that's what I thought he was doing. It was hard to tell with the large pair of shades covering his eyes.

His lips twitched into a small smile. "Sorry if I scared you." He tugged on the drawstring of his hoodie. "I wasn't sure if you'd come here after what you said last time."

I wiped my sweaty palms along my legs, finding it impossible to ignore how good he looked. His untamable hair curled around a cap tucked under the shade of the hoodie over his head. It was the same type of sleeveless hoodie he'd worn that time he'd visited the bakery. Chino shorts and tennis shoes completed the ensemble. He appeared strangely normal. Nothing gave away that this was a star tennis player, not that he could have fooled me.

Focus, Sere. You're not here to ogle him. "I didn't think I'd come here either," I told him. "But someone made the mistake of challenging me, and I wanted to prove him wrong, so"—I waved a hand over myself—"here I am."

Aiden chuckled, a low, pleasant sound that warmed my stomach. "You're here just to prove me wrong?"

"I also didn't want to be a coward anymore."

Rocking back on his heels, he lowered his head, avoiding my eyes. "About that. I'm—"

"Wait! Can you let me speak first? Please?" Otherwise, I wasn't sure if I would chicken out on what I wanted to confess.

Aiden's head snapped up, eyebrows furrowing, but he nodded.

"Thanks." Okay, I could do this. Technically, I'd already done the harder stuff last weekend and on Monday, making up with Liz and quitting work. This, in comparison, would be a cinch.

I fixed my gaze on his face so I could catch his reaction. "I resigned from my job."

"You—*what*?" Though I couldn't see his eyes, I could almost imagine them widening under his raised eyebrows behind the sunnies.

"You were right," I went on. "I knew working full-time at a law firm wasn't what I really wanted to do, but I convinced myself that I didn't have any other choice. Like you said about me not wanting to come here—I was a coward."

Aiden took a step closer to me and raised a hand. "I didn't mean to call you a coward. I was angry at myself and —"

"It's okay. You don't have to explain. I understand." He might not have meant for his words to come out that way, but they had. I didn't need him to make me feel better. As much as his words hurt, they held a measure of truth.

"But—"

"I *was* a coward. You saw it before I ever wanted to see it for myself. Sorry it took me so long to realise." I shot him a sad smile. "You were right. We only get one life, and I want to spend it doing something I like."

"You... You're actually quitting then?"

"Yep. I already handed in my resignation letter and everything." I squinted up at him. "It's hard for me to tell your reaction when you've got those huge sunnies on."

Aiden laughed, adjusting his sunglasses so that I caught a glimpse of his eyes, crinkled in amusement, before he moved them back into place again. "Sorry. Precautions."

"Oh, right." He probably didn't want fans to recognise him, or for the media to take photos of us together like last time; not when he was dating someone. That made sense. Him not wanting to make his girlfriend jealous, that was. Not the whole him getting a girlfriend after our awkward kiss. My lips pursed at the remembrance of Isabelle, and a burning sensation ignited in my chest.

"So." Aiden scuffed his shoe along the concrete, drawing my attention back to him. "Are you ready to open up your catering service, become incredibly successful, and retire early?"

I tried to laugh, but it came out half-hearted. "Not that fast. I'm going to take it one step at a time."

Speaking of early retirements, was he still going through with that? I hadn't heard a peep about it from the media. Questions desperately bubbled up inside me, wanting to escape. *Are you still retiring after the Australian Open? Or did you change your mind? Who was that guy you practiced with? Is he your new coach? Have you talked to your dad yet? Has he stopped bothering you?*

But the question I wanted to ask him the most would hurt me too much if I heard the answer. *How did you move on so quickly?*

I'd thought he'd liked me as much as I liked him. Or had it only been a fleeting spark of attraction that had dissolved the moment a pretty, blonde tennis player had shown him more interest? I hadn't thought of him as that type of person after getting to know him, but...

A tap on my cap made me look up. I stared at my reflection in Aiden's sunglasses, my confused face blinking back at me. "It'll be fine, Sere," he said. "I know you'll do great, however you plan to tackle it."

What? Oh, right. He was talking about my future plans. My neck grew hot at his unabashed belief in me. "What if I plan to tackle it by hiring you to work for me?" I joked. I was no longer certain I could be serious. If I let myself acknowledge the truth of him moving on, my heart would break into a million pieces.

"Then I'd say thanks but no thanks," Aiden said, "and maybe question your eye for baking talent."

A real laugh burst out of me, even as I hurt on the inside. "But I thought you said I'd get anything I wanted as my prize for winning the challenge."

He rubbed his nose with the back of his hand. "True. You could ask me for anything. To invest in your business, or even give you money. But you would rather hire me?"

"Those other ideas honestly never crossed my mind." And I didn't need or want his money. "Also, I'm only joking about hiring you."

"Hah. Yeah, I thought so. What do you want as your prize then?"

What did I want? That was simple. I wanted another chance. A chance to tell him how I really felt. But because that opportunity had already come and gone, and I couldn't change that now, I would ask for the next best thing. "Do you want to spend the day together?"

Aiden stood there, silent, the slight parting of his lips the only indication he'd heard me.

Crap, crap, crap. That came out more horrible than it had sounded in my head. "I mean, as friends." Then, because I couldn't help it, I had to dig a deeper hole. "If you want to be friends. You don't have to. I can enjoy the Australian Open by myself. I just thought that..." That it would be my last chance to spend time with him, potentially, before he quit tennis. That if I didn't ask for this, I would soon be long forgotten in his life. "That my dad would want me to have fun with a friend," I finished lamely, immediately wincing.

Way to play the sympathy card, Sere. Surely he wouldn't refuse me now, but the guilt would torment me for the rest of the day for putting this on him.

As expected, a look of concern—or was it pity?—touched Aiden's face. It was easy to tell, even with the sunglasses on. He placed a hand on my shoulder and squeezed it. "Of course I want to be your friend, Serendipity. I thought we already were."

My heart shot up to my throat, and my body couldn't help itself from feeling the silly, fluttery butterflies when he grinned at me. "All right, then. Your reward is my command." He jabbed his thumb at Melbourne Arena. "Let's go enjoy the Australian Open."

CHAPTER 29

"Aussie, Aussie, Aussie! Oi, oi, oi!" the crowd cheered inside Melbourne Arena, and I joined in on the catchy, patriotic chant. "Aussie! Oi! Aussie! Oi! Aussie, Aussie, Aussie! Oi, oi, oi!"

When the shouting finally subsided to excited murmurs at the end of the match, I took the opportunity to guzzle down a mouthful of cold water, soothing my parched throat. Ah, that hit the spot. Thank goodness for the existence of water refill stations at the Aus Open.

"Hey." Aiden's breath tickled my ear, eliciting shivers down my spine. "Having fun?"

"Yeah," I whispered. I shifted around to face him, my eyes taking him in. He currently had his hoodie and sunnies off, but the cap on his head still cast the top part of his face in shadows. Seeing as we were sitting toward the back of the stands, he probably deemed himself safe enough from the prying eyes of potential fans.

"That's good." He smiled, then turned to look at where Vincenzo Monetti, the winner of the match, was being interviewed on the court.

I leaned closer to Aiden. "How about you? Did you have fun? Or was it boring and made you wish you were on the court yourself?"

He chuckled. "No, thanks. I'm already scared about potentially going up against Monetti later. He's a tough opponent."

"I'm sure you could beat him again." Although Monetti was seeded higher in this Grand Slam, Aiden was still the overall better player, having won three out of five of their previous matches.

A thoughtful look settled over Aiden's face. "It's hard to say who would win. I'm still coming out from a slump."

That was true, but he was playing really well in comparison to the second half of last year. "Don't write yourself off yet. You're into the fourth round. That's not an easy feat."

"I'm just lucky I haven't faced any of the top seeded players yet. I could go down in straight sets next round."

"Don't say that. You're not giving yourself credit where it's due. The way you're playing now, I bet you could take out a top ten player."

Last year, his US Open run ended in the second round in straight sets to a qualifier. I hadn't seen the match, but I'd looked at the statistics. More than forty unforced errors.

So far, his Australian Open matches were much better, statistically speaking. It made me wonder why. Was it because he was playing without the pressure from his dad? Or because this would be his last Australian Open, like he'd suggested on social media?

As much as I wanted him to keep playing, I understood his situation more now. He deserved to choose his own future. And if he'd prefer a normal life, away from the spotlight and the gruelling demands of this sport he'd grown up with, then so be it. I knew more than anyone that not all jobs were as glamorous as they appeared to be.

Aiden flashed me a smile. It wasn't the cheerful, confident smile he wore in public. It wasn't even the usual amused smile he showed me. Nope. This was an entirely unsure smile, half hesitant, half grateful, but one-hundred percent sweet. "Thanks, Sere. I'm glad I met you."

Heat crept up my neck, making my face flush hot. I couldn't even blame the summer sun for this. "I'm glad I met you too." Even though there were other things I wasn't so glad about.

You messed things up. You can't blame him for moving on. I made sure to repeat that to myself as the day went on. It didn't do much to dull the aching pain, but it did stop me from starting my own pity party.

We ended up staying in Melbourne Arena for almost six hours, watching the women's match next that lasted for three sets. It didn't feel that long though. Time passed so quickly to me, and spending time at the Australian Open again made me realise how much I loved watching tennis live. The anticipation of not knowing who would win the next point, the next game, the whole match... Sure, a part of me would always hurt when I thought about Dad's absence, but another part expanded until I felt fuller than life itself.

"Ugh, I'm so tired." I covered the yawn that escaped from my mouth, trudging alongside Aiden as we exited Melbourne Arena after the women's match.

"Oh yeah?" Aiden rolled his neck in a semi-circle motion. "I guess it's been a long afternoon."

That was definitely an understatement. How did he not look as tired as me, if not more? His third-round match yesterday had been a four-setter, and he'd also practiced in the heat today. I mean, in terms of how hot it could get during summer, he'd probably experienced worse, but it still must have had some sort of toll on him.

"Do you want to call it a day?" I asked, even though I never wanted this day to end.

He slipped the top of his hoodie off his head and rubbed the back of his neck. "Nah. I'm fine. Just feel a bit stiff. What do you want to do now?"

A giddy feeling shot through me at the knowledge that he also didn't want to leave yet. "Are you sure? I feel bad that I took up so much of your time today. Don't you need to be well-rested for your match tomorrow?"

Eyeing a cluster of people passing beside us, he adjusted his cap and pulled his hoodie back up. "It's fine. I only practiced for about an hour today, and it wasn't even that hot."

Um, had we been standing under two different suns? "Seriously? I thought I would die in this heat."

His lips quirked up in an amused smile. "It wasn't that bad."

"You're crazy," I muttered. Or I was weak.

At least the heat had thankfully waned to an irritable, but more bearable, temperature. The sun cast a vivid orange glow on the horizon. Sunset soon. Eventually, I'd have to find the hotel I'd booked for the night. My stomach gnawed at my insides.

Okay, and I would find a cheap meal too. It took all my willpower to resist asking Aiden if he was hungry. As much as I wanted to spend more time with him, I had to draw the line somewhere. I wasn't going to torture my heart any more than I needed to. "You know, I'm actually feeling quite tired, so..." I pointed in the direction of the nearest exit. "I think I should probably get going."

His eyes widened, the smile wiped clean off his face. "Oh, okay. Where are you off to? I'll walk you."

My stomach did a little happy dance. Why did he have to be so nice? "No, you don't have to do that. I'm just going to a hotel in the city."

"It's fine. I'll walk you," he said. "Come on."

Before I could refuse again, he draped an arm over my shoulders, urging me forward.

Panicked thoughts overtook my mind as we slowly made our way toward the exit. Why was he being so touchy with me? In fact, why was he going beyond what a guy would do for another girl when he was already seeing someone? Maybe I was overthinking it, but I didn't want to be *that* girl. The one who tore a relationship apart. Even if I did really like him.

Decision made, my sneakers screeched to a stop. I spun around so his hand fell off my back. "I'm sorry. This was a mistake."

"A mistake?" His voice came out in a husky rasp. "What's a mistake?"

"This." I gestured between the two of us, my heart feeling like it was caving in on itself. "I shouldn't have asked you to spend the day with me. You're dating someone now, and I—"

"Wait." Aiden clamped a hand over my shoulder. I jolted, looking up at him. "What makes you think I'm dating someone?"

"I, uh," I stammered, averting my eyes. "I thought you were seeing that tennis player, Isabelle."

"You thought *what*?" He exhaled loudly and let go of my shoulder. "You should know me better than that, Sere."

My heartbeat stuttered. He wasn't seeing Isabelle then? I had thought it was weird. But then, weirder things had happened to me before. Weirder and more hurtful. And it wasn't like Aiden had been my boyfriend to begin with, so he hadn't owed me anything.

"Come on." He angled his head, looking around us at the people ambling about. "It's too crowded here. Let's go somewhere else to clear things up."

He took my hand in his, and I just about internally combusted. I numbly let him pull me along, his hand enveloping mine. I didn't dare let myself hope, but...

CHAPTER 30

A couple of tram stops and a short walk later, we arrived at what appeared to be a small park, concrete pathways paved on an area full of greenery. The smell of nature mixed with the greasy scents of what smelled like a barbecue nearby. It seemed like the perfect place to have a picnic or walk your dog. Or in our case, have a conversation without anyone else listening in.

"How did you know about this place?" I asked.

Aiden's eyes swept over the area before landing on me. "I found it one time when I went out to get some fresh air during the Australian Open. It's kind of been my go-to place ever since, when I want some quiet time to myself. There's usually hardly anyone here."

He steered me to an empty bench in front of a thick cluster of trees. I collapsed onto the wood with a solid thump, and he sat down beside me. As he took off his sunglasses and the hood of his hoodie and cap, I took deep, steady breaths through my nose. *Calm down, Sere. Calm. Down.*

Sure, I had already spent most of the day sitting next to him in a loud arena, but having him sit beside me now in a quieter and more secluded area felt ten times more intimate—especially without him having to hide his face.

I made the mistake of locking eyes with him as he swivelled around to face me, preventing me from escaping his sharp gaze. "Okay, now where were we? Do you have something to confess? Something like reading fake gossip articles about me?"

The slight upturn of his lips cued me in that he wasn't angry about it if I had, so I mumbled, "I might have accidentally read something like that."

"I knew it." He shot me a look of exasperation. "I'm not seeing Isabelle. Or any other person I happen to meet up with. One lunch together and the media thinks we're dating?"

I winced, realising that I'd jumped to conclusions when I should have known better. "Sorry. I shouldn't have assumed without asking you first."

His expression softened. "It's okay. I just don't want you to get the wrong impression of me."

"So you don't like her?" I blurted out.

"Not in that way. She's just a friend." His eyes narrowed on me. "It's funny. You almost sound..."

"S-sound like what?" I stopped to heave in a lungful of air as he continued to stare at me.

But then he shook his head. "Never mind."

Jealous? Had he been about to say jealous? If only he'd finished that sentence. All I would've had to say was, *Yes, I am jealous*. A simple, four-worded response that would have made my feelings crystal clear to him.

But of course it hadn't worked out like that. It was like I was being punished for lying about how I felt. Stupid me had believed if I avoided a relationship, that my heart would be safe. Nope. Wrong. Even without a relationship, my heart had already been stolen by Aiden Andale. It wasn't because he was famous. Not at all. If anything, his fame had been a turn off, had made me mistakenly believe that he would be stuck up or fake. Someone belonging to a different world. But I'd been wrong. Completely wrong. He'd proven to be the opposite. He'd surprised me, again and again, going as far as publicly challenging me, of all things. Which reminded me...

"Hey, Aiden."

"Yeah?"

I fidgeted with the hem of my tank top. "I've been wondering about something you said in that interview you challenged me in. You said that I had some kind of impact on you."

He hummed thoughtfully. "You don't know?"

"No. What did I do?" I didn't remember doing anything life-changing for him or to him on that day, besides our obvious awkward first meeting.

He sighed, a glazed look in his eyes as he stared off into the distance. "That day we met, I wasn't in a good place. I'd lost myself somewhere. Had thoughts about whether tennis was something I actually wanted, or if my dad had pushed the idea onto me." He paused, his throat bobbing.

"Winning the junior boys Australian Open that year made it worse. I rode on the high of that win, but it also made my dad think I had a shot at being a top professional player. Like the top of the top. He kept saying how I'd soon be winning a Grand Slam. I know I said that winning a Grand Slam had always been my childhood dream, but..." His chin dipped low. "That sort of changed as I grew older, and my dad kept pushing me to train harder. Honestly, I don't even know how I managed to convince him to let me stay at my mum's that December when we first met. But even then, he wouldn't completely let up on my training.

"So there we were, practicing some boring drills, when all of a sudden..." His eyes fixed on me. "I'm whacked in the head by a stray tennis ball. And when I turned around to see what in the world had happened, this pretty girl started apologising to me."

My face grew hot at the memory. To me, it would forever be imprinted in my mind as one of my most embarrassing moments, but to him...

"It was like fate. No, not fate. It was serendipity." Aiden grinned, his cheeks puffing up. "You made such a lasting impression on me. You were my good thing that happened by chance. That's why I think your name is perfect for you. I think you pretty much proved it for real when I found out about you by chance again."

"Through the Millers?" I guessed, my mind spinning from the influx of new information. He never did end up telling me how he found out about my family's bakery.

"Yeah. Rose had a magazine lying on the dining table, and I found a photo of you in it."

Oh my gosh. *That* embarrassing magazine? "But I still don't get it. How did I make an impact on you that day? And please don't say it was because I physically impacted your head when I accidentally hit you with the tennis ball."

His laugh came out as a half-snort. "No, I'm being serious." His eyebrows pulled together. "Do you remember when I asked how someone would know if they really liked something if they'd been doing it their whole life?"

My throat clogged up as my brain pieced everything together.

He hadn't really known if he actually liked tennis or not, and he'd asked me—a complete stranger at the time—for advice.

"You told me the best way to know was to try to live without it. That if I ended up still thinking about it a lot, that meant I really did like it. So that's what I decided to do. I told my dad I wanted the rest of December off from tennis, or I was out for good. I actually missed playing tennis during that time, so it made me decide to stick with it."

I never would've guessed that had made such a profound effect on his life.

"I've always wondered though," he said. "You said your dad taught you that. Did you not know whether you liked something or not? Was it to do with baking?"

"No." Well, that wasn't completely true. "I mean, it was to do with baking, but my dad never gave me that advice. Not directly." I gulped, thinking back to the reason why I'd told Aiden it was because of Dad. "It was...it was a few months after he passed away." The pain had still been so raw back then, the gaping hole Dad had left in our lives a wound that couldn't be healed. "We'd been thinking of selling the bakery. My mum didn't think we'd do a good job running it without my dad."

"What changed her mind?"

"Me." I'd woken up one day with the urge to feel flour under my fingers, to open the oven and smell freshly baked tarts and buns. So I baked. Mum followed soon after seeing me do it. We baked and baked and then cried together.

We'd realised that however painful it was to live without Dad, we also couldn't live without our bakery.

Reciting all of this to Aiden was a different kind of pain altogether. Like talking about a broken leg long after the incident had happened. I could remember feeling the deep ache so clearly. But presently? I didn't know how to describe it. Only that what I felt now was different. The pain of Dad's passing, of him not being here, would never leave. It was something that didn't adhere to time healing all wounds, something I'd just learned to accept. Something that had become a part of me. But Dad's memory, his wisdom—it lived on in me.

It was why I could say to Aiden with utmost certainty, "My dad would've liked you. I mean, he would've liked you anyway as a tennis player, but I think he definitely would've liked you as a person too. He would have loved your sense of humour and how hardworking you are."

"Serendipity," Aiden said. The way he said my name sparked something to life inside me. It ignited my soul, unfurling that same feeling over my whole body. All along, I recognised this feeling. Recognised it, but refused to believe it. But with him in front of me now...

I shivered at his laser focus on me. Before, I would have looked away. Now, I stared back into those hazel eyes, the familiar butterfly flutters coursing through my stomach. "Yes?" I whispered.

"There's something I need to tell you." He bit his bottom lip. "The challenge. You should have won it, not me."

"What do you mean? Didn't I win?" Wasn't that why we'd spent the day together?

"I'm not talking about this challenge. I mean the last one. In December."

That made no sense. "Why should I have won? I thought we agreed you won by default since your dad never replied." The old grouch. Unless... "Wait. Are you saying he finally replied to your email?"

"No." Aiden's eyes darted over me, then he grimaced and glanced away. "That's the thing. I never sent him the email in the first place."

What? It took a moment for his words to sink in. Had he purposely lied to win the challenge? "Why?"

A pained look overtook his face. "I guess some part of me doesn't want to forgive my dad for what's done, even if he ever shows remorse for it. He—I feel like it's been a long time since he's treated me like his son. For once, I want him to worry about me as a person, not me as a tennis player."

I gaped at him, wanting to say something to comfort him. But any words I might have conjured up were lost to me. Though he'd divulged some details about his dad's actions last year, I'd never really known the extent of injury they'd had on him. How much he had really felt.

"Also..." He cringed. "I think you had the wrong idea about something I did. The day I got mad at my dad, I posted a bunch of stupid stuff online to scare him into thinking I would quit tennis. That's why you challenged me, right? But that was never really the plan. I like tennis, and I want to continue playing. I just don't want my dad to be involved in it anymore. I want him to act more like my dad, you know? Hopefully, as soon as I can find myself a new coach, he'll have no other choice but to stop coaching me."

His revelation hit me like a tennis ball to the back of my head. "You never planned on quitting tennis?" I'd basically challenged him for nothing. "You—why didn't you tell me?"

"I'm sorry," he murmured. "I had so much fun doing the challenge with you, I didn't want it to stop. And I was so annoyed at my dad. I wasn't ready to bare my soul to him."

An ache sprung in my chest as I looked into his sorrowful eyes. In spite of him withholding the truth from me and lying, I couldn't find it in myself to be angry.

Before I could think twice, I wrapped my arms around him in a tight embrace. The heat of his body engulfed me, the earthy scent of his cologne teasing my nostrils. "It's okay. It's okay to feel mad at your dad and not want to forgive him. What you want matters. If he really doesn't care about you and refuses to see it, then he doesn't deserve to be in your life."

His body trembled, then his arms looped around my middle and squeezed. "He might not deserve me, but I don't deserve you." He buried his face in the crook between my neck and shoulder. "How can you forgive me so easily for lying to you?"

My pulse picked up speed like I was running down a steep hill. The words tumbled out from my mouth. "Because I lied to you too."

His hold on me loosened. "What do you mean?"

I worked my jaw, but hesitation took hold of me.

This wasn't easy. Not like baking. You followed the recipe, and voilà. Done. If you messed something up, then you could start the recipe again from scratch.

Love, on the other hand, was not so easy. You didn't really know what you were getting yourself into. There was no recipe to follow, no exact measurements. Sometimes there were no opportunities to start over. But you didn't know until you tried. I'd been afraid of trying, for fear of being rejected again. Of finding out I wasn't good enough. It took me a while to realise that it had never even been about me. Nothing had been wrong with me, except for this fear holding me back.

Suddenly, Aiden's catchphrase came to mind—*embrace the unknown*.

I remembered pondering over the meaning of those words. How could I embrace something I didn't even know? But it all made sense now. Embracing the unknown meant to stop being so afraid of a future I didn't have complete control over. To take chances so I could live my life with no regrets. And with all the chances I'd taken during the past week, I hadn't regretted any of them.

"Sere? What did you lie about?"

I opened my mouth to speak. *I lied when I told you that you were mistaken about my feelings.* That was all I had to say. So why did my tongue lock up and refuse to say it?

Tugging myself free from his embrace, I pulled away so that we were no longer pressed flush against each other. Instead, I had the perfect view of his face. Eyebrows knitted together, hazel eyes filled with concern, his lips pressed in a thin line. Seeing him like this undid me, letting loose the torrent of feelings I'd bottled up inside myself.

Gathering my courage, I closed the distance between us. "This," I said, and kissed him.

It was everything I remembered and more.

His lips pressed against mine, soft but firm. My eyes fluttered closed, and my hands found their way to his hair, fingers weaving through the tousled strands. His own hand moved to cup the back of my head, preventing me from pulling away. Not that I'd want to ever pull away. My heart yearned for more.

As if sensing that, Aiden moved his lips more urgently on mine. His free hand skimmed over my back, sending shock waves rippling across my skin. Heat pooled in my stomach, my entire body melting from his touch. His hand continued to trail upward, leaving behind a molten pathway of heat in its wake.

When we finally pulled apart, panting for breath, awe filled his rounded eyes. "You lied about your feelings?" Uncertainty lingered in his voice. "Why?"

The truth came out of me, unbidden and raw. "I was scared of getting into another relationship. I thought it wouldn't end well. And...I thought you might have been mistaken about your feelings for me."

He huffed loudly. "I'm not mistaken." He took my hand in his and gave it a gentle squeeze.

My body stilled at his touch.

"You're like nobody I've ever met, Sere. You challenge me in so many ways. You made me realise I should be happy with what I have instead of being upset at what I don't have. Except..." He squeezed my hand again. "I still can't believe it." He lifted his other hand, his thumb gently brushing my cheek. "I'm not dreaming, am I?"

I smiled and hugged him tightly, pure joy suffusing every fibre of my being at his confession. "If you're dreaming, then I'm dreaming too. Just embrace the unknown."

Aiden laughed, a loud chuckle that sounded like music to my ears, as he hugged me back. "We'll embrace it, Serendipity. Together."

EPILOGUE

ONE YEAR LATER
(24 YEARS OLD)

"Thanks for offering to drive, Gor Gor," I said, buckling my seatbelt.

"Meh, it's fine." Max turned the key in the ignition, letting the car rumble to life. "Who else would drive you? Ma's so emotional right now that she'll probably start crying."

I looked out the window to see, true to his word, Mum sniffing into a tissue, gazing forlornly at us. With the way she was acting, people would've thought I was leaving her forever instead of only a few months. But this would be the longest I'd ever been away from home.

Max let out a wistful sigh. "I still can't believe you're going to New York."

"Don't forget Mexico and Miami." Travelling with Aiden to his next few ATP tournaments was going to be my big holiday away from work.

Starting my own business from nothing and trying to make it something? Not easy. Creating an online shop with an enticing selection of goods and promoting it all had taken its toll on me. I was intent on including original recipes of my own, like the strawberry-choc custard tarts. That meant baking a lot with trial and error.

Business was slowly coming together now, but it was also time for a well-deserved break. And, okay—I *really* missed Aiden.

A loud rap on the car window made me jolt upward.

Mum peered in through the glass. Her mouth moved, but the words were muffled by the car engine. I pressed the button to roll down the window.

"Did you remember to bring everything? Passport, mobile phone, charger?" she asked.

"Yep. I got everything."

"Everything except a boyfriend who'll drive you to the airport," Max butted in.

"Hey!" I elbowed him. He didn't sound grouchy about it, so I knew he wasn't actually upset at having to take me there. But I'd pretend to be offended for Aiden's sake, even if he wasn't around to hear it.

Mum shot Max a stern look. "Don't be rude, Max. Aiden is a good boyfriend. He's just busy. I'm only sad he couldn't make it to our reopening day."

I hummed in agreement. Aiden had spent almost every day with me last month, but I'd convinced him to go to

Melbourne a week ago, ahead of the Australian Open, to give him time to practice and prepare for the Grand Slam.

"It's not like he won't come back to see the bakery later. In fact, he'll probably bring in more business for us." Max mimed taking a photo with a camera.

"Ugh, don't remind me." Though we'd been discreet about our relationship, the media had eventually caught wind of it. Now pesky paparazzi wandered about whenever Aiden returned to Sydney. As much as I initially disliked photos of my face on the internet, I was weirdly getting used to it now and made sure to steer clear of most public places whenever Aiden was here.

"It's okay," Mum said. "More business for the bakery is good. I don't care if they take photos since everything looks so nice now."

Yeah, that was one positive way to see it. The bakery looked almost like a brand new shop now that renovations were done. Max and I had grouped our sizable savings to pay for the renovations, making Mum the happiest she'd been in years.

"We better get going," Max said. "Wouldn't want you to miss the plane."

Mum gave me an awkward half-hug through the open window. "You take care, sweetie. Call me when your plane arrives in Melbourne."

"I will, Mum. Bye! See you in a few months!"

We waved to each other until Max pulled out of the parking spot and drove off. I eyed her in the passenger-side mirror, watching her dab at her face with a tissue. Poor Mum. Sometimes she got emotional like that. At least she had both Max and Ming to keep her company while I was gone.

Soft music trickled out from the car speakers, filling up our silence for most of the ride. I recognised some as Disney songs Ming liked to hum while baking. As the last notes of *A Whole New World* faded out, our car slowed to a stop at a traffic light.

Max drummed his fingers against the steering wheel. "So, Dippy. You're happy with Aiden?"

Uh, was that even a question? "Yeah, of course I'm happy." Happy didn't even cover half of what I felt. I was elated. Treasured. Loved.

Long-distance relationships were definitely hard, but it also made me appreciate the time we did have together. Maybe people would say that magic wouldn't last forever, that we were still in the honeymoon phase. That wouldn't stop me from enjoying every moment I had though. I'd worried enough about potential bad things happening to me. As Aiden would say—embrace the unknown.

"That's good." Max cleared his throat, readjusting his glasses. "I'm proud of you...and Ba would be proud of you too."

My mouth fell open. Was I hearing him right? "Um, what? Where's my gor gor, and what did you do with him?" My older brother declaring he was proud of me was as likely to happen as him giving up early in a challenge.

He rolled his eyes. "I'm serious. You've turned your life around since last year. Ba would be proud of how far you've come."

I melted at the rare praise. "I think he'd be prouder of you. I mean, you've come a long way since your computer-addicted days."

"Hah. Thanks. High praise from you, Dippy."

"You're welcome." We both laughed. Then, because I couldn't help teasing him, I added, "But I think Ming deserves most of the credit."

A huge smile split across his face. "Yeah, I'm lucky to have her. You know, I think I lucked out a lot really, with following through on my promises to Ba."

"*Promises*?" More than one? "What—"

Beep! A loud honk from the car behind us broke the conversation. Max stepped on the accelerator, causing me to lurch back into my seat.

I ended up holding my tongue for the rest of the trip, not wanting to cause an accident. Before I knew it, we'd arrived at the airport.

Max eased the car to a stop at the departures section. I hopped out and stretched my stiff legs while he grabbed my luggage from the back passenger seat and deposited it at my feet. "Well, guess I'll see you in a few months, Dippy."

"Wait a sec." I jabbed a finger at his chest. "What was that about following through on your *promises*?" I had to ask him now while I had the chance. "I thought you only promised Dad to keep the bakery alive."

Max winced. "Nope. I, uh, also promised to make sure you and Ma are happy."

No way.

I wouldn't have guessed that at all. But it made sense. Max was the eldest, and the only man left in the family. Basically the one who should hold all the responsibilities in the household, according to Chinese tradition.

Max toed the ground with his sneaker, avoiding my eyes. "I know what you're going to say. That I did a crap job of upholding my promise."

"No." I sighed. "You didn't do a crap job. You looked after the bakery when I didn't." He'd also helped Mum hire Ming and worked during weekends to ensure the bakery didn't close down. "Plus you helped me make a website for my business. You've done more than you realise."

"Geez. Thanks, Dippy." He flashed me a grateful smile, then glanced at his watch. "You better get going."

"Right." I pulled out the handles of my luggage bags. "Thanks, Gor Gor. See you in a few months."

"Bye." He took a step forward and patted my head. "Don't have too much fun without me."

I laughed and swatted his hand away. "Don't worry. I'm sure I will."

"Game, set, and match, Andale. 7–6, 6–4, 6–3," the umpire announced.

I leapt up in my seat and clapped along with the raucous cheers of the crowd. Aiden raised his racket, waving it to the audience.

From beside me, Aiden's coach, Duncan Dunham—or Dun for short—let out a loud whoop. He high-fived Mike, who stood next to him, and then me, followed by the rest of the team. With Dun's blonde hair and blue eyes, it was easy to see the family resemblance with his niece, Isabelle. She'd been the one to introduce Aiden to her uncle last January after he'd mentioned needing a new coach. So far, Dun was doing a great job. And thankfully, Aiden's dad had agreed to stop coaching him and had since moved on to training kids at a tennis academy.

"Congratulations, Aiden." The male interviewer's voice boomed over the microphone. "You've officially made it past the first round of the Australian Open. How do you feel?"

"I feel great, thanks," Aiden said.

"That's good to know. A straight-sets win for you is a brilliant start to this Grand Slam. But I think we're also interested in who's sitting in your player's box today. Specifically, your girlfriend?"

"Ah. I was wondering when you were going to ask about that." Aiden rubbed the back of his head, smiling sheepishly. "Yeah, that's her."

I resisted cringing at the interviewer's nosy line of questioning. Instead, I schooled my face into the perfect picture of passivity. Thank goodness my sunglasses gave me extra cover too. I was slowly growing used to the random stares whenever someone happened to recognise Aiden in public. But inside a tennis arena? That was a whole other level of attention.

"I know you're really secretive when it comes to your personal life," the interviewer said, "so what made you decide to bring her today?"

Could this interviewer get any nosier?

Aiden chuckled. "I didn't decide anything. The decision was all hers, not that it was easy. She didn't want any attention, actually. But now that she's got it..." He turned to face me in his player's box. "Thank you for being here and supporting me, Sere." He paused and tilted his head up, his lips pressed together. "You're the best thing that's ever happened to me. Everyone should know that I've only continued to play tennis to this day because of your support."

Oh. My. Gosh.

My face heated up like an oven. I bit the inside of my cheek in a poor attempt to keep a straight face. The last thing I wanted was the media capturing live footage of me getting cheesed-out by my boyfriend's sweetness.

I managed to contain my emotions well—until Aiden continued.

"That's why I want to celebrate you being here. So for every ace I hit during the Australian Open, I'm going to donate one thousand dollars to Gifts of Gold, a charity that's close to your heart."

I quickly cupped a hand over my gaping mouth. What in the world? He hadn't mentioned this to me at all.

Applause echoed throughout the arena, pounding heavily in my ears. The sound still followed me when I left, my heart thumping wildly along with it as I made my way to meet Aiden.

I quickened my pace as soon as I caught sight of him.

A smile lit up his face. "Did you like the surprise?" He slipped an arm around my waist, pulling me close.

A strong whiff of his deodorant filled my nostrils. "Yes! I can't believe you did that."

"I'm glad I did."

I reached up to tap his nose. "But you've got such a good serve. I wouldn't be surprised if you hit more than ten aces in some matches." He'd already hit eight in this match alone.

"That's fine." He grinned. "I'm living my life with no regrets."

"Ha ha. Smarty-pants." Using my own mantra against me.

His grin widened before his expression slowly softened as he stared at me.

I held his unwavering gaze. "What are you thinking about?"

The green flecks in his eyes twinkled. "Serendipity."

Wait. Serendipity as in me, or serendipity as in something good that happened by chance?

Before I could press him further, he bent down to kiss me.

I kissed him back, putting all my love for him, for how he made me feel, into the kiss.

When we finally broke apart, he leaned in to nuzzle me. "And what are *you* thinking about?" he whispered.

What was I thinking about? How could I put it into words?

I rested my cheek against Aiden's chest. His heart thudded, steady and solid. My own heart filled with an overwhelming rush of happiness. "I'm thinking that I'm glad I took the chance."

And from now on, despite everything unknown in my future, I would take each and every chance that came my way.

Afterword

Thank you for reading! Did you enjoy this book? Don't forget to leave a review wherever you can! As an indie author, word of mouth is the best way to help spread the joy of our books.

And as special thanks for getting a physical copy of the book, please read on for an exclusive extra scene I wrote. It's in Aiden's POV when he finds out about Sere's family bakery!

No Longer Unknown

I woke up to a persistent rumbling in my pants pocket—my damn phone. Again. Thought the stupid thing had finally stopped blowing up today. No such luck.

Where was I again? I slowly pried my eyes open and massaged my stiff neck, blinking away the haziness of my surroundings. My personal trainer's head came into focus, poking up above the driver's seat in front of me. Oh, right. Inside Mike's car. My personal trainer had come to rescue me again. Saving me from all my life's problems. Trying to, anyway. Not sure how it would all work out, but I would cross my fingers (and toes too if that was possible). *Stay tuned for tomorrow's episode of* Why you Shouldn't be Aiden Andale *to see if I make it out alive.*

Yawning, I stretched my arms and peered outside the back passenger window. A blur of small lights and houses whipped by. The endless expanse of dark night sky blanketed above, stars twinkling distantly as though laughing at my current predicament. *Well, join the party, stars. You're not the first one.* But guess what? I would have the last laugh when they found I'd escaped them once and for all. *If* I managed to escape them, that was. A very big if.

"FML," I said, hitting my head against the windowpane. I watched as my breath slowly fogged up the glass.

"Free my life?" Mike jokingly guessed. Oh, he definitely knew the F did not stand for free.

My dad had done a perfect job drilling into me not to speak the profanity from a young age, so this was my sad little workaround. Good on my dad, you'd like to think, teaching his son to be a saint. That was where you'd be wrong. He hadn't taught me for the usual reasons parents encouraged their children not to curse. Nope.

Dad said swearing that word by reflex could be the difference between me getting away with being angry on the tennis court, or copping an unwanted warning from the umpire. Not that I had grown up with a big temper problem anyway. I was pretty chill if anything. Probably the only proud thing I had going on for myself at the moment with tennis.

"Forget my life?" Mike pretended to guess again when he realised the first wouldn't earn a response from me.

I lifted my gaze from the window and turned to face my personal trainer. His reflection in the front mirror grinned at me with his full set of pearly whites. The car swung left, veering a sharp corner. My whole body jerked right, my seat belt digging into my shoulder. I shifted back on the headrest, letting the belt retract into a more comfortable position.

"Fudge my life," I said, the closest I could get to saying the damn word. Seriously? With or without Dad, I was too much of a goody-two-shoes to cuss like a normal twenty-three-year-old. And why shouldn't I right now? Too many crappy things had happened. Even though it was officially off-season, I didn't feel the supposed relaxation I was meant to be feeling. Hopefully that was about to change. Which reminded me... "Are you sure your wife won't mind me staying over, Mike?"

He snorted as though I'd asked him if he was a superhero—which, by the way, he totally was. Just minus the tights and cape, but plus the saving my worthless ass. "Do you even need to ask? Of course she won't mind. Isaac is on his best behaviour whenever you're around."

I chuckled, remembering his shy but easily excitable son. The last time I'd seen him was during the Sydney International a few years ago. Every moment during my free time, he'd wanted to spend it with me. Back then he'd been nine years old. "Isn't your son almost eleven now?" I tried to remember how I'd behaved at that precarious age, but all I could conjure up were boring tennis drills. The sad story of my life. "Are you sure he hasn't outgrown me?"

"Nope. He tells me he's still your number one fan."

"Hah, good to know." At least I had one fan who hadn't abandoned me yet.

"We'll be arriving soon so you better prepare yourself," Mike warned me.

Prepare myself for what? I wanted to ask. But then memories of his chatty wife, Rose, rose to mind (full pun intended) and added with Isaac's fanboying... *Okay, mentally preparing it is.*

A few minutes later, the car slowed to a stop up a steep driveway. I hopped off the car, landing on a manicured front lawn. Mike led me up a pathway flanked by neatly trimmed bushes. Despite meeting his wife and son several times before, I'd never actually set foot in their home until now.

How did Mike feel, being away from his family most of the year? I mean, he did get the occasional week off to fly back whenever I was off, but what was that compared to how long he was absent for? Sometimes I felt like I was stealing Mike from his family by hiring him as my full-time fitness trainer. Though he had yet to complain or quit, so I guessed he was happy where he was. That or he loved the money my dad had paid him. Which Dad would not be dictating anymore. The guilt of Dad's behaviour still clung to me like sweat on the back of my shirt during a long tennis match. Yeah, very gross. Needed to change to a new shirt ASAP. Unfortunately the same couldn't be done for a new dad.

"Come in, come in," a sweet feminine voice ushered at the front door and I was all but shoved into the Miller household.

A fresh homely smell filled my nostrils as soon as I stepped through the entrance and into the hallway. A boy partially hid behind one of the two big pillars bordering the walls. Isaac.

"Hey, man," I said, dipping my head in acknowledgement as I bent down to untie my shoelaces.

"H-hi!" he squeaked, and it took all the effort I possessed not to laugh at his shyness. Not to be mean or anything. The kid was just too adorable. He was pretty short for an almost eleven-year-old. Hopefully he'd gain that extra height during his teenage growth spurt.

"Welcome, dear," Mike's wife said, giving me a gentle pat on the shoulder. "You must be tired. Do you want some tea? Water?"

"Some tea would be great. Thanks, Rose."

"Hey," Mike said to me, slapping my back. "I'm going to pop out for a bit. Buy some groceries. You make yourself at home, okay?"

"You got it," I said, waving him off. "No worries. If you have time, can you get me the usual stuff too? I'll pay you back."

"Yeah, sure." Mike flashed me his notorious grin again. "Can't have your cover blown already."

I huffed, trying to think of a clever retort, but by the time I had one in mind, he was out the door again.

Got to let my superhero have his screen time, I should've said. Because the matter of fact was I'd never be caught dead (or alive) in a regular supermarket. That would be like me walking around with a "Hey, world. Here I am. Come get me paparazzi" sign. The man really was my superhero for doing my shopping.

Rose wore an amused expression at our exchange, but said nothing about it as she guided me to the dining room —a neat little space with a table large enough to seat four people—and then disappeared into the kitchen. Seeing as I would be waiting for a while, I picked out a random chair and plopped onto it. A moment later, Isaac scuttled into the room and sat opposite me. He grabbed a stack of paper cards on the table and started going through them.

"What's up?" I asked, curiosity taking hold of me at whatever he was doing.

"Um, this is for you." I took the card he held out in between us. My name was written in golden, neat cursive. I flipped it over.

You are formally invited to Isaac Miller's 11th Birthday Party.

It stated the party theme was tennis (of course) this Sunday at 1 p.m. at his home.

"Cool. I'll probably be in the house most of the time, so count me there."

Isaac beamed and I couldn't help but return the smile. The kid's happiness was infectious. "Mum organised it to have tennis-themed everything. And Dad's setting up a net in the backyard too. And, uh..." He clasped his hands together and twiddled his thumbs. "You can join in too...if you want. My tennis club friends are coming."

"That'd be fun." Though I usually made it a habit to practice daily, this past week had been tennis-free. Mainly because Dad hadn't been around to force the habit, but still. A brand new first for me. The strangest thing about it all? My hands constantly itched, imagining the familiar feel of a tennis ball ricocheting off my racquet... Damn, maybe some tennis would do me good. Or some light workout. I'd ask Mike about it later. Sitting still all the time for the next few weeks would just drive me crazy.

"Isaac, can you help me wash the dishes?" Rose called from the kitchen.

The young boy's eyes darted between the kitchen and me. With a little sigh, he leapt off his seat.

I laughed. "Have fun."

He shot me one last smile as he ambled to the kitchen.

All my amusement was wiped clean when a buzzing vibration shook my pants pocket.

My phone. I'd almost forgotten about the darn thing. Jamming my fingers into the pocket, I pulled out the device that had plagued me since my big fight with Dad. I tapped it on—only to see the bajillion missed calls and texts from the man himself.

Anger roared in my ears at the first message I read in the long list.

Dad: Where are you right now? Have you come to your senses yet?

Come to my senses? Oh, get lost. I pressed hard on the power button and swiped the toggle, switching off my phone and effectively cutting off his only way of communicating with me. I didn't want to talk to him right now. Or today. Or maybe even ever. *Try again next lifetime when you're not senselessly dictating my life, Dad.*

Unfortunately, there went my main form of entertainment, too. My eyes searched the table for a distraction. Maybe I could find a newspaper (with no news about me). I picked up a magazine in the pile of catalogues. *Local Food Delights and Treats.* That'd do it.

I began to mindlessly flip through it, more occupied with the feeling of the thin pages between my fingers than looking at the contents. But every few pages, I would silently salivate at something that looked rather delectable —and highly forbidden in my diet. Cupcakes, blueberry pie, a triple value hamburger... Things I'd eaten enough times in my life to tally them all on two hands.

Were they really forbidden to me now though? Without Dad around, I could do whatever I wanted, really. I'd never been much of a foodie, but that was because I never had much to look forward to when it came to meals. Besides the rarely allowed cheat days when I won a tournament, I never had much opportunity to eat outside my usually strict diet. Well, not anymore.

With that settled, I challenged myself to go and eat the next piece of nice food my eyes landed on. I flipped to the next page. *Violet's Vegan Treats*, a shop that sold vegan desserts. Muffins, pies, pancakes. Healthy, but not what I was aiming for. Next page.

Tsang's Bakery, for all your sweet and savoury cravings. The accompanying photos didn't look like everyday buns you'd find in a bakery. *Authentic Hong Kong buns*, the subtitle claimed. My eyes roamed over the food, but then quickly caught on the centremost photo. A girl with straight, long black hair and dark brown eyes. She held up a tray of vaguely familiar-looking yellow tart pastries.

What the... Was I seeing what I thought I was seeing?

"Aiden," Rose called. She asked me a question that went in one ear and out the other. "Aiden?"

"Sorry, just give me a moment..." I breathed deeply, let the magazine drop onto the table, and pulled out my wallet from my pants pocket. Hands trembling slightly, I withdrew the old instant photo from within the front see-through pocket and placed it beside the magazine photo. My eyes flickered between the two, comparing. Not that I needed to. I'd known as soon as I saw the photo it was *her*. Serena.

Well, not Serena. A year after we met, Dad had surprisingly allowed me a short break to fly back to Sydney on a weekend trip to see mum on her fortieth birthday. That was when I'd dropped by the sports centre and asked after Serena.

The first girl had said it was strictly against centre policy to give away private information about their members. The second receptionist had been a big fan of mine and had agreed to see if there were any Serenas under the tennis club list. To get around the privacy rules, they said they would contact all the Serenas on file to ask if they knew me. My attempt was proven fruitless. There was only one Serena listed under the sports centre and she didn't know about any Aiden, nor was she even part of the tennis club.

After that day, I'd given up on finding her, considering she probably had given me a fake name. If she wanted to know me, she could find me herself at a tournament or something. I wasn't completely oblivious to my rising fame. Not when people started asking for photos and autographs on the street. So obviously she didn't want to know me.

I could never get rid of the nagging feeling in my head that she *hadn't* lied though. Her curly-haired friend had called her Sere. Maybe she'd no longer been part of the club—or had never been in the first place. Well, whatever.

I'd soon stopped worrying over it, with tennis occupying all hours of my life.

Now the memories all came tumbling back into my mind. A big jumbled mess.

I had found her. After all these years. When I hadn't even been looking. Just great. What did I do with this information now?

The scuffed sound of footsteps disrupted my train of thoughts. I turned to see Rose as she approached me, her face scrunched with concern. "Is everything okay, Aiden?"

"Yeah, everything's fine," I said automatically.

She gave me a yeah-right look. "I asked you how you'd like your tea three times."

Crap. She had? "Sorry. I was a little distracted..." My eyes drew back to the two photos of Not-Serena.

Rose's gaze followed mine. "What were you—" She gasped, startling me, and snatched the instant photo off the table. Her eyes bugged out as she analysed the photo of sixteen-year-old me with the girl whose name I didn't know. "How do you know Sere?"

"I—" What? "You know her?" This was quickly becoming weirder and weirder. "How do you know her?"

Rose shot me a look that made me realise I asked the very same question she had asked me. But she answered, "Of course. Her family owns a bakery that I go to. Isaac loves their buns. Now how do *you* know her?"

"Uh, I actually don't." She shot me a look of disbelief. Yeah, that sounded stupid considering she held a photo of the two of us together. "I met her a long time ago at a sports centre. She said her name was Serena, but I don't think that was her real name. We didn't exchange contact details, so we lost touch after."

Rose burst out laughing. Whatever reaction I expected from her, it hadn't been this. "She did the same thing to me! Saying her name was Serena, I mean. But I learned from her mum later on that Serena wasn't her real name."

"What's her real name then?"

"Serendipity. Her mum said it's because it was a miracle she was born. She'd been told after her first child that she wouldn't be able to conceive again." When Rose noticed my eyebrows furrowing, she explained, "Serendipity means a good thing that happens by chance."

Serendipity. This girl I'd been thinking about over the past seven years finally had a name to her face. *A good thing that happens by chance.* That was suitable, considering how meeting her had been the one good thing that had turned my life around at the time.

She didn't know it, but that day, I'd had thoughts of running away. Of quitting tennis. Of telling Dad that I'd wanted out. Only I never ended up doing that. I had listened to her advice. Had asked Dad for a break from tennis instead, to set my mind straight. And after all that, I realised how much I loved the sport, despite Dad forcing me into it as soon as I'd been old enough to walk.

I owed Serendipity. Meeting her had changed my life. But a strange, bitter taste coated my mouth at the thought that maybe my meeting with her hadn't meant anything to her if she'd lied about her name.

I had to see her again. She at least owed me an apology for giving me a false name. With my mind made up, I decided on my plan of attack.

Tomorrow, I would walk into that bakery first thing in the morning and see how she reacted to me. That would be fun. Now that she was no longer unknown to me, there was no escape for her.

ACKNOWLEDGEMENTS

Growing up, I unfortunately didn't get to read that many books with Asian representation in them. So that was how Sere came into existence. She's supposed to represent me —an Australian born Chinese. Don't let that fool you though. In most ways, I'm not like Sere at all. I, for one, wouldn't have the guts to challenge a professional tennis player! Sere also encompasses what I wish to be and hope will encourage everyone else to be too. Braver. More willing to take chances. Someone who embraces the unknown.

It's funny how things don't always go as planned though. When I first plotted this book, it was only meant to be a novella written as practice for my writing. But somewhere along the way, it grew into something bigger and better. It was definitely a journey to get to the finish line, but I'm so glad I stuck to it. However, this wouldn't have been possible without a lot of people.

To my parents and brothers—thank you always for your love and support.

To my aunty, Biyi—thank you for being the original number one fan of my writing. I will always remember your excitement at reading my very first fantasy stories.

To Eric—thank you for your endless support and for reading the chapters of this book as I wrote them. You were able to reassure me that my ideas weren't too crazy and that people out there would actually want to read them.

To my beta readers—Kirsty, Leslie, Liana, Linda, Melissa, Patricia and Rachelle. Thank you all for volunteering to read my book and for taking the time to give me so much valuable feedback. This book became so much better because of all your help.

To Mish—thank you for answering all my questions about studying a law degree so my information about Sere's studies and career would be as accurate as possible.

And to you, dear reader—thank you for buying my book and reading it.

ABOUT THE AUTHOR

Natalie is a big daydreamer who spends her days imagining fantasy worlds full of magical mysteries, action and sweet romance. When she's not working on her next story, you can find her buying too many books, binge-watching anime or drowning in her accumulating pile of unfinished video games. Natalie lives in Sydney, Australia, but you're more likely to see her lurking around Bookstagram.

You can connect with Natalie through the following:

Instagram: @nataliechung.writes

Website: www.nataliechungbooks.com

Lightning Source UK Ltd.
Milton Keynes UK
UKHW011933270622
405020UK00003B/963